D1310854

Something Begins

J.D. Burk

DISCLAIMER

1 Monday	1
2 Tuesday	6
3 Wednesday	9
4 Thursday	17
5 Friday	25
6 Saturday	37
7 Sunday	46
8 Monday	50
9 Tuesday	56
10 Wednesday	65
11 Thursday	76
12 Friday	87
13 Saturday	91
14 Sunday	97
15 Monday	107
16 Tuesday	115
17 Wednesday	124
18 Thursday	138
19 Friday	150
20 Saturday	158
21 Sunday	164
22 Monday	169
23 Tuesday	178
24 Wednesday	185
25 Thursday	191
26 Friday	198
27 Saturday	203
28 Sunday	209
29 Monday	214
30 Tuesday	218
31 Wednesday	225
32 Thursday	230
33 Friday	235
34 Saturday	241
35 Sunday	252
36 Monday	261
37 Tuesday	265
38 Wednesday	268
39 Thursday	274
40 Friday	277
Epilogue	283

1 MONDAY

Pat walked into the break room and saw her co-worker staring off into space over a cup of coffee. "Lindy, what are you doing here? I thought you were off camping this week."

Looking up with a wan smile Lindy answered, "John broke up with me. So a week at his parents' cabin seemed a bit awkward."

"I'm sorry, dear." Pat settled into a chair next to the young woman. Plump and matronly, she knew others found her presence comforting. "Do you want to talk about it?"

Lindy seemed to struggle with words for a moment then blurted out, "We were doing so well! I felt such a connection and thought we would be happy together. We were talking about the future and he told me he had two kids living in Maine so I told him about the accident and that I can't have children. I never imagined he would get angry!"

Tears pooling in her eyes, Lindy whispered, "He called me a useless mouth. Said people who don't have kids are a waste of resources."

Pat tried to rein in her anger before she spoke but finally let loose, "What a twat! Sorry dear, but when you've had time to think about this you will know that his twisted logic is his problem, not yours. As if his being a sperm donor made him superior to anyone. Humph!"

Watching Pat tapping her fingers on the table with a determined look on her face made Lindy feel decidedly apprehensive. "You aren't thinking about doing anything to John, are you? I don't want any more to do with him!"

"What? Oh no. He's not worth the hassle." With a chuckle she admitted, "I was thinking of ways to distract you. If you're still packed why not come stay on the farm for a few days? There's plenty of room and I'd love to show you what the kids gave me for my birthday."

It took very little to convince Lindy that a change of scenery would be welcome and they agreed to meet up after work.

Lindy leaned back contentedly on the wide seat of the '68 Ford Galaxy. Pat called it 'the Tank' and admitted it ate gas but it had been her late husband's car and she was attached. The wind from the open windows made talk difficult but felt good in the late June heatwave. After fifteen miles on the highway, the car turned off onto a well-maintained gravel road. Another five miles and Pat pulled into a driveway and rattled across a cattle guard. A slow curve and the farm came into view: a large pole barn on the left with open doors showed a flash of machinery as they passed. Ahead, an old barn obviously in the middle of receiving a new coat of red paint and to the right a large rectangular farmhouse with a wrap-around porch, pale yellow trimmed with white.

As Lindy climbed out of the car with her backpack her gaze was drawn up by the chattering of a squirrel in the massive cottonwood that shaded the house. The shimmering leaves whispered in the breeze and in that moment the tension eased from her shoulders.

"Bang!" The slamming of the screen door pulled her eyes back down. Her head jerked in surprise at the appearance of the man who stepped out: short with a weight-lifter's build, bald, neatly trimmed beard and, over jeans and t-shirt, a very pretty, light blue apron. Movement in the corner of her eye drew her attention to a garden area where another man was leaning on a hoe and settling a straw hat onto his head. Then a metallic clatter had her swinging around to see someone pushing a motorcycle out of the pole barn. Before she could gather her thoughts, the old barn door swung open and yet another man stepped out with a paint can.

Helplessly, Lindy fell back against the car laughing, and asked Pat if they danced with axes. Chuckling herself, Pat replied, "It can be overwhelming when they are all here, but the twins have found summer internships in the city so you're getting a light dose. They try to arrange their vacations so we can all be here at the same time."

"Only the six then?" Lindy asked with a twinkle.

"Yes," smiled Pat proudly. Then, suddenly becoming serious, added, "Lindy, they're all adopted. Matt and I couldn't have any of our own."

The message was clear, and Lindy looked at her friend with gratitude.

"Michael, is there enough for one more?" Pat called to the house.

"I'll see what I can do." He turned back inside as Pat explained, "He's a chef in the city. We've tried to get him take a proper vacation, but he loves cooking too much to stop. It's a relief how it worked out; the twins stay at his apartment - he keeps an eye on them and they are company while he deals with losing Amelia. Oh, sorry. You don't know what I'm talking about. His wife died last year in a hit and run accident. A tragedy, but I think he's coping. Now, would you like to get settled in your room?"

Without waiting for a reply, Pat bustled inside. Lindy hurried to catch up, almost tripping over an ancient spaniel snoozing on the rug. Pat had paused to pet a wriggling German shepherd puppy before waving her forward.

"You should be comfortable in here, but let me know if you need anything. It's directly under my room so won't be too noisy."

Lindy had to smile at the idea of noise being an issue. Her apartment had thin walls and sometimes shook from the movements of the family above her. This room looked delightful with cream colored walls, a pair of twin beds under pink chenille covers and a vanity with a large mirror. A round braided rug made a colorful accent on the hardwood floor.

"It's lovely. Thank you for letting me come." It wasn't hard to feel safe and at ease in a room that looked so much like the one she used when visiting her grandparents as a child.

Later that evening, while eating dinner at a table designed to seat eight, Lindy studied Pat's family and thought about what she had learned so far. Michael, the oldest, was clearly the rock of the family, steady and admired. Steve, the gardener, was tall, lean and taciturn. He had moved back home to help with the farm when their father had died but kept working as a software engineer. Jeffrey looked like a classic bad-boy with attitude; slightly long black hair, earring and the Harley. It was a surprise to discover he was a tenured professor of mathematics. Finally, there was James. Thin, short, with a shock of red hair he was, frankly, ugly...until he smiled. It was like watching the sun come out and light up everyone around him.

When asked what he did, James answered, "I'm a starving author in a family of success stories." Steve promptly threw a bread roll at him and chaos reigned briefly around the table.

When the laughter subsided Michael said, "Don't believe him. He has a fine job as a tech writer and has published romance novels. He's just pouting because he would rather write something deep and meaningful."

At this very moment, many miles away, an angry young man slammed the door shut behind him. "I'll show them. I'll show them all!" he snarled while shoving books aside until he found a portable hard-drive. Holding it almost reverently, he whispered, "Firesale."

"You're not local, are you? I don't remember seeing you around." James deftly dried the plate Lindy handed him.

"I started out here, but then my family moved and moved and moved. Never more than three years in one place. When I finished high school I just wanted to stop so I came back to where I began." Her hands stilled as she glanced over and asked, "How is it you are all so welcoming to a complete stranger pushing into your family time?"

The chuckles that bubbled up with James' crooked smile were so infectious that she couldn't help grinning in response. "Oh, we've had lots of practice. Mom couldn't resist offering a nest to every stray girl that wandered into her clutches. Everything from runaways to troublemakers to girls who needed a safe place to regroup.

"Dad recognized the danger early on and sat us down to explain that anybody that stayed here would be treated as a sibling with no exceptions." With a wry twist of his lips he continued, "He was right of course. Imagine what would have happened when six hot-headed boys all tried to catch the attention of the same girl!"

Lindy sighed contentedly, "That explains why I feel so safe; I've just acquired four brothers." Unable to hold a straight face, she began to giggle helplessly while James put on a face of mock offense before he also broke down with laughter.

Pat paused in the doorway, then moved on nodding to herself. This was the best place for Lindy to begin healing.

2 TUESDAY

The next morning the two women discussed options for the remainder of the week; finally agreeing that they would go to work then stop at Lindy's apartment. She could pick up a few items more suited for a farm and get her car so she would be free to come and go at will. Pat gently encouraged her to take the rest of the week off and do as little or as much as she felt like on the farm.

"And if you're wondering why I'm not taking this week off, it's because I like the boys to settle back into their home first. Then I can enjoy them full-time next week after they've gotten all the little rivalries out of their systems." With a firm nod she went inside to finish getting ready for work, leaving Lindy on the porch soaking up the morning peace.

"A benevolent queen," mused Lindy to herself. "And this her kingdom."

Only one person knew that war had been declared, not with explosions and death, but with code that slipped unnoticed into a tablet in a coffee shop.

It had been an unremarkable day at work and soon after getting off Lindy was at her apartment, jiggling the key to get it to catch. Just as it unlocked her neighbor across the hall poked her head out. "Hey, your boyfriend was here last night looking for you. Mickey had to threaten to call the cops to get him to shut up."

"Oh!" Lindy could feel the tension and shame tightening up her shoulder and neck muscles. "He's not my boyfriend anymore and I'm going to be away for a while so if Mickey needs to report him, that's what he should do."

Her neighbor nodded in understanding, "Okay. You take care of yourself and we'll keep an eye on your place."

Inside, Lindy sank onto her sofa as tears welled up and spilled over. The happiness she had felt proved to be a very thin and brittle veneer covering a storm of emotions. Some time later, she gave herself a shake and got up to sort out clothes she could get comfortably dirty in. She didn't know why John was looking for her but was determined not to let him ruin her vacation. She couldn't resist a smirk at the thought of how annoyed he must have been that her cell phone had been off since their fight.

Glancing around her apartment for anything she might be forgetting, she grabbed a couple Elizabeth Peters novels for comfort reading and headed out. In the parking lot her white Ford Focus waited; older and uncomfortable, at least it was paid for and staying out of debt was important to Lindy. She had watched too many co-workers struggling to last to the next paycheck when so much had to go to pay for purchases they had made and long since forgotten.

Finally, Lindy headed out of town towards the farm and the family she felt she was escaping to.

'Virus' didn't come close to describing what had been released. "Inconceivable!" would be the expected response. The only one

7

capable of not only conceiving the concept but creating it was a very twisted genius. And even he couldn't stop what had begun.

----

3 WEDNESDAY

Wednesday morning found Lindy and Steve in the farmyard. The understanding was that everyone was free to do as much or as little as they wanted but she couldn't imagine sitting around while the rest were busy. Steve had offered her a tour and they set off climbing the hill behind the house.

"The farm was in Dad's family for generations and when Mom's parents passed she wanted to invest so they bought land. 1920 acres total. The fields are rented out now, but we kept the pastures for the cattle and haying. The shelterbelts, those are the stretches of trees and bushes, were planted during the Depression. Some farmers have been ripping them out to get the extra growing space, but Dad insisted on keeping ours. His parents remembered the dust storms too well. He was even thinking about planting buffalo grass in some of the fields and raising bison, but ran out of time."

Reaching the top of the hill, they turned and Lindy could see the entire farm. Spotting some small buildings she hadn't noticed before, she asked about them.

"The little one by the house is the old outhouse; it's no longer functional, the hole was filled in years ago. Next to the barn is the chicken coop and the farrowing house. The brick building behind the pole barn used to be a smithy. It's just used for storage now."

Lindy's eyes darted around, eager to see it all. The tallest item caught her attention. A metal windmill was turning lazily in the breeze. "Is that a working windmill?"

"Yeah, the folks both had a thing for antiques and keeping them functional. That's pumping water for the cattle." While Steve's voice was calm, something about it spoke volumes of his pride in their home.

"What projects can I help with?" she asked.

"Maintenance is always big. Last year we painted the house and planted more fruit trees to replace those getting older. The year before that all the small outbuildings were painted and got metal roofing. James is working on the barn and Michael helps when not cooking. After I get caught up in the garden I'll help them since it's the biggest job. Jeffrey is working on some old farm machinery - stuff Dad had parked outside that he thinks can be renovated. If the weather holds, next week will be haying. Since the twins couldn't get time off, we'll have a job getting everything done."

"Okay, can I start by helping you in the garden? Understand I haven't done any since I visited my grandparents as a kid."

"Sure. I'll introduce you to the animals first, then we can get to work." With that, they set off down the hill.

First they stopped at the chicken pen where a mad rush of birds dashed for the fence. Steve raised his voice to be heard over the clucking, "There are about thirty hens and two roosters. I'm not sure how many chicks so far. Normally they have free run of the farm but we lost a couple to a hawk last week so I'm keeping them in the pen for now."

Lindy looked up and realized there was netting over the entire pen. A very loud crowing startled her and pulled her attention back down. The bird eyeing her seemed enormous, yet some of the others were tiny in comparison. "Are they different breeds? None of them look alike."

"Yes. We've always had a wide variety of chickens and they intermix freely. Every few years we bring in an outside rooster for a fresh bloodline. As you can imagine, we get way more eggs than we need so I sell the excess at the farmer's market on Saturdays. Ready to see the pigs?"

It was hard to tear herself away from the chickens. Lindy was feeling both overwhelmed and fascinated by the constant movement and noise. As they moved over to the pigs Steve explained, "The farrowing house can hold twenty sows, but we've removed most of the barriers and just have Susie and her litter. We keep a couple for meat and sell the rest."

Susie proved to be a massive pink beast with floppy ears. Ignoring the indignant squeals of her offspring, she heaved herself up and grunted at Steve. He indulged her with a vigorous back scratching over the fence while keeping an eye on Lindy who had squatted down and was attempting to get a piglet to come closer. One with black spots came almost close enough to touch before dashing back to its siblings, leaving her laughing in delight.

"It looks like the cattle are out in the far pasture. Probably won't be in until evening. Are you still interested in gardening?"

"Oh, yes!"

"Let's grab some gloves then."

Cell phones were easy to infiltrate and smartphones became a gateway not only to computers, but also to the companies behind the communication industry. Verizon, Sprint, O2, T-Mobile, MTS, MegaFon, ZOPO; all were unaware they had been compromised. In fact, not only did the Virus slide past all virus software, it searched for and destroyed other viruses. Systems around the world became more efficient.

Lindy scooted back further down the row, reaching over to pinch out the young weeds and saplings from among the sturdy onions. She had begun by bending over, then tried squatting, but protesting muscles finally had her sitting in the dirt. She decided weeding onions was a Zen-like job, much more relaxing than the yoga she had once attempted. Glancing over she noted that Steve was still pushing the wheel-hoe between rows on the far end of the garden. When asked about the size of the plot for two people, he had explained that they preserved large quantities and he took some of their extras to the farmer's market as well. Focusing back on the task at hand, she didn't even notice that she was humming to herself until a shadow passed over.

"Ready to take a break?" asked Michael, handing her a tall glass of lemonade. "That's how I always did the onions too."

"Thanks." Pushing back her straw hat revealed a sweaty, dirt-smeared face.

"Hey! You need to get out of the sun. Why don't you come keep me company inside?" Michael was alarmed by how drawn she looked.

Lindy looked behind her at what remained of the onion rows and got a mulish look. "No, I'm going to finish this."

"Hmm, well I've got plans for you this afternoon, so don't expect to come back out here today." With that he crossed the garden with her empty glass and a full one for Steve. She saw them looking at her while they talked and knew the decision was out of her hands.

An hour later, she levered herself upright, groaning but incredibly proud of the pristine rows she had done.

"Will you ever look at vegetables the same again?" chuckled Steve, joining her.

"It's wonderfully satisfying. I wish I had a garden of my own."

Studying her expression, he saw the possible birth of another garden devotee and made a decision. Holding out his hand he said, "I'd be happy to share mine with you. Come out anytime; then, when you have space for your own, you'll know what to do. In the meantime, lots of fresh veggies!"

"Great." Lindy shook his hand firmly.

A quick shower and she joined the men for lunch. After a few bites she paused to ask, "How much of this is from the garden?"

Michael's eyebrows arched up. "All the main ingredients were raised here on the farm. Spices, flour and sugar are bought."

James began to laugh. "Do you remember that year Dad refused to buy anything? We had to grow enough grain for the livestock and for us. Tubers for the pigs. The sugar beets were a complete failure."

"And we had to trade for honey and maple syrup. Otherwise, no sweets." Michael looked thoughtful. "I think helping Mom experiment in the kitchen that year was what got me hooked on cooking."

Lindy was confused. "But why? Why did he make you?"

Her companions suddenly seemed incapable of meeting her gaze. "Well..." "Um."

Jeffrey spoke up, "It was because we were ungrateful asses. Complaining about how easy the town kids had it and how cheap Dad was. It seems a backwards way to teach us a lesson, but I felt ten feet tall when we had enough to last all winter."

The rest were nodding in agreement when suddenly Michael froze, his eyes focused on Jeffrey's left hand. Softly he asked, "Jeff, where is Melissa?"

Jeffrey rubbed at the pale flesh on his ring finger for a moment before speaking. "We decided on a trial separation and she moved out. Except," he paused to take a ragged breath, "she moved in with Kramer in Physics and filed for divorce. I put my stuff in storage and the house on the market. I can't teach in the same department now so I took a year sabbatical. I don't know what I'm going to do. Now you know everything and I don't want to talk about it anymore!"

With that he shoved his chair back and slammed out of the kitchen. There was a breathless minute as nobody moved, then Michael very quietly spoke, "James?"

"Yeah. I'll try." Even his red hair seemed dimmed as he followed Jeffrey.

Michael glanced at Lindy and answered the question in her eyes, "James can talk to him. And listen, which is probably more important."

Lindy chewed on her lip as she struggled with her thoughts before blurting out, "I should go home. He doesn't need a stranger around now."

Steve put his hand on her shoulder. "Lindy, Jeffrey wouldn't have spoken in front of you if he minded you hearing. He's a very private person. You fit here and I think it's safe to say we're all comfortable with you. If he thought he had driven you away it would be even harder on him. Please stay."

Michael set the plates he had been gathering back down and sat across from her. "Mom always wanted a daughter. They had made all the arrangements and were only weeks away from adopting one when they got the call about the twins. They had been abandoned by a distant cousin of hers and nobody else in the family would take them. So she said yes, but at
that time six was the maximum they were allowed to adopt and they lost their chance for a daughter.

"If you feel you need to leave, okay, but you should know that you've already brought happiness here."

Tears sprang to Lindy's eyes. "I seem to cry so easily lately. Sorry. Yes, I want to stay. Thank you." Impulsively, she jumped up and ran around the table to hug Michael.

Through the open window came clattering noises and the sound of singing. All three peered out to see Jeffrey climbing the scaffolding at the barn while James handed up paint, both singing loudly.

"Fie on Goodness? Isn't that from Camelot?" she asked.

"Yeah," Steve answered. "It's our venting song; something you can sing loud and let out anger without busting up your knuckles. I'm going to go help."

Lindy volunteered for afternoon kitchen duty so Michael could be with his brothers. From what she could see through the window, they didn't seem to be talking much, but there was something harmonious about how they worked together. After cleaning up the lunch debris, she shelled peas and peeled potatoes. Searching the cabinets confirmed that there wasn't an apple/potato peeler gadget hiding somewhere and she decided to buy one as a thank you gift.

Afterwards, she curled up on the sofa with a book. Mellow, the old spaniel, sprawled on the floor next to her, snoring softly; the dog's rather unfortunate smell the only detraction from a perfect afternoon. Soon, the gentle humming of the ceiling fan combined with the aftereffects of unaccustomed physical labor had her drifting off to sleep as well.

When Pat drove in she saw Jeffrey waiting for her. She had known something was wrong since he came home; apparently now he was ready to talk. It was so hard not to rush in and try to fix things for her sons, but she had learned that it was best to listen, offer advice when asked and just be there for them.

It was a good hour before they finished and headed inside. She was feeling more tired than usual but had one more serious discussion to have. Finding Lindy in the kitchen, Pat asked her to join her on the porch.

"Dear, the police came to work today to do a wellness check on you." Holding her hand up to stop Lindy's protest, "It's okay, you're not in trouble. Your apartment was broken into and badly damaged. An officer is going to stop out tonight to take your statement and verify that you're fine. Okay? Okay.

"Now, I feel very strongly that you shouldn't go back to town until this is resolved. Please consider staying here while the police do their job." Pat's expression was such a combination of anxiety and hope that Lindy couldn't resist reassuring her.

"I'll stay. I'm not brave or strong enough to face John on my own." Lindy paused, "I'm feeling very uprooted though. It's like everything stable in my life has unraveled."

Pat nodded thoughtfully, "I felt like that when Matt died. I was adrift and nothing made sense. When my thoughts got too frantic, I'd lie under that cottonwood tree and listen. Somehow, it helped.

"I think I'll have one of the boys dig out the lawn chairs." With another of her firm nods, she patted Lindy on the shoulder and headed inside.

When the policeman came round later that evening, he explained the incident as they knew it. An upstairs neighbor had been up with a restless baby and heard sounds of things crashing and breaking from her apartment. He called it in and was waiting on the balcony when he saw the glow from a fire below. Because he was still on the line with emergency services, they were able to respond in record time and nobody was hurt. But, between the vandalism, the fire, and putting the fire out, everything she had was ruined.

Lindy answered all the questions she could and requested that her location be kept confidential. Then, she gave the officer her phone and its battery, asking that he not install the battery until back in town. The phone had been a gift from her ex and she was afraid he might be able to track it.

When he had left she went to her room and did the only thing she had enough energy to do - she cried herself to sleep.

The Virus had infiltrated every system connected in any way to the internet. Many that should have remained isolated and secure were compromised by human error or stupidity. Stage 1 complete, it now went dormant except for passive scanning for previously unreachable equipment. Unnoticed, it was copied into backups around the world.

---

4 THURSDAY

Lindy sat on her bed, frozen in a miserable moment with a pounding headache and on the verge of being smothered by a cloud of depression. There were so many things she needed to do: calls to her parents, the insurance company, the apartment management, arrangements for her mail, replacements for lost documents; but all she had managed so far was to get dressed.

A light knock sounded on the door followed by it opening enough to allow the entrance of an extremely pregnant calico cat. The cat spared her one haughty glare before heading to the corner behind the vanity. Curiosity overcame Lindy's inertia and she rose to investigate. Curled up on a faded towel, the cat was clearly settling in and meant to remain. Lindy sank onto the floor nearby and cautiously began petting her.

"For the first time I'm glad I can't have children. What a mess if I were in your condition right now!"

Some time later there was another knock on the door. This time James poked his head in and spotted Lindy sitting on the floor. Placing a sandwich and glass of water on the vanity, he sat down next to her. They sat in companionable silence until Lindy asked, "Why aren't you a therapist?"

He shook his head. "It's one thing to help people you care about. To do it for money? And all the time? No."

Then he set a cell phone on the floor next to her. "Mom keeps a few of these prepaid phones around for emergencies. It's new so nobody else has the number. When you need a break come find me; there's something I want to show you."

"K, thanks."

After he left, Lindy ate a bite of the sandwich, surprising herself with how hungry she was; though it didn't hurt that Michael made a killer sandwich. Then, cross-legged on the bed, she entered a number into the phone from memory. "Hello, Mom?"

It took two hours to get through the things she could do over the phone. After checking on the cat, fast asleep, she headed outside to find James. Before she even made it off the porch the door opened behind her.

"Hold it, young lady!" Michael wore a stern look on his face as he held out the straw hat she had worn yesterday.

"Thanks." Slipping the hat on, she smiled. "And thanks for the sandwich, it was delicious."

As he turned back to the house, Lindy wondered when he found the time to maintain his muscle mass. She had friends who spent hours in the gym every week who didn't look as bulked as he did.

Walking past the parked cars, the heat seemed to shimmer over the gravel. It hadn't been noticeable inside but she was glad to have the hat on out here. She could hear James' distinctive throaty voice and followed it around the side of the barn where he was painting the trim on a window and singing to himself.

"Hi." He smiled at her. "Just give me a couple minutes to finish this."

While waiting, she leaned on a fence post and watched what had to be the cattle walking in from the pasture and heading for the water tank. At least Lindy assumed they were cattle although she had never seen any like these before. Not very large, they were incredibly shaggy with red fur that flopped over their eyes. The calves were adorable, but the horns on some of the cows made her glad she wasn't on the other side of the fence.

"How do you like our Scotties?" James was next to her, watching the herd. "They're very hardy, from the Scottish Highlands."

"I've never been around cows before; they're kind of scary."

"That's okay. These are pretty low maintenance so there shouldn't be a need for you to work with them. Ready to go for a walk?" For someone who had been working in the heat, he seemed as energetic as ever and they headed down the driveway.

James kept up an easygoing prattle as they walked, telling stories about growing up on the farm and misadventures he had gotten into. Around the curve, they entered the welcome shade where the thick shelterbelt marched in both directions down the road. He turned away from town, pointing out the wild plums and chokecherry bushes as their shoes kicked up little puffs of dust from the gravel. Across the road from the farm wasn't a formal shelterbelt but enough volunteer trees and bushes had grown up in the fence line to make the view of the fields speckled with leaves. After a half mile James gestured to a break in that fence line where a driveway appeared.

Lindy gazed around with interest. It was clearly a vacant property, but not in bad shape. The house was a simple, white rectangle with a sagging front porch yet had touches of beauty in the stained glass over the picture window and rose bushes that had run wild along the side. The barn was smaller than the one James had been painting and needed some replacement boards but the roof looked sound. There was an outhouse, a single car garage and a dilapidated chicken coop.

"This was the Andersen farm. Nice old couple; their kids moved away and put it up for sale when Mrs. Andersen died. Mom and Dad bought the whole place for the land. About all we've done here is keep the roofs repaired. I've wanted to fix it up and live here ever since." With shining eyes he pulled a key from his pocket and asked, "Want to explore?"

Poking around in an empty, old farmhouse might not be fun to all women but it sounded like an adventure to Lindy. When James unlocked the front door she was ready to rush right in but he stopped her. Digging in the leg pocket of his cargo shorts he pulled out two disposable masks, little led flashlights and lightweight leather gloves.

"Just to be on the safe side. Nobody has been in here in years and I don't want to take chances on anything like Hantavirus."

Something about putting on the gear made the exploration feel more serious to Lindy yet she was still eager to begin. Stepping inside, her eyes darted around the hallway with dark paneling and a staircase; the door on the left was closed and that on the right was ajar, letting in a little light.

"Oh." Lindy couldn't keep the disappointment from her voice.

"You expected something fancy, didn't you?" James eyes were sympathetic, but also amused. "Remember this was built to house a large family of hard-working farmers; built by hand and meant to last. Look closer."

Momentarily resenting his tone, Lindy curbed her temper and used her flashlight this time. A close examination exposed the quality of craftsmanship in every detail. Expecting the years to have loosened the joints, she was especially surprised to find the banister solid under her hand. A rueful expression and nod acknowledged his point and they moved on.

Pushing open the right hand door revealed what would have been the living room with the picture window. A nice sized space with a brick fireplace; it was difficult to see past the peeling wallpaper and water stained ceiling. James didn't hesitate to pull up the carpet in a corner, letting out a whoop "Hardwood floors!"

The grin crinkling up his eyes and his enthusiasm were infectious and Lindy found herself joining him in seeing the possibilities. "Teal walls? And maybe a round, braided rug in blues and greens."

He bounced up, grabbed her hand and pulled her after him as they continued exploring. The dining room was across the hall, opening into the kitchen which also opened back into the hallway. Across from it was a dark room paneled with oak and begging to be filled with bookcases. They tried to open the back door but it had warped and wouldn't move.

"No bathroom?" asked Lindy.

"Aha!" James flung open a narrow door under the stairs, exposing the tiniest half-bath she had ever seen.

"What about the basement? I didn't see any other doors."

"That's outside by the back door. One of those entrances you have to pull up to open. I think I'll enclose that in a back porch. Imagine having to go outside to get to the washing machine in the winter!"

"Let's go up next."

At the top of the stairs was the full bath. They exchanged glances and comments: "No shower." "The sink can go." "The tub has to stay." "Pink and green tiles?" "Gone!"

Laughing, they looked into the master bedroom and four smaller rooms.

"James, did you notice there aren't any closets? In the entire house!"

"I think there was a coat tree by the front door and I suppose there were wardrobes in these rooms. I wish they were still here. Modern furniture wouldn't feel right but antiques will cost a fortune." He reached for the cord that would pull down the attic access. "Stand back."

Pulling hard, he leaped away, expecting a crash. Instead, the stairs unfolded as smoothly as they had been designed to do, so many years before. Climbing cautiously, he peeked over the edge hopefully. "Damn. It's been cleared out too."

Dusty and tired, they agreed to check the basement another day. After locking up, they shucked off the gloves and masks and sank down onto the front porch steps.

"Why did you wait until now to start on this?" Lindy asked, fanning her hot face with her hat.

"Because I know my limitations. I can handle the electric and I'm so-so with woodworking, but a job like this done right needs more than that. Jeffrey has offered to help; he's brilliant at carpentry and this is a challenge that will keep him occupied. I'll have to hire a plumber..."

"Ahem." Lindy interrupted.

"What?"

"Did I ever mention what my dad does?"

"No, I don't think so." James looked puzzled.

"He's a plumber and I spent every summer helping him until I finished high school."

James grabbed her hand and started shaking it vigorously, "Lindy, you're hired."

Laughing, she pulled away. "You can't pay me! I'm not licensed. But I'm volunteering. I want in."

When Pat got home from work that evening she was surprised not to find anyone outside. Instead, everyone was gathered around the dining table with pads of paper, busily scribbling notes.

"What's all this?"

Jeffrey raised his eyebrows at James who responded with a gesture that released responsibility to him. Turning back to his mother, Jeffrey explained, "We're working on the to-do list for the Andersen farm. And budgets, schedules and plans. Since I'll be on site, I'll be the project manager. Everyone else is basically limited to weekends after next week except for Michael. Unless he changes his mind about taking a rat in and getting the restaurant shut down..."

Hoots of laughter followed this old joke but Pat knew they would all genuinely miss Michael when he returned to his hectic schedule as head chef. He spoke up then, "I'm serious about funding all the plumbing costs though. I'll give you a check for $2,000 to start with and Lindy can let me know when she needs more."

James protested, "Michael, you don't need..."

"Stop. You know I want to be here helping more than anything. Just wait until the twins find out you've started this when they can't be here either."

"Ha! At least they'll get some free time between the end of their internships and before classes start up again. Jeffrey, make sure you save up some hard labor jobs for then." James had relaxed again.

"Wait a minute. I'm confused." Pat rapped on the table firmly. "Why is Lindy doing the plumbing budget?"

After explaining her experience and willingness to tackle the job, Lindy leaned back in her chair with a very satisfied smile. She had noticed that Pat never questioned her inclusion in the project or if she would be around. For the first time in her life she was experiencing something she had only imagined; she was putting down roots in a real home.

The conversations split then as everyone discussed and decided on what would be done the next day. Steve and James were leaning over a sketch of the property and decided they would walk back over after dinner to verify placements. It was too late in the season to start a garden (and nobody would have time to tend it), but Steve would till up a plot and plant a cover crop of comfrey. He had also been experimenting with grafting fruit trees onto hardy root stock so had a nice selection to plant. What was left of the apple trees there were old and splitting, badly needing replacement.

Michael scooted closer to Lindy and handed her a list. "All of these are included in the plumbing budget."

She scanned the list with interest. "Are you sure? These are going to add up fast."

"Do you think my money will give me more satisfaction sitting in the bank?" he asked as he stood up and headed for the kitchen. Lindy followed to help bring dinner to the table.

After dinner Pat relaxed on the porch, watching Steve and James walk down the driveway. Even with the troubles afflicting Jeffrey and Lindy, she hadn't felt so happy in a long time. Every year she worried a little more about the boys growing apart and losing the ties that drew them back to the farm. With Michael and the twins four hours away in the city and Jeffrey's university three hours in the other direction it was impossible to feel the same closeness they had grown up with. Even James she didn't see as often as she would like although he was less than an hour away. Now, though, they would be home every chance they could and when the Andersen house was livable, Jeffrey and James would bach in it until circumstances changed again.

Jeffrey stepped through the screen door and sat next to his mom; a damp dish towel slung over his shoulder. "I heard today that Melissa is being offered the position of Dean of Math and CompSci."

His shoulders seemed bowed under a heavy weight as he gave a sardonic chuckle. "Maybe I should try for alimony."

"Are you...?" she paused. They had never interfered in the boys' finances before, so how to ask?

"No, I'm fine. We always kept separate accounts and the house will sell fast. The rumor is that I'll be offered a hefty settlement to walk away from my tenureship. I can't believe I won't be teaching. I've always wanted to teach more than anything else." Straightening his back, he drew a deep breath before continuing, "You know how that foundation has been after me to write a mathematical theory text? I think I'll take them up on it this winter.

"And next summer I'd like to build my own place, maybe a cabin." Stretching his arm around her shoulders for a hug, he kissed her on the cheek. "I'm okay, Mom. Don't expect me to be happy, but know I'll be fine." And he headed back inside to finish drying dishes.

5 FRIDAY

The harsh roar of motorcycles in the yard broke the stillness of the night, reverberating through open windows and jolting everyone out of deep sleep. By the time Lindy opened her door the men were already peering out the front windows. They had obviously rolled out of their beds, into the nearest footwear and came straight down. She would have been amused by the sight of them all in boxers, t-shirts and untied shoes except they were also each holding a shotgun.

By now the bikes had shut down and the expressions on their faces had acquired varying degrees of exasperation.

"Who is it?" Lindy asked.

Steve replied, "It's the twins."

"Why are you still holding the guns like that then?"

"Because we don't know if someone is chasing them yet."

"Now, Steve. Michael said they've been behaving themselves." Pat spoke from the stairs.

"Ha!" he grumbled.

By this time two tall, leather-clad young men had entered and were shucking backpacks off. As the first one strode past to hug Pat, Lindy started to get an inkling of why there might be trouble following. Blonde, gorgeous, with a confident stride and easy charm, he made Hollywood stars seem like posers. Then his brother joined him and the effect was doubled...if one could ignore the two black eyes and a swollen nose that was clearly broken.

"Alex! Your face!" Pat looked dismayed as she studied the damage.

"It's not that bad, Mom. There was a little problem at work but it's over. Can we talk about it in the morning?"

As fascinating as this drama was, Lindy was more intrigued by the reactions of the men she had become friends with this week. Steve looked fed up and was already moving past to go back upstairs; Michael seemed disappointed but was shrugging it off. Jeffrey was leaning against the wall wearing a bemused smirk and James looked angry. When he met her eyes she shrugged, mouthed 'nite' and slipped back into her room. As the noise from the hall died down and she eased back to sleep, Lindy wondered how this would change the family dynamics.

Lindy woke to some strange noises in the corner of the room and when she padded over to investigate found Mama Cass (as she had been informed the cat's name was) had four new kittens: a calico, one dark orange, one orange and white and a black and white. Mama looked quite contented and the babies were as cute as babies always are. Lindy couldn't resist curling up next to the little family and watching, so was later than usual leaving her room.

The sound of raised voices slowed her even more as she approached the dining area. Tempers were clearly flaring so she ducked into the kitchen for a glass of orange juice and to wait for a quiet moment. Michael's voice cut across the others and silence fell. That was her cue. As she entered, she ignored the tension and told them about the newest additions to their cat population.

Pat seemed relieved to see her; something about the way she pursed her mouth and rolled her eyes reminded Lindy of her preference not to be around when the 'boys' were adjusting to each other. Then she stood, stating that it was nearly time for her to go, but first, "Lindy, this is Adam and Alex, looking a little worse for wear. Boys, Lindy is my friend. I'll see you tonight and everyone stay safe."

Adam half stood and leaned across the table to shake Lindy's hand. He turned on a full smile and met her eyes but she was relieved to feel no spark. Hopefully John had left her immune to the charms of handsome men. After she greeted Alex, the conversation turned to plans for the day. It was quickly agreed that they would keep the arrangements settled on the evening before. James and Lindy would take his car to town to run errands, visit the DIY center and kick off the shopping to get started on the house repairs. Jeffrey and Michael would use Steve's truck and trailer to fetch everything Jeffrey had left in storage. Mostly, he wanted his tools, but felt it was ridiculous to keep the storage locker when he wouldn't be moving back. Steve was going to do his normal Friday routine of harvesting and prepping for the farmer's market on Saturday. And Pat had already informed the twins that 'since they were there' the back of the barn needed scraping.

"I'm nervous about maybe running into John in town," Lindy confessed as they were splitting up in the yard.

Michael pulled her into a hug, "It's unlikely he hung around after the fire and James won't let you out of his sight. I'm more worried about one of Alex's jealous husbands showing up." This was said with a wink as he stepped away.

"Hey! She wasn't married, just...well, um...involved. Say, Lindy, we could come along today in case you need backup."

"Thanks, but I wouldn't want to take you away from the barn." The expression on Alex's face had her helplessly giggling as she got into James' car. She sobered quickly as they drove towards town. The low-hanging grey clouds seemed to reflect her uneasy mood and the very atmosphere felt like it was bearing down on her.

"Incredible how the change in pressure from a weather front can affect us, isn't it?" James asked sympathetically.

"That obvious?" Lindy hugged herself.

"Some people are more sensitive than others. You might end up being one of those wise old folks who can predict the weather. I've always thought they must be handy to have around. Did you know during WW2 there were no weather forecasts given in England? They didn't want to give the Germans any advantage in planning attacks. Years of not knowing if it was supposed to rain or storm."

James' easy conversation was like a balm to her frazzled nerves. Lindy closed her eyes and let his voice flow over and silence the worries that had been clamoring in her mind. It wasn't until they had parked in front of the post office that he stopped. And that began their day of errands; at every place she was nervous and alert until she became focused on what she was doing. James stayed by her side throughout and kept a careful eye out for trouble. It wasn't until they arrived at a diner for lunch and she happened to glance over while he was exiting the car that she identified the profile at the back of his waist.

"James!" she hissed, trying not to shout. "Do you have a gun?"

He sat back down in the car. "Of course. I always carry one in town. I have been at the farm too lately. Does it bother you?"

Lindy's mouth twitched and her fingers pulled on her purse strap for a moment before she burst out, "Can I shoot it?"

At James' surprised laugh she explained, "I've got my concealed carry permit, but I've never even held a gun. I was going to take a handgun safety course, but I had to get my car fixed and other stuff came up.

"Did you see the movie RED? Helen Mirren's character, so elegant and deadly." With a mischievous smile she added, "That's what I want to be when I grow up."

James just looked at her, as though he was reevaluating what he had thought, then nodded. "You're in luck. Steve is an NRA instructor. I'd take you shopping for your own gun but it's really his area of expertise."

With that, they headed inside for lunch and the rain began to fall.

Back at the farm Steve slipped through the gate next to the water tank. As he worked his way through the small herd he watched for any problems: a matted eye, favored hoof, sign of mastitis or someone hanging back but they all looked fine. A couple of the older cows shoved their wet noses against him, demanding attention so he obliged by scratching their backs. Lindy would have been surprised to see him like this, relaxed and peaceful, but it was unlikely that she or anyone else would. He never let down his guard when people were around. The time spent in the National Guard had left him with jagged scars on his back but it was the invisible scars that affected him the most. The therapy sessions had been worse than useless because he was left frustrated and unable to talk about it at all, not even with family. Moving home turned out to be a blessing; in these peaceful environs the nightmares had lost their potency then stopped entirely.

Past the cattle he leaned on another gate, this one kept the herd out of the pen behind the barn. He could see the twins had put their time to good use that morning. The barn was scraped clear of old peeling paint as high as they could reach from the ground, the scaffolding had been set up and they were well on the way of getting the middle section done as well. The taunts and jokes were flying back and forth in a good-natured manner. Steve was grateful they weren't trying to sing; unlike the rest of the family these two were tone-deaf and painful to listen to when they did try.

Finally, he interrupted to ask if they were ready for a break and they came flying down recklessly. Inside the house, eating a quick meal of sandwiches and raw veggies, Steve asked if they would keep on if it rained.

"Depends on the wind and angle. If the wood is getting soaked, we'll stop and help you." answered Alex. "Tell us about Lindy?"

"Why? What do you think?" Steve countered.

Adam and Alex shared a glance then spoke together in a way that disconcerted strangers, finishing each other's thoughts and sentences so easily that it was difficult to keep track of who said what. "Nice, but not insipid. Pretty, but not vain. She seems to fit here. She might cause trouble, but not on purpose. Mom would kill anyone who made her uncomfortable. And she's not the only one. Unless someone royally screws up, she won't be moving away again. And she's not into either of us."

"Hmm," mused Steve, thinking that the twins had a tendency to see and understand more than people gave them credit for. He then proceeded to tell Lindy's story.

By the end of the tale, both young men were on their feet and pacing the length of the room. "Well! Has there been any sign of this John tracking her here yet? It's only a matter of time once she returns to work. Especially if his relatives get involved. Shouldn't we be closing the driveway gate? At least at night. And we should dig out our radios so you can reach us if anyone shows up while we're out of sight. Shame the dogs are both at awkward ages to be any use; one too old and the other too young."

Steve was startled by their reactions and intelligent suggestions. Then his eyes narrowed as he considered why they sounded so experienced. "How many husbands?"

"None! That we knew of at least. A few fathers, brothers and boyfriends though. And the odd girlfriend."

Steve sighed. He hated their cavalier attitude towards women, but still understood how it happened. Girls and women, even those old enough to know better, had been flinging themselves at the twins since they hit puberty. And with the advent of hormones, the boys hadn't been fighting them off.

"Check the closet junk box for the radios. There should be plenty of fresh batteries in the pantry cabinet. I've got heaps of produce to get sorted so the rest we can talk about tonight."

James and Lindy spent three hours at the DIY store that afternoon. She chose a basic, yet ample selection of plumbing tools because there were none at the farm. They then proceeded to arrange to have a massive amount of goods delivered: lumber, water heater, toilets, sinks, windows, siding … the list went on.

Finally, Lindy drew him aside. "James, even with Michael's help, the cost of this is huge! How are you going to pay?"

Seeming to change the subject he asked, "Are you familiar with Biddie Newell's books?"

"Ugh, yes. They're all over the place. I can't stand them, but some of my friends love her. Why?"

"Lindy, you're wonderful for my ego. That's my pen name. I've been writing that drivel for the last eight years. I've even considered writing full time, but I'm afraid my brain would explode. It's paid well for a hobby though; so I can't go crazy spending, but I won't go into debt either."

"I'm... You're... But..." she sputtered to a halt, trying to work out what to say first. "Why didn't your brothers say anything?"

"They don't know. Never asked." He shrugged. Actually, he had let them believe he was a self-published indie writer. Even in a close-knit family it was nice to have some secrets.

"Shall we finish this? Luckily all the windows other than the picture window are standard size, but we need to special order it. I'm afraid the stained glass will have to come out, but maybe we can use it somehow. I'd hate to lose it entirely." James was still talking as he headed back to the counter. Lindy stared after him in shock before shaking herself and hurrying to catch up.

It was after four when they had loaded down the trunk and back seat of his car with tools and hardware. As they sank into their seats with tired sighs, James asked her if she still wanted to swing by her workplace before going home.

"Yes, I'd rather talk to them before Monday morning."

They both smiled when they saw Pat's tank of a car in the parking lot. Lindy said she wouldn't be long. She just wanted to make sure they knew her situation and check on the security. It was forty minutes before she came back out and threw herself into the car.

"Lindy," he got no further before she burst into tears. Seeing the workers begin exiting the building, James drove out of the lot and down the street before parking. Then, leaning over and wrapping his arms around her, he held on while she cried herself out. Finally, the sobs eased and she sat up, pulling tissues out of her purse and struggling to regain her composure.

Looking out the window, she spoke in a monotone, "They let me go. So very sorry but it's too dangerous to keep me. Here is a nice severance check. Good luck."

Now her voice started to rise, "Anonymous letters, harassing calls, graffiti, tires slashed, an attempted arson; why is he doing this? He broke up with me!"

"You didn't stick to the script. He expected you to crawl to him; begging him to take you back. Then he would have you helpless and dependent forever. You weren't supposed to escape and have family to turn to. You don't have many friends here, do you?"

"Not really. My close friends are in towns I used to live in, here it's more friendly acquaintances. You think he targeted me because I was alone here?"

"Almost definitely." His lips pressed into a thin line as his fingers tapped on the steering wheel.

"Can we go home now please, James?"

"Of course."

Farther away, Jeffrey was not having a good day. Somehow the rumor mill had found out he was in town and the Dean's secretary called, asking him to stop in for a meeting.

"Howard. What's the problem? Since I'm on sabbatical you don't need my input on university issues." Jeffrey came straight to the point even though he knew the Dean would twist and slither around the conversation for as long as he could. When Jeffrey finally got the facts he learned that the Dean wanted him officially gone so they could replace him immediately. That would have been okay, but the severance offer was a blatant insult of two months' salary and he exploded. Pulling out all the stops, he threatened to spend every day of the next year in his office and wandering the department wearing cut-off shorts and a crop top. Then, he swore, he would come back to his position and make Melissa's time as department dean as unpleasant and disruptive as only an ex-husband could. And with the magic word 'tenure' there was nothing they could do to stop him.

After a solid two hours of shouting, Jeffrey walked out a free man with a check for two years' salary. He had known he had the upper hand, but hadn't realized quite how obsessed the Dean was with keeping up appearances. Wasting no time, he went to the bank to deposit the check; although everything was on paper and legal, he didn't trust them. After which, he drove back to the storage unit where Michael had finished loading the trailer and was calmly waiting. Together they made quick work of fitting the rest of his possessions into the back of the truck and began the three hour drive home.

That drive was cathartic for both of them. They talked about the effects of becoming suddenly single again and the differences and surprising similarities between reaching that state through death and divorce.

Rain pattered down, windshield wipers thwapped rhythmically, windows fogged up and two brothers reforged bonds that divergent lives had withered.

Pat had stopped at the grocery store to pick up some bananas and fresh pineapple before heading home. James ran out to help carry the bags and fill her in on what had happened. She was so startled that she stood in the rain with her mouth open.

"How did they keep all that out of the company gossip?" she exclaimed. "I chat with the night security guard every morning. He couldn't keep a secret to save his life. Impossible! I don't believe it; there's something else going on."

"Well, either way, Lindy is out of a job and frightened," James replied.

Sympathy replaced the indignation on her face. "Oh, that poor girl. Where is she?"

"On the sofa with the twins. They're 'consoling' her." James expression was carefully neutral while Pat's displayed consternation.

Hurrying inside, she stopped short in the living room. Adam was massaging Lindy's shoulders at one end of the sofa while Alex rubbed her feet at the other.

"Hi, Pat," Lindy called. "I would be very annoyed at being given a 'mandatory spa treatment' if it didn't feel so good. But now that I have two little brothers, can I boss them around? I have a lot of resentment from being the youngest to work through."

"Please do," Pat said dryly. "You can start by sending them to the kitchen to put away the groceries and prepare dinner."

As the twins sheepishly filed past James, relieving him of the bags, Pat sat next to Lindy to talk.

Lindy began, "I assume James told you my latest. I'm wondering if I should go back to my parents and work as an apprentice plumber."

"Dear, you do whatever you want, but don't rush into anything when your emotions are high. Will you stay for at least another week? I was really looking forward to your company."

While they were talking Steve had come through the front door with two very wet dogs. He and James grabbed towels off wall hooks and were rubbing them dry before they tracked mud in. Lindy watched and knew that although part of her wanted to run to her parents, a much larger part wanted to stay. Emotion welled up as she turned back to Pat and threw her arms around her. "I can't go yet! I would miss you too much."

Tears ran freely as they clung to each other while the men stood by the door feeling awkward. Interruption came when the puppy jumped onto the sofa and tried to force his way in between them.

"Biff! Down!" The dog was much too excited to listen as it wiggled all over trying to lick both their faces at once. Laughter replaced the tears as Lindy ended up on the floor, wrestling with the energetic bundle of damp fur. Mellow gave up on dignity and attempted to join in by sitting on her.

At dinner the family agreed to postpone serious discussion until Michael and Jeffrey returned. Instead, the twins talked about school and their plans. They were both going into their third year at university that fall; Adam wanted to be a large animal vet and Alex was going for a combination of Ag Science/Business. Both admitted that choosing summer jobs so they could work at the same company was a mistake although Alex had compounded the problem by dating the boss's girlfriend.

"Will losing your jobs make it hard to pay for next semester?" Lindy asked.

"Not really. We both have basketball scholarships and work on campus during the school year. If things are tight we can pick up extra by tutoring."

As they cleared the table, James asked Lindy what she was thinking. "I was feeling sorry for all those unsuspecting college girls that must fall for them every year."

"Hmm, I suppose they could wear bags over their heads…" He pretended to duck as she punched him on the arm. "Don't borrow trouble. They are experts at letting people down gently."

"People…men, too?" she looked startled.

"I've never asked," James replied with an unconcerned shrug.

The family settled in the living room to wait. Mama Cass had decided to take a break from the kittens and was draped across Pat's lap. Mellow slept across Steve's feet and Biff leaned against Adam's leg while nursing a scratched nose.

"Do you need help in the morning, Steve?" asked Pat.

"Well, if the sun is out, the market will be packed. I could use Adam." Adam's easy-going nod acknowledged that he would be a draw to pull in customers. "If the truck is full, can I use the Tank, Mom? And since James hasn't unloaded his car yet, can we take your car too, Lindy? I'll be loading at 5:30 if any volunteers are available."

It was after eight before the truck turned into the driveway. Michael pulled right into the pole barn and parked. When he and Jeffrey went into the house, Alex grabbed a jacket and ran down to close and lock the gate across the driveway. Conversations flew around the room as everyone caught up on the day's events. At last, discussion turned to the future.

Steve started in on security, "The risk is still low while he doesn't know where Lindy is, but we won't know when he does find out so should plan on being cautious going forward. Tomorrow afternoon I'll begin training Lindy on gun safety. Mom, I'd like you there as a refresher. You haven't done much shooting for a few years. And, Jeffrey, you too.

"I'd like Adam to pick up more radios tomorrow so we can all keep in touch here and at the Andersen farm. Only two of our old ones still work.

"James, will you consider adding a driveway gate over there as your first project? It would be good as protection from potential vandals also."

Everybody nodded in agreement and Lindy asked, "What are we doing in the morning?"

"It will be too wet to do anything outside," replied Pat. "So we'll be canning produce. That will easily keep us busy this weekend."

6 SATURDAY

It was still dark when Lindy woke. Peering blearily at the bedside clock showed it to be after five. Dressing quickly, she joined the others in the kitchen. She wasn't the only one still yawning and Michael was pouring cups of coffee. All too soon Steve began herding them to the basement door. Directing the twins out to load the folding tables into the Tank, he led the rest of them down to where rows of baskets of neatly bundled vegetables and herbs waited in the cool belowground atmosphere.

With so many willing helpers, everything was quickly loaded and Steve and Adam drove away. Lindy lingered in the basement, gazing in consternation at the buckets and baskets still remaining. She turned to Pat. "All this?"

"We're having a good year. Tomatoes and beans are coming in strong now so that's what we'll concentrate on this weekend. Peas are almost finished so those will mostly be used fresh. Would you like to see what I call my deep pantry?" Pat led the way to a wooden door and flipped the light switch to reveal a large room filled with rows of metal racks. Each one holding dozens of quart jars or empty spaces where jars obviously once sat. "I aim for two years' worth of produce. We use from the front of the shelves and load new jars from the rear. Over there are jams, jellies and fruit. Back by the wall are meats."

"But you couldn't use so much with two people!"

"Oh, no. Lots go home with the boys whenever they visit." A pensive look crossed Pat's face. "Something has me nervous this year. I want to fill this room to bursting."

They each paused to pick up buckets of beans before returning to the kitchen where the delectable odors from Michael's cooking swirled around them. "We can snap beans on the front porch after breakfast and I'll tell you stories about raising six boys on a farmer's income.

"Sometimes I threaten to have the old wood-burning cook stove that Matt's mother used brought back in just to see how Michael could handle that." A muttered 'ha!' could be heard from the stove area. "Which reminds me; I heard that propane was probably as low as it's going this summer so we should get the tank filled. James, you should call about having a tank put back in at the Andersen's. Theirs was rented and is long gone."

"Good idea. Thanks, Mom." James flipped open the little notebook he was carrying around to keep track of his to-do list.

At breakfast, after recovering from the explosion of flavor that was Michael's version of French toast, Lindy was staring off into space with her fork in midair. The others were glancing at each other with concern by the time she began speaking, "I think...James should quit his job and concentrate on writing, but not that crap he writes now."

Everybody looked at James, only to see him sitting with his chin in his hand watching Lindy with a bemused smile.

"A space opera or historical fiction, something completely different. And if we put in a workshop then he could learn to build his own wardrobes, made properly so they would be right for the house. Not frilly, but solid and lasting like the banister." Lindy focused back on her companions and realized everyone was staring at her. "Oh! Sorry. Ignore that."

"But you're right. I should try writing something I would enjoy and if it didn't work out finding another tech writer position would be easy enough. I'm not sure how good at cabinetry I'd be though."

Stepping around the table he paused to plant a kiss on the top of her head then announced he was going to do chores.

Michael prepped for canning in the kitchen while the rest hauled buckets of beans and bowls onto the porch and began snapping. With four busy pairs of hands working there were soon enough to begin the first batch. Rows of freshly washed jars were lined up on the island; James joined Michael and washed the beans while Michael filled the jars. All the burners were full on the stovetop; two held pressure canners and two had large kettles of steaming water. Even with the windows and doors open it began to feel a bit like a sauna. As the morning wore on, the rows of empty jars were replaced with hot, full jars. The workers rotated out of the kitchen to take a break from the heat; Pat and Lindy took over canning then they were replaced by Jeffrey and Alex.

By eleven all the beans had been snapped, washed and waited on the canners. Alex and James began shifting some of the jars out onto the back porch to finish cooling and free more counter space.

Michael stretched and asked Lindy if she would like to do a milk run with him.

"I don't know what that is," she replied.

"Three miles from here is a semi-retired farmer who keeps some jersey cows for milk. He hates chickens so we trade eggs for milk then he sells the extra eggs to his other customers."

"But what vehicle can we take?"

"Ah, good question. Jeffrey, would you mind if we unloaded the truck?"

"No problem," answered Jeffrey. "We can leave the trailer in the shed and store the truck load in the smithy."

All four men went out to make the changes while Lindy and Pat kept an eye on the timers and filled more jars. Pat had years of experience, but Lindy found it hard to wait for the canners to depressurize before they started another batch.

"If we had more canners, could we move the finished ones off the stove to cool and start the others?" Lindy asked.

"Sure, but canners are expensive and heavy to move when full. Although with all the extra help now, we could handle the weight. Hmm, I wonder…"

When Michael came to get Lindy, Pat stopped him and asked, "Will you ask Hansen to spread the word that we're looking for used pressure canners? Some of his customers might have one tucked away after they stopped gardening."

"Sure, Mom. Lindy, are you ready?"

Twenty dozen eggs were already loaded in the back of the truck so they were quickly on the road.

Michael drove slowly, enjoying the freshly washed countryside. The afternoon promised to be hot and steamy, but for the moment it was still comfortable. He realized Lindy was looking at him and when he met her eyes she asked, "Is it hard to leave the farm and return to a normal life?"

Knowing she wanted a serious answer, he took his time. "When I was young, I couldn't wait to get away. Everything was new and exciting; I was following my dream. Then, later, it was great to visit but going home meant Amelia and I could be alone again and that's where we were happiest.

"Now," his voice dropped to a level that hurt to hear. "It's the hardest thing to leave here. And it's empty again." The truck had rolled to a stop and Lindy reached over and squeezed his arm. She didn't know what to say.

Michael looked at her and patted the hand on his arm. "It doesn't help that everyone else gets to be here getting to know our new little sis better." Then he winked to reassure her.

"Would it be any good if I came to visit? I haven't been there before. In fact, if you could handle it, we could all take turns visiting. Pat and Steve never have time away. And if you were the one who called and said you would like some company it wouldn't be an imposition."

"I…that might work. Let me think on it first." Turning his attention back to the road, they moved on.

They returned home triumphant; carrying in not just the half gallon jars of milk, but also an old pressure canner and dozens of dusty, empty quart jars.

"Bob Hansen had these in his basement. He wanted $50 for the lot but I got him to throw in some cheese too." Michael was looking very pleased with himself.

"A Presto. Someone call Adam and have him check at the hardware store for a new gasket. Oh, good. They put the pressure weight inside." Pat smiled at Michael. "Another one and…"

"I told him we wanted three more," he interrupted.

"Three!" she exclaimed.

"The Andersen house was stripped bare. We should start going to auctions too. It's going to take a lot to make it a working home again."

When Steve came home it was obvious that he was tired; dealing with crowds of people was always a strain on his nerves. The others pitched in to unload the unsold goods and tables. Adam arrived not long after with his shopping and they sat down to a late lunch.

The conversation centered on the morning and some of the more entertaining characters who frequented the farmer's market. Then Alex asked, "Why don't Adam and I take over the market side for the rest of the summer? We've both helped with it before and we're at loose ends now."

"Can I help next week?" Lindy asked.

Adam and Steve exchanged glances before Steve quietly asked, "Lindy, do you know a blonde woman, very tanned, who wears western clothes?"

She stiffened, "That would describe John's sister or his mother. Where did you see her?"

"She was working the market, showing your picture around and asking if anyone had seen you. I called the police, but she was gone before they arrived. They suggested you stay away from town if possible."

Adam pulled out his phone and showed her a picture of the woman in question.

"His mother." Lindy's face flushed and she dashed from the room. James caught up with her in the front yard where she was striding back and forth swearing angrily.

She whirled on James and said, "I'm sick of being scared. I don't want them controlling what I do and where I go. I want...I want to send them a message to leave me alone!"

James gripped her arms to hold her focus. "Okay, let's start by sending a letter through a lawyer. We can threaten a lawsuit if the harassment doesn't end."

"Oh, they would hate that." Then she sagged. "But John will still be out there."

"We will keep you safe. Always."

Trusting that James would deal with the crisis, Steve, Pat and Jeffrey went to the study to get the gear for the gun lesson that afternoon. It was a cozy room with bookcases, heavy drapes and a roll top desk. This was where they kept the farm records and did paperwork. On one side, what appeared to be a built-in cabinet swung open to reveal a large gun safe. The left-hand side contained the hunting rifles and shotguns that had accumulated during the growing years of six active boys. On the right were four AR-15s; two were Steve's and the others belonged to the twins. The center shelves held a variety of handguns and these were what Steve selected from today.

"Does anyone know anything about John's family? Are they likely to escalate?" Steve asked as he worked.

"Not really," Pat answered. "They aren't local so the police didn't have anything on them. They were clean of outstanding warrants. I doubt Lindy saw any of that side of them."

"Humph." Steve grunted as he efficiently filled two bags with guns, boxes of ammo, magazines and ear protection. Reflecting on how little she had with her, he added a baseball cap and lightweight goggles.

"Ready?" Receiving nods, he handed one bag to Jeffrey and asked Pat to bring a tarp. Out front, he asked James if he was coming too.

"No, I'm going to cut down thistles in the pasture. Have fun."

The group headed behind the house and over the hill. At the bottom was a flat space with a tall berm of dirt at one end. Pat tacked up paper targets on a wooden rack in front of the berm while Jeffrey laid out the tarp with rocks to keep it down. Steve went through the safety rules for gun use patiently and thoroughly. Lindy was clearly nervous and excited when he finally let her load a revolver and take her first shot. When she swung around he quickly disarmed her and went through muzzle awareness again.

After trying three different sizes of revolvers, Lindy sat in the grass with Jeffrey and watched Pat draw and shoot the small pistol she carried in a belly band under her shirt.

"What's the tarp for?"

Jeffrey pointed to the brass falling down as Pat fired. "It makes cleanup easier."

"Why did you stop shooting?"

"Ah, well, Melissa hated guns. Wouldn't have any in the house and gave me grief if I went shooting here. It was just easier."

After Jeffrey took his turn, Steve had Lindy try a 9mm. Her arms and shoulders were beginning to ache from the unaccustomed activity when she had shot through two magazines so he called it quits after that. On the walk back over the hill, he asked for her opinions on what she had tried.

"I loved how the 357 felt and the accuracy. It didn't push my hands up either. But I don't know how easy it would be to carry around all the time. It's pretty big. The last one..."

"The Beretta."

"Yes, that was nice but I'm not comfortable with the slide. Can I practice more with it?"

"That would be best. I'm going to ask you not to practice without someone else with you for now though. I don't want you developing any bad habits. We can give you a day to recover then try some more on Monday."

Back at the house, Lindy watched Steve set out the guns on the long table in the laundry room and had her first lesson in gun cleaning.

Adam leaned on his scythe and gazed over the far pasture. "Isn't it funny how satisfied you can feel at the end of a dirty, sweaty job?"

He and Alex had decided it was too humid to prime the back of the barn and joined James in his fight against the thistles. As long as they got to them before the noxious weeds blossomed, they were ahead of the battle.

"You won't be too tired for the race tomorrow?" teased James. Each year they cut the smallest hay meadow by hand, competing to see who was the fastest with a scythe. Steve was always a clear winner, but that didn't stop the twins from trying their hardest.

Alex looked hopeful, "If either of us beat Steve then we'll both enter in the County Fair race. I wonder if Mom would make us kilts."

"You're not even Scottish!" James said in exasperation.

"Doesn't matter. The girls would love it."

As they hiked back to the farm, the discussion continued on how they would look the most impressive until James finally interrupted. "Don't you ever want more than a fling? Something real like Mom and Dad had?"

The twins both shrugged, "No, not really. Not now at least. We're only 21 after all. We both work hard at school to keep our grades up and we don't want to have to work hard on a relationship too. What about you? You're almost thirty."

"I've...come close a couple times. Remember, I dated Cindy for three years. It just didn't work out."

Adam laughed. "I remember you moved in with Laura and couldn't move back out fast enough."

"Yeah, well, some people you get along fine with until you're always together; then you drive each other crazy."

A screech pulled their eyes up to where a hawk circled high above in the pale blue sky. Denied its easy meal of chicken, it searched for gophers, mice or rabbits. The sight returned their thoughts to the present while an echo tied them to every other hot summer day spent on the farm.

"Anyone want to go fishing in the morning?" Adam asked hopefully.

"The lake? Yeah, but we should ask Steve first. If it's not safe for Lindy but she wanted to go..." Alex looked pensive.

It turned out that Steve thought it would be fine as long as they stayed on the north end where there wasn't much boat traffic and no amenities to attract people. Lindy hadn't been fishing for years and protested that she didn't have a license.

"You're not the only one," Pat reassured her. "But they're easy to get online. The boys will want to get an early start so we can get those taken care of while they gather up all the gear."

"Is every day this busy when they're all home?" Lindy asked.

"Mostly until the last three or four days of their visit when they slow down. I'm not sure how it will be this year since only Michael is leaving next weekend. If Jeffrey and James treat their renovation like a job, then it will probably be like every other year."

7 SUNDAY

The pre-dawn lightening of the sky found the family loading up the Tank and the truck. The chickens and pigs were startled to be woken for such an early feeding and Biff was very upset at being left behind but all the people were in a great mood.

It was an eight mile drive to the deserted end of the lake and they continued until the track disappeared into the grass. Piling out, everyone grabbed armloads of gear and set off down a faint trail leading to the water. The trail cut down through the edge of a bank overhung with trees and onto a mud and rock shore. Michael stopped there with the cooler while James, Pat and Lindy turned right and the others headed left. If they were successful then Michael would be frying fish for breakfast, otherwise it would be a more prosaic meal although still cooked over a campfire.

Spreading out, fishing spots were chosen. It took quite a bit of wiggling to get the folding camp chairs steady between a tendency to tip on rocks or sink into the mud, but finally they were all settled with lines cast. Then the sun rose grandly and spilled an orange glow across the shimmering gray of the water. Birds that had been disturbed by the arrival of people began to call out and bugs were visible skittering upon the surface.

While the sensible side of Lindy knew this beauty happened every morning, the side of her that craved serenity was in awe that she was in this place at this moment. Dimly aware of the others reeling in lines, replacing bait and recasting, she was content to watch the morning happen.

Not until the smell of bacon and eggs wafted across and woke her hunger did she look around and notice how late it was. Reeling in her line and empty hook, she joined the rest for a breakfast for unsuccessful fishers. After a vigorous discussion led by Jeffrey and Alex, it was agreed that they would try for a while longer and they spread out again. Something had changed in the interval because barely had the hooks sunk before the bites began. They each had no trouble catching two or three decent sized fish and were triumphant as they hauled everything back to the vehicles.

Everyone was expected to help clean fish and while her first try was messy, Lindy soon got the basics down. Even though breakfast had been more of a brunch, they were all ready for another meal with Michael grilling fish and fresh vegetables.

"Why does fishing make me so hungry?" asked Lindy between bites.

"Fresh air, an early start, anticipation, our own private chef..." Adam rattled off and started a round of applause for Michael.

"As long as you're so appreciative, you can clean up." And laughing good-naturedly, they did.

Soon after, all six men had gathered with their scythes and they headed to a small fenced-in meadow. Pat had Biff on a lead to keep him safely out of the way while Mellow opted to take a nap instead.

At the meadow James explained, "This was another of Dad's passions; he was champion at the fair most years until his back began bothering him. So we keep it up for him. We line up and race across the meadow and whoever finishes first wins."

"How do you keep from hitting each other?" Lindy asked, eyeing the wicked looking blades nervously.

"Oh, we space widely out, then on the way back we cut the in-between swathes. The whole meadow is only about an acre so six of us finish fairly quickly." He looked rueful for a moment. "Jeffrey and I are usually pulling up the rear; too much time sitting at desks these days."

Pat and Lindy moved to stand outside the fence on the far end and prepared to cheer them on while the guys stripped off their shirts and lined up. Pat chuckled, "Tradition."

Then, taking a deep breath, she shouted "Go!"

Lindy climbed the fence to get a better view as the men began sweeping through the waist-high grass. The twins pulled ahead quickly but Steve was close behind and gained on them as they passed the midway point. While they were fast, his movements were smooth and controlled. He reached the fence line one slice ahead of his pursuers and waved at the applause. Michael followed the twins; his build was designed for strength, not speed but he wasn't even winded. James, then Jeffrey joined the others, laughing and panting. Taking the time to sharpen the blades, each lined up again at an unmown section and began the return.

Lindy gasped as her eye caught ragged scar tissue. "Steve's back! What happened?"

Pat gripped the fence rail tightly and said, "Afghanistan. That's all I know. He won't talk about it."

Lindy slipped off the fence and hugged Pat. "He's here now," she murmured. And Pat knew exactly what she meant.

Taking their time walking back around, they found Michael waiting for Lindy. "I think mine will be the best fit for you and everyone should try it once."

She felt very slow and awkward, swinging the scythe around, but nobody teased and she kept going until her shoulders ached. Resting, she watched Adam, Alex and Steve finishing up the cutting. "How long does it take to get any good?"

"Quite a while," answered Michael. "But if you want to try again feel free to use mine. Just keep to the grass."

"What will happen to this grass now?"

"In two or three days we'll come down and rake it over to finish drying. Then we haul it up by the barn and make an old-style haystack. Ours never look as good as Dad's did but they seem to do okay at shedding the rain."

"But this can't be enough hay for all the animals," protested Lindy.

"Oh, no. Tomorrow we'll be using the windrower on the large hayfields. And the farmer who rents from us will come around and bale it all. Some years there's enough extra to sell, but Mom always waits until mid-winter to do that." Looking at Lindy's flushed face he said, "I think you've done enough out here. Will you help me with dinner?"

"I will...for a glass of ice water."

"Sold." Michael carefully swung the scythe over his shoulder and they headed back to the house.

Five minute cool showers were enough to refresh them and they were busy in the kitchen when the rest of the family returned. Dinner was a relaxed affair with everyone feeling tired yet cheerful from the full day. Plans were made for Monday with options and suggestions flying back and forth across the table. Adam and Alex were going to start on the hay. Jeffrey was going to unload the trailer and James' car. James would be calling the family lawyer, his boss and his apartment to make arrangements, then tackle the pile of laundry. Michael and Pat planned on an entire day of canning; while Steve and Lindy would be in the garden. Everyone said goodnight early and sank into well-earned slumber.

8 MONDAY

"Lindy," called James as he approached the garden.

Straightening from the tomato plant she was stripping of ripe fruit, she turned. "Yes?"

"I talked to Mr. Harris, our lawyer, and he wants to visit with you in person. He understands the problem with you coming to town so I invited him to join us for dinner tonight. Is that okay?"

"That's fine with me." Lindy paused, studying his face. "What's wrong?"

"Oh, nothing serious. My publisher called and wants to meet with me about the new release. I just don't like going to the city. Anyway, I put her off until next week. I have an idea about that, but it involves Michael.

"By the way, where's your laundry? It wasn't in the downstairs hamper."

"Oh! But…" Lindy flushed.

James chuckled, "How about if I promise not to tell what size you wear?" He ducked as she threatened him with a tomato.

"Seriously, though," he continued. "If it really bothers you, you can do your own. It's just not necessary."

"Well, okay then. They're in a pile at the foot of my bed. And I'm trusting you."

Snagging a bright orange tomato, James backed out of the garden. "Your socks are safe in my hands!"

After getting a load started in the washing machine, James went looking for his mom and Michael. "Do you know how little Lindy has? Two pairs of jeans, some shorts and t-shirts, a jacket, hiking boots and tennies. Did she get her insurance check yet?"

"I think she got an interim check from them," answered Pat.

"Okay, I have an idea. What if she goes to the city with Michael on Sunday? She can shop Monday, then I'll bring her home on Wednesday."

Michael frowned, "What if she wants to stay longer?"

"Then someone gets her when she's ready. Do you mind being invaded again?"

"No, I liked the company. I just don't want her to be rushed or feel like a prisoner."

"Okay." James turned to his mom, "Well?"

"Let me ask her." Pat held up her hand to forestall the objection. "It should be her decision and you could talk a snake into slithering backwards. Let me."

Before anything could be said, the door slammed open and Adam stomped in. "That $*%!*^# machine! Just when we were transitioning from alfalfa to brome, the belt snaps and we're dead. The weather is perfect too!"

"Adam…"

"Sorry, Mom. But it might be hours before we can get back to it even if Alex finds a replacement belt. Why on earth does he want to be a farmer? Something is always breaking down."

"Well. Why don't you go rinse off? You're covered in dust."

Still muttering, he headed upstairs as the sound of a motorcycle roaring to life and driving away filled the room. When Adam came back down, he had changed into old, paint-splattered shorts and announced he was going to spray primer on the barn.

Michael told him to stay on the ground, but James stepped in and offered to help after he got the current load hung out to dry. Knowing James would keep the reckless behavior to a minimum, Michael nodded.

It was nearly lunchtime before Alex made it back with a new belt. He and Adam wanted to get right to work on the repairs, but knowing their obsession would likely keep them out until they couldn't see, they were convinced to eat first. After lunch, Steve insisted that Lindy stay inside and out of the oppressive heat. She counter-argued that she could at least take over the rest of the laundry and won.

Another discussion was taking place between James and Pat; she was worried about him being on the scaffolding alone and he was adamant that he was cautious enough. Their compromise was that he would keep his radio on broadcast. Lindy couldn't resist listening to the odd thumps and humming noises interspersed with muffled swearing. Every so often she was rewarded when he would break into song. Curiosity finally drove her to ask Pat, "What is he singing? I've never heard of any of those songs and he knows them all by heart."

Pat laughed, "It's a band from Britain called Take That. James decided years ago that he sounded like one of them and has been singing along ever since."

"Does he?"

"Oh, I don't know. But when he gets his brothers singing along it sounds nice."

Lindy was a bit taken aback by this until she realized that Pat was proud and embarrassed at the same time; she decided it must be a viewpoint of the older generation and went to gather in some dry clothes.

It was going on three in the afternoon before a 'whoop' from the radio heralded the twins' success at getting the windrower functional again. Lindy had finished hanging out another load and wandered over to the pole barn to see how Jeffrey was getting on. She found him stretching a tarp over a pile in the far corner.

"Will it be alright out here?" she asked.

"It should be. Anything delicate I took up to my room and the more valuable things are locked up in the smithy. I'm going to run

James' car over to the Andersen place and unload it there. Want to come along?"

"Sure! I'll let the others know where I am." Pulling the radio off her belt, she passed the message on.

"So," Lindy began. "What's your view of James' singing?"

Jeffrey smiled. "You've been talking to Mom. Honestly, James is right. He sounds remarkably like Mark Owen. The rest of us? Not so much. You won't find another Robbie Williams or Gary Barlow here. But we can carry a tune and blend together nicely."

Lindy waved her arms around. "I have no idea who any of those people are!"

"Well, since this is his car…" He turned on the cd player and music blasted from the speakers. 'Get ready for it…'

"Wait! I've heard this song. It was in the Kingsman movie."

Jeffrey looked startled, "You saw that?"

"Of course. It was a hilarious spoof of the Bond movies. And Colin Firth kicked."

Shaking his head as he pulled up close to the front porch, Jeffrey said, "Lindy, you are full of surprises. Where do you want your plumbing gear?"

"Let's put everything in the dining room for now. That should be one of the last spaces that gets worked over. I can sort out my tools as we go."

It wasn't a large car so didn't take long to unload. The house was too hot and stuffy to be comfortable for long and they were soon seeking fresh air on the front porch.

"Is there anything in the barn?" Lindy asked.

"Ha! There isn't anything left on the farm that wasn't nailed down."

"That might be good. The deliveries should start coming tomorrow. Can we store the supplies there?"

"Let's have a look."

The sliding double doors only opened half-way before jamming. Lindy peered at the rusty rollers at the top of the doors while Jeffrey kicked at the weeds and dirt clogging the rails. They both began speaking at once, "WD-40" and "I'll need a tool…"

"We could look inside while we're here." Jeffrey led the way into the dim interior. The floor felt spongy with years of blown in dirt and decaying bird droppings. High above, pigeons shuffled along the rafters, murmuring complaints about the humans. He sighed. "We really should shovel this clear before storing anything here."

"Wearing masks," Lindy agreed. "It's a nice open space but we'd have to keep everything under tarps."

"Yeah. Bird proofing the barn isn't going to be high on our priorities for quite a while. Should we go back and get James?"

"Might as well. I need a ladder and you two have a lot of shoveling to do." Laughing she ducked back out the door and jogged to the car.

James had finished the priming and was cleaning the sprayers when they returned. This time they loaded the truck with a ladder, wheelbarrow, shovels and the other odds and ends they suspected might be useful and drove back to the Andersen farm. After donning their dust masks, the men went inside the barn and began investigating the best way to clear the floor. They forced open the single door at the rear but it was too narrow for the wheelbarrow. Agreeing that all of the debris would have to be hauled out the front door, they started shoveling.

Meanwhile, Lindy set up the ladder to one side of the opening and applied a generous stream of lubricant to the rollers above the door. Trying a number of different tools on the overgrown track at the bottom, she settled on a long-handled crowbar for scraping it clear. About twenty minutes of diligent work and she was able to open that door completely. An extra spray of WD-40 to encourage smooth motion and she moved over to the other side.

The men had been working steadily, taking turns dumping the wheelbarrow in the area Steve had marked out for the garden. With the dust hanging in the air around them, they both heartily wished they had thought of goggles. They completely lost track of time until the radios chirping brought them back to the present with a dinner reminder. After gazing around what was left to do, they stepped outside and stripped off the masks.

James sighed, "I really don't want to clean up for dinner, knowing I'm coming back to this."

"Let's finish now instead," Jeffrey countered. "We can eat later with the twins."

He notified Michael of their plans and that they were sending Lindy back in the truck. She looked momentarily rebellious, but gave in.

It took nearly three hours to finish the job and both were more than happy enough to head for home. At the Andersen driveway, Jeffrey pulled James aside and showed him two sturdy gate posts cemented into place.

"When?" James asked in surprise.

"Saturday morning. Alex covered for me with the canning so I could work on them."

"So we can hang the gate tomorrow?"

"I think we should give it an extra day since this isn't really something I've done before."

"Okay. We could pull the cattle grate up after the delivery truck has gone for some security."

When they arrived home, the twins were just starting on their late dinners. One glance and everyone agreed James and Jeffrey should clean up first. In the living room, Steve was explaining to Lindy the different options for holsters. They had managed to fit in a quick lesson after dinner and she had decided to use the Beretta for her carry gun. He suggested she talk to Pat about what she did and didn't like about the different styles. As he pointed out, his mom probably had a drawer full of holsters that she didn't use.

9 TUESDAY

At 5:30 a.m. Lindy woke with the sun and full of energy. Dressing quickly, pausing only to check on the kittens, she grabbed her gloves and headed outside to her new favorite hobby: the garden. Not wanting to sit down in the heavy dew, she alternated pulling weeds from around bean plants and using the hoe in the space between rows. Pausing to stretch her back, movement out of the corner of her eye caught her attention. Swinging around she discovered five sheep had joined her in the garden with more heading that way. They weren't after the weeds though. Shouting loudly and waving the hoe she ran at them. The nearest sheep scattered while those farther away stopped to decide what to do. Back and forth she ran for what felt like ages but was only minutes before reinforcements arrived.

Alarm at hearing Lindy's shouts had quickly turned to anger when they discovered the reason. Steve's fury was palpable as he surveyed the damaged crops.

"Where did they come from?" Lindy asked Alex as the others herded the flock down the driveway.

"A bad neighbor to the west. He's cut our fence again. It's the only way they could have got here."

"But why would he do that?"

"Sheer cussedness. He wanted the Andersen land but Dad outbid him. We can only plant hay in the fields bordering his land. He finds too many ways to damage other crops. Before we always drove the sheep back onto his land, but not this time. They're going to push them east down the road." Alex was smiling with delight at the thought of the unpleasant neighbor having to chase his sheep down himself.

Forty minutes later the others came back looking very pleased with themselves. Over breakfast they explained how they had taken the flock to a very large sheep farm where the owner was happy to help by putting the strays into an empty paddock. That prevented them from damaging any other crops and kept them off the road. He also promised to call the sheriff if the owner didn't find him that morning.

Steve looked at Lindy with a grave expression. "If you hadn't been out there and raised the alarm we could have lost most of the garden. What they didn't eat they would have trampled."

"Oh!" gasped Lindy. "My radio! If I had been wearing it I could have told you right away. I'm sorry."

"Why don't you go get it now?" requested Steve. When she left he shrugged to the others, "Anything that gets her to wear it."

"Man! I completely forgot about Mr. Harris coming to dinner last night," exclaimed James. "Did that go alright?"

"Yes," reassured Pat. "We fed him well then they talked in the study. He is going to email her a copy of the letter before sending it."

As Lindy returned, Steve was standing. "If no one needs me this morning, I'm going to go buy an electric fence for the garden. I've put too much work into it to risk a disaster."

"What should I work on?" she asked.

With an approving smile, he answered, "Would you mind doing the chicken chores?"

Lindy was beaming with delight as he left. She felt like she had just received a promotion.

Following the actions she had observed during the past week, Lindy gave the chickens fresh water, checked the feeders then took a scoop out of the bag of three-grain scratch. As she moved out into the pen to scatter it, she found herself surrounded by eager birds. When she paused, two hens stood on her shoes and another tried jumping for the scoop. Laughing, she shuffled through the flock, sprinkling widely so all would have a chance at the snack.

Even knowing she was technically done with the chores because the eggs weren't gathered until afternoon, Lindy couldn't resist staying to watch. Noticing a dark brown hen with golden speckles had returned to her shoe, she tentatively reached down and stroked the soft feathers. "That's Grace," said James, who was standing outside the pen watching. "She would follow you all over the farm and into the house if she could. Just loves people."

"She's beautiful," murmured Lindy. Reluctantly rising from her crouch, she left the pen. "Who needs help today?"

"Mom and Michael are canning soups today. The twins are finishing painting the barn. Jeffrey is going to an estate auction this morning. Steve will be setting up his fence when he gets back. And I'm going to help you in the garden; the beans are probably ready to be picked again and my deliveries aren't due until this afternoon."

"Already!" exclaimed Lindy.

"Well, there won't be as many as from the first picking, but yes, beans grow fast."

"I had better get my hat then." Lindy headed inside. "Wow! What is that smell?" she asked, poking her head into the kitchen.

Michael turned from the stove with a smile. "Chef's secret recipe. You can try some at noon, though it's best in mid-winter. Could you bring me a dozen good-sized onions from the garden, please? Are any peppers ready? And I'll take the beans right away too."

"I'm on it." Lindy slapped her hat on and hustled out to work.

While Lindy pulled onions and brushed the dirt off, James gathered an assortment of bell and hot peppers. She carried the basket back to the kitchen and he settled into the rhythm of pushing aside the canopy of leaves and plucking out the long, slender bean pods. Alternating between bending over and squatting, James reminded himself of what a good workout this was until he glanced over and saw Lindy sitting on an up-ended five gallon bucket as she worked two more bean rows. Chuckling, he took mercy on his screaming muscles and fetched another bucket.

Meanwhile, thirty miles away, Jeffrey was checking out the items up for sale at an auction. It was another situation where the younger generation was selling everything when their parents could no longer live alone on the farm. He gazed sorrowfully at the well-maintained farmhouse and flower beds. Most likely it would become yet another vacant and decaying home as the land was taken over by other farmers.

Concentrating on the kitchen items, he was pleased to spot a pressure canner and boxes of jars. Some of the furniture were beautiful antiques, but he knew those would be far out of their budget. Jotting down notes as he went down the line, he tried to prioritize; Steve had already left in the truck when Jeffrey found the auction listing so he had borrowed James' car again. He was regretting not having his own truck instead of the beloved Harley, but without an income he wouldn't be buying one now. He decided if he did find something large that was too good to pass up he would call Steve and ask him to bring the truck. As he shifted his attention to farm tools, he began taking photos and texting them to Steve and James to get their opinions on usefulness.

Suddenly, he spotted something too tempting to walk by. It was a gorgeous, antique, wood-burning cook stove. As Jeffrey was checking it over, opening doors and turning handles, another man walked up. "Beauty, isn't it? Shame the market's dropped out. Two years ago I could have made six grand profit easy. Now, I've got three in a warehouse I can't shift."

"What changed?" Jeffrey asked.

"Who knows? Some rich people suddenly decided it was out of style and dealers are begging me to take them back. Darn heavy too. They always were a pain to ship." The man wandered away grumbling to himself and Jeffrey got busy snapping pictures.

James called, "Are you crazy? Do you know how to cook on one of those things?"

"I know. I know. I can't help it. I really want this. Please?"

"I know I'm going to regret this. Okay, if you can get a deal and you arrange for the firewood."

"Yes! Agreed. Thanks, Jimmy." Jeffrey was grinning with delight.

Three hours later and $600 poorer, he was the proud owner of the stove, canning supplies and some tools Steve had suggested he bid on. Jeffrey had seen the dismay on the auctioneer's face when not a single dealer had been willing to bid for the stove. Now he just needed to call for the truck and enough muscle to load it.

Back at the farm, Steve had finished setting up and testing the garden fence. As the first type of solar powered equipment on the farm, he was tempted to find more gadgets they could use. That desire was tempered by awareness that if this hadn't happened in his busy season he would have been building a fence instead. After showing Lindy and James how to tell if the fence was on and the shut-off switch, he helped carry the beans as they headed inside for lunch.

Michael had placed a pot of his secret spicy soup and loaves of fresh crusty bread on the table and the mood was cheerful as they sat down. The twins teased James by insisting they needed him to serenade as they painted; Pat reminded Lindy to check her email and James and Steve fielded texts from Jeffrey at the auction. They all cheered when he won the stove until they realized hauling it home would take much of the afternoon. After vigorous discussion it was agreed that Steve would stay at the farm, James had no choice but to await his deliveries and the other men would take the truck to Jeffrey.

After lunch, Lindy used the computer in the study to log onto her email. The letter that Mr. Harris had attached seemed straightforward enough: all contact from John's family had to go through him as her lawyer and any attempts to find or contact her would be considered stalking and prosecuted as such. With relief she authorized its distribution and turned to emails from friends and family. One of her young cousins was complaining about being bullied online. Lindy wrote back suggesting she stop using those sites although it was unlikely the teenager would listen. Once again Lindy was grateful her parents had taken an immediate and intense dislike to social media so she had never used it. Finished in the study, she joined Steve and Pat on the front porch to snap more beans. Pat told stories from her grandparents about homesteading in the area and the time passed quickly.

Down the road, James had all the windows in the house open and was working his way from room to room taking measurements and jotting more notes. The kitchen was a generous size, but he suspected the stove would take up quite a lot of it. Going back outside, he circled around and studied the back of the house, finally deciding to ask Jeffrey if it was possible to expand the kitchen and enclose the basement entrance in one modification. The sound of a horn alerted him to the arrival of the lumber delivery. Directing the driver to the open barn doors, James supervised the unloading of this and the other two trucks that arrived later. He had managed to forget about the stove until Steve's truck pulled into the yard. Everyone worked together to unload it into a corner of the barn and cover everything with tarps. It was a weary group who closed up the house and barn, pried up the cattle grate and headed for home that afternoon.

Arriving home, they found Pat and Lindy in the living room with their feet up. "I needed a break from canning," Pat announced cheerfully. Thoughtful looks crossed the faces of her sons as they spread out around the room.

James spoke first, "Mom, why don't you come over with us in the morning? I've got some ideas and I'd like your opinion."

Pat's eyes sparkled with pleasure. She had felt a bit left out of the planning up 'til now. Before she could reply Alex broke in, "Why are you pushing so hard on the canning anyway? Most years you're more relaxed about it. You've already got enough to fill all the shelves in the basement and you haven't slowed down at all."

"Oh, well." She hesitated. "Maybe it's just nerves, but I have a bad feeling. Remember the stories about my great-grandmother? How she felt worried one year and made her husband load in supplies and it was the worst winter ever? They didn't see another person for three months and if they hadn't been ready, they would have had to eat the horses. Well, I feel all jittery like we need to be ready for a terrible winter. So, even if I have to store the extras in your basement, James, I will."

Lindy realized, looking from one brother to the next, that they were all taking Pat's forebodings seriously. James took out his notebook and flipped to a blank page. "Okay, what else do we need to do?"

Steve said, "If we use the woodstove regularly, we can stretch the propane tank for the whole winter, but we don't have enough firewood."

"I promised to get wood for the other place, I'll see if I can find a supplier with seasoned wood for here as well," Jeffrey offered.

James spoke up, "I've got someone coming to look at the fireplace chimney at New Farm (I'm tired of calling it the Andersen farm). I'll have them come sweep the chimney here at the same time."

"We should get enough chicken feed and straw for the winter," Alex said.

"And dog and cat food," added Adam.

"I can get bulk foodstuffs from my restaurant suppliers and send it back with James next week," said Michael.

Pat was smiling at her family and added, "Lamp oil in case we get one of those awful ice storms taking down the power lines."

"Is that it?" asked James. "Okay then. Adam and Alex can take the trailer when they do the farmer's market next Saturday and load up on animal feed. Mom can make a list of how much and what types. Michael and I will get people feed next week. Jeffrey has firewood and Steve straw."

"And I'll get the lamp oil next time I'm in town," said Pat firmly, ending the impromptu family meeting.

After a quick meal, Adam, Alex and James left to finish painting the barn; they were determined to get one project finished. Pat asked Lindy to help her dig some things out in the attic and they headed upstairs. Instead of pull-down steps, this attic was accessed through a narrow door and steep stairs. The air was still, hot and slightly musty smelling, yet there was an atmosphere of treasure seeking adventure to Lindy. At some point in the past the ceiling studs were covered with boards to turn the attic into storage space and generations had obviously been making use of it.

Pat carried a battery lantern to augment the dim light bulbs and led the way to a stack of boxes. Lindy was shamelessly exploring and discovered piles of old sports equipment, a dressmaker's dummy, amateur watercolors, a set of encyclopedia books and furniture from the 70s before Pat called her back.

"There are a couple generations of clothes for young women here that might fit you. Mine from the 70s and my mother's from the 50s. I don't know how daring you are in fashion..." Pat trailed off as she held up a pair of skinny trousers that were predominantly lime green. Lindy chuckled delightedly as she dove into boxes of crocheted tops, beaded vests and peasant skirts. Ignoring the odor of cedar sticks and mothballs, she pulled out dresses from her grandmother's generation.

"But these are vintage!" she cried. "You could sell them."

"I could," Pat replied. "But I'd rather they went to family."

Lindy stood and hugged her hard. Together they packed up the boxes and began carrying them down to the laundry room.

When the painters trooped in they found the others gathered in the living room. Steve had called around and found two farmers with small oat straw bales for sale. When asked where they would store it, he suggested closing off the north end of the farrowing house where it would provide extra insulation for Susie.

Jeffrey had been busy checking craigslist for firewood. "The tree trimming company will deliver dump truck loads of green wood cheap, but we would have to cut and split it ourselves. There's also no guarantee on the quality of the wood. At that cost I think we'd be foolish not to get a few loads at New Farm for future use. I found a couple places that sell dry wood which we would need for this winter. We can save some money by hauling it ourselves and more if it's not split. I think we should consider getting some split and some not.

"As for storage, the barn at New Farm has a lean-to or the garage is close to the house. Here, I think we need to put up a wood shed."

Everybody looked to Pat for a response, "We've never kept more than a couple cords on hand before but if we're going to try heating with wood, we should be serious about it. I'll go to town tomorrow and get the building permit. This might be our busiest vacation ever!"

James spoke then, "Don't forget we'll be raking the meadow tomorrow. We should get on that as soon as the dew is off." This reminder was greeted with groans as they shuffled off to bed.

10 WEDNESDAY

Lindy woke early again and full of energy. Bouncing up, she dressed quickly and went straight to the basket beside the back door where Michael had begun leaving a list of vegetables he would need for meals. Marching briskly to the garden, she checked that the electric fence was running and shut it off before stepping over. Confidently, she filled the basket with his requests. Not ready to go back inside, she then puttered around, pulling the odd weed and drinking in the fresh morning air. When the radio chirped at her waist, she retrieved the basket, turned the fence on and returned to the house.

Breakfast was a cheerful meal as they tucked into omelets amid chatter about the coming day. Steve gave Lindy the go-ahead to take over morning chicken chores for as long as she wanted. Pat announced that she was going to town first thing and asked if anyone had any errands for her to run. Michael requested fresh rosemary since it was probably too late in the year to replace the dead plant on the porch and Lindy had a small shopping list of necessities.

Lindy and Steve did the chores while the others cleared the table and gathered the rakes. As they walked to the hay meadow, Biff gamboled excitedly around their legs while Mellow placidly followed behind. Lindy asked about the rakes and James handed his to her. "Nice, aren't they?" he said. "Dad helped us each make our own when we turned ten. Then we replaced the handle after we stopped growing."

She turned it over to inspect the wooden teeth. "Is it just for hay?"

"Yes, we'll rake it into rows now and use pitchforks to throw it onto a hay wagon that we borrow in a day or so. I've got a surprise coming on the day we make the haystack." James was clearly looking forward to something.

At the meadow, they spread out and began steadily raking; there was no competition involved today. Lindy kept one eye on Biff as he chased random scents and barked at the butterflies. She chuckled when James started singing 'I'm a Lonesome Polecat' and three of his brothers joined in.

When Adam stopped for a breather nearby she asked about him not singing. "It was the gift from the fourth fairy godmother that we are completely tone-deaf," he replied with a grin. "Nobody should be flawless." And he dove back into the work.

Lindy took a turn with Michael's rake and found it a much more peaceful process than scything although her shoulders began to ache too quickly. When she handed back the rake, she asked how long it would be before she could do a fair share of normal work.

Michael shook his head. "You do understand that there is nothing normal about this work? If you had lived a hundred years ago then you would be used to the physical labor. Now, if you keep active, then next summer you'll be pulling alongside us."

This idea sparked a desire within Lindy to work hard and become truly useful.

Finished with the meadow, they called Biff back and woke Mellow up to return to the house. Pat had finished her errands in town and waited for her family's arrival. She had left a case of quart bottles of lamp oil in the car and placed Lindy's shopping in her room. On the kitchen table next to a packet of fresh rosemary was a feeble looking rosemary plant in a tiny pot. Unloading her other purchases from the hardware store resulted in a small pyramid of boxes of wooden kitchen matches and another of a couple dozen boxes of canning lids.

The family swept in with a rush of fresh air that smelt of warm summer sun. Good-natured teasing greeted Pat's purchases while she protested, "They were on sale!" As it wasn't quite eleven, the entire family decided to walk over to New Farm and discuss the plans on site.

First Lindy, Pat and Steve wanted to see the stove for themselves, then they poked around the barn lean-to, the garage and chicken coop while debating the merits of each for firewood storage. The garage was the clear winner for convenience to the house plus a decent amount of space. The next discussion focused on the size of the kitchen and the obvious fact that it had been built before refrigerators became a common appliance. Michael pointed out that none of the outlets in the kitchen had a ground plug.

"I know," said James morosely. "The entire house has to be rewired. I daren't even turn the power on for the fire hazard."

"It only seems fair considering all the pipes need replacing," countered Lindy, thinking of the massive job ahead.

Everyone turned to look at Jeffrey. "What?" he asked.

"We want to know if you can expand the kitchen out the back of the house," answered James.

"Hmm." Jeffrey went outside and around to the rear. He heaved open the basement door and disappeared. When he came back up, putting a tiny flashlight in his pocket, he walked all around the house. "Okay, here's the situation. The foundation is sound and I don't want to mess with it so an addition would go onto a crawlspace. That will be faster but also not as warm in the winter. We would have to hire out that part because none of us has any experience or time to learn now. I suggest expanding across the entire back side of the house while we're at it and move the laundry up to the ground floor. We're going to need another building permit."

Lindy was looking around the backyard thoughtfully. "Will they use a backhoe? Could we get them to dig a trench out to that open space?"

"What for, Lindy?" James was puzzled.

"I'd like to run a water line out there and maybe next year we can put in a summer kitchen."

"Oh, yes!" said Pat, thinking of her steamy kitchen in canning season.

"Mom, do you know of any good contractors around here?" asked Jeffrey.

"Wilson's has a good reputation. I'll give Pete a call." She sounded a little smug, but nobody noticed. The group split then with most heading back home while James, Jeffrey and Lindy stayed to fine-tune their plans. They agreed to begin with replacing the windows; Jeffrey showed them how rotten most of the trim had gotten and that it would be best to do it all at the same time. Lindy said that she wanted to start demolishing the upstairs bathroom and asked what they were planning on using for a toilet while working. The guys didn't want to admit that they hadn't thought of needing more than a handy tree but were stumped for a solution. The original outhouse was falling to pieces and completely unusable.

"Maybe we should do a few things before starting on the house," admitted James. "The driveway gate is still top priority, a new outhouse can be next and I completely forgot about arranging for dumpsters to get rid of all the rotten stuff we'll be ripping out."

"It wouldn't hurt to get the septic tank checked out and the pipes from the rural water line to the house as well," offered Lindy. Seeing James' wince, she pulled out the list of approved plumbing expenses and nudged him with her elbow. "Don't worry. Michael included the septic system. Does he really have this kind of money available? I mean, even as a good chef, he is still a cook."

Jeffrey explained, "He's not just good, he's very good. It's because of him that the restaurant is always booked five weeks in advance. And Amelia put some of his better recipes into a fancy cookbook that's still selling well. She was a pharmacist so that was two high incomes and this is where they spent their vacations, so they didn't throw money away."

"What was she like?" asked Lindy.

"Feisty," James said emphatically. "She told me the first time they met she had been on a bachelorette party with college friends and tripped getting out of the limo. He caught her and she knew instantly that he was the one she wanted."

Jeffrey was laughing. "His version is she was too drunk to walk, but by the time he turned around she had disappeared in the crowd and he would never have found her again if she hadn't left him holding her purse. I suspect he was a bit thunderstruck himself. She was a curvy red-head and they really were two halves of a whole."

"I think they didn't have kids because they already made a complete family together," James added. "They were married for nearly ten years."

"That's so sad," Lindy murmured. "Was Steve married?"

"He had a fiancée when he deployed to Afghanistan. He didn't when he came back; sometimes love isn't enough. What about your family? You mentioned being the youngest."

"My sister is in California. Her husband manages a hotel. My brother is in D.C. with his girlfriend and her kids, but he likes to move around so I'll get a postcard eventually with their latest address. And my parents just moved from Tulsa to Toledo a few months ago."

"Do you miss them?" Jeffrey asked.

"Yes and no. I love them, but I think I'm a throwback to some ancestor that needed to settle down instead of roam. I'm happier now than I ever remember being before."

"Aw, shucks." James winked at her until she dissolved in laughter. Then he stretched and asked, "Anyone else ready for lunch?"

Michael and Steve were leaving the garden when they walked up the driveway. Their favorite chef had wanted more time outside, so the twins had taken over lunch duties. They served a simple meal of salads and grilled cheese sandwiches but nothing was burnt and no-one was inclined to complain.

Jeffrey explained about the projects they wanted to work on that afternoon and asked for suggestions for the gate. As the debate became heated, Steve gestured for silence and announced, "Anyone really determined could go around through one of the fields. There's nothing we can do about that now so let's concentrate on making it inconvenient. A cattle gate chained shut and removing the grate will be enough to fend off petty thieves and meth cookers. Two of us can get that mounted in a couple hours, leaving the rest for other jobs."

Alex waved his hand, "We can dismantle the scaffolding and get it moved over pretty quickly. Then I volunteer to dig the outhouse hole."

"Me too," added Adam.

"Pete Wilson is going to stop out later this afternoon. He said a job got cancelled when his customer declared bankruptcy, so he could squeeze this project in." Pat looked justifiably pleased with this announcement. Contractors were notorious for being booked months in advance.

"That's amazing luck!" exclaimed Jeffrey. "We better not count on more of that though. Let's try to have things planned out from now on. After I talk to Pete, I'll get the extra supplies we'll need on order."

"I've been making a schedule of when things are expected to happen," Lindy offered, pulling out her notepad. "So, contractor comes today. Tomorrow is chimney sweep, dumpsters delivered, hayfields baled. Anything for Friday?"

"The septic tank guy will be here either Friday or Monday. Rural water said they won't check the pipe until we're ready to turn it back on," James replied. "And we arranged to borrow the hay wagon on Saturday for the meadow."

Jeffrey flipped through his own notes. "I almost forgot. We can pick up the dry wood anytime. I reserved four cords already split and ten unsplit. And the trimming company will start delivering green wood sometime next week."

"Straw is coming Saturday morning," added Steve. "I'll stay here this afternoon and set up the farrowing house for that." Unspoken was that his instincts were telling him not to leave Pat and Lindy alone on the farm although he wasn't sure why.

As the men scattered to get to work on the various projects, Lindy and Pat cleared lunch and started going through the boxes of clothes in the laundry room. Sorting them into piles of unusable, washable and those that would be aired out for now, the women chatted.

"I forgot to ask if you needed any monthly products, Lindy."

"No, I don't." She looked over shyly. "Would you mind hearing about the accident?"

"Not if you don't mind talking about it, dear."

"It happened when I was fourteen; my dad was taking me for ice cream to celebrate a good report card. I don't remember the accident itself; one minute I was happy, then I woke up in the hospital. A drunk driver had hit my side of the car. Dad had a broken collarbone and concussion. I was a mess: broken legs, ribs, arm, internal bleeding. The surgeon had to remove my womb and some of my intestinal tract. And the driver walked away without any injuries." Lindy shook her head at the memories.

Pat was silent for a few minutes, not working, just thinking. "Something like that must have altered your entire family."

Lindy looked at her in surprise. "How did you know? Everything changed. Not just how they acted with me, but how they treated each other too."

Pat smiled back, "They're human. It would have been strange if they weren't deeply affected. I understand because I have feelings that I'm not proud of myself." With a sigh she kept talking. "It's only now that I find myself able to let go of a kernel of resentment I've always felt towards the twins. On some level I *needed* a daughter. Amelia couldn't fill that hole because she and Michael were completely intertwined in each other and Melissa was just impossible."

Impulsively, Lindy threw her arms around Pat and both were laughing and crying at the same time. Peeking through the door, Steve decided not to ask for help at that moment and went back to struggling with the panels on his own. Two hours later the clotheslines were full of an eclectic collection of colors and styles flapping in the breeze. Pat was puttering inside the house while Lindy ran around the farmyard with Biff when a large, red pickup drove up. The door decal said Wilson Construction and a stocky man with gray hair stepped out. Steve had started towards the house when he heard the truck but Lindy drew back into the shadow of the barn and watched. As the front door opened, Lindy noticed that Pat had changed from her laundry spotted top into a pretty blue blouse and was smiling warmly at the visitor. After shaking hands with Steve, he directed his attention to Pat.

"Oh!" said Lindy to herself and wondered if the boys knew their mother had an admirer. She was grinning as she watched the man who had to be Pete Wilson help her friend into his truck and drive away. Steve looked slightly puzzled but when he spotted Lindy he only asked if she would give him a hand.

Pat was enjoying herself. It had been four years since Matt had passed away and she missed the companionship of a man her own age. Pete had made it a habit to stop by for coffee every few months to chat and check up on her. She knew very well that he had plenty of jobs he could have filled in his schedule with and if he did this one it was as a favor for her.

At New Farm, Jeffrey came forward to greet them and spoke easily about their plans. After voicing her thoughts on some of the details they were going over, Pat left them to it and went to check on the outhouse build. Pete measured out the proposed addition and staked the outline. After a thorough discussion of options and preferences, he stepped aside to make calculations. Although his eyes were following Pat's progress around the farm, it didn't take him long to return to Jeffrey.

Handing over a sheet of paper Pete said, "This has the quote for the foundation. My crew is clearing off the site we were on today and can pour here tomorrow. The rest of the work I have quoted you can let me know about on Sunday. It includes framing, shingles, insulation, windows and doors. That leaves siding, drywall, trim and the fine details for you. I know you were planning on doing it all, but I don't see how you can get all that and the other work you have lined up here done before winter."

Studying the amounts listed, Jeffrey's eyebrows rose. He recognized that they were being offered a very good deal. "I'll have to talk it over with James, but I can't imagine we will pass this by. Thank you."

Shaking hands again, Pete strode off to give Pat a lift back to her house. Taking advantage of their brief time alone, he asked her out for dinner Friday evening and she accepted.

Lindy was absolutely filthy when she went inside the house again. After moving the pen panels to make room for the straw bales, they had scooped out the old straw and mess made by the pigs. That was hauled to the compost pile then they moved on to clean the chicken coop. Steve threw down a bale of old hay from the barn loft to spread on the cleared floors and they were finished. She went straight for the shower and felt like a new person coming out. In her room she found all of the new old clothes in the closet. Gleefully, she began trying on various combinations before settling on a pink-striped dress from the 50s. It was a little loose but wearing the epitome of ladylike attire was the perfect contrast to her afternoon of labor. She couldn't spoil the effect with the shoes she had, so chose to go barefoot instead.

In the living room James was sitting halfway on a chair arm while petting Mama Cass. When Lindy walked in, he glanced up to say hello and did a double take so perfect that he slipped and landed on the floor. Laughing, she twirled around, "Isn't it pretty? Your grandmother had wonderful taste."

"Beautiful," James agreed.

Chattering on about Pat's generosity and the joy of having options to wear, it took Lindy a few minutes to realize James was still on the floor. "Are you okay? Need a hand?"

"Fine, fine. Just bruised my dignity. You should show everyone in the kitchen." As she slipped out he met the cat's sardonic look and muttered, "Don't you start," while levering himself up.

Later that evening, Alex and Michael were sitting on either side of Lindy teaching her how to crochet, Adam was on the floor playing with Biff and the others were reading when James entered. "I may have solved a little mystery. I remembered how surprised Mom was that her bosses could keep all those problems a secret from the workforce. So I called the police to see if anything had been reported. Nothing. I did some digging online and discovered something odd: the owners are cousins of John's family."

Everyone began talking at once except for Pat, she sat there and fumed. Finally she exploded, "Lies! It was a pack of lies they told Lindy to frighten her! And if I confront them they will know I've been talking to her and tell John about it. Damn! I can't go back there without losing my temper but if I up and quit that would look strange." Pacing back and forth did little to ease her fury as she searched for a solution. "I know! I'll call in that I've been unwell and my doctor told me to take it easy for a few weeks. When I don't go back, they'll have forgotten all about me."

This statement caused some skeptical expressions but nobody chose to argue against her idea. Lindy protested Pat losing her job because they took her in, but Michael reassured her that Pat had only been working because she was bored during the day when Steve was telecommuting.

Everyone was too tense to settle down so when Adam challenged Alex to some moonlight soccer they all went along to watch or play.

74

The exertion was an effective distraction and they went to bed in much better moods.

11 THURSDAY

Steve leaned against his hoe in the early morning light. There wasn't much to do in the garden other than harvesting now; many hands really made a difference when it came to weeding. Today he had opened up the drip lines that ran down each row; the plants had been drooping in the daily blast of dry heat and for good results it was vital that the tomatoes and cucumbers got ample moisture.

His thoughts turned to the recent changes in the family. These were certainly interesting times for them, yet everything seemed to be working out well. The twins being fired was bad, but they were undoubtedly useful to have around. He felt no remorse for Melissa leaving the family; she was an ambitious, cold-hearted woman whose beauty truly was skin deep. If only she had left a year or two earlier then maybe Jeffrey would have been open to seeing Lindy as more than a sister. Steve laughed at himself and shook his head; matchmaking wasn't his thing.

Hearing a shouted 'hello', he turned and saw Lindy approaching. Wearing jeans and a t-shirt again, she looked natural and comfortable. She asked about the watering and he explained the reasoning behind drip irrigation as opposed to sprinklers and the needs of the different plants. After that the discussion turned to insects, beneficial and not. Lindy was genuinely interested which made her a keen student while Steve was passionate about gardening, thus the best type of teacher. Both had to be reminded of breakfast by radio.

Lindy came close to mutiny at the table that morning when she learned they expected her to stay home. The explanation that there would be too many strangers at New Farm to keep her presence a secret did nothing to calm her.

"I'm sorry, dear. I know you're probably sick of canning vegetables by now," Pat began.

"Oh, no! It's not that!" Lindy interrupted. "I just want to be part of what's happening over there. I'm happy to help you."

"Would you be interested in a lesson on long guns?" asked Steve. "And you could help me get started on the wood shelter."

"I could leave my radio on so you could listen in today," offered James.

Lindy's mulish expression was fading fast by this time. "Steve, yes to both. James, will this radio show include singing?"

"That depends if singing is an incentive or not."

"Singing is a bonus, although I don't know how you're going to get the contractor's crew to join in." Mischief was sparkling in her eyes.

Adam was leaning forward eagerly, "When are you going shooting? Can we come too?"

Steve answered, "If James will give me a warning when he's bringing the chimney sweep over, we'll go then."

"Probably later this afternoon then," said James. "Does everyone realize tomorrow is the fourth? Any errands should be done today if possible."

"Say, James, shouldn't you have emptied your apartment already?" asked Jeffrey.

"No, I have one more month on my lease and it was easier just to keep it for July instead of trying to get out early." This explanation brought nods of agreement and everyone rose to get the day's work underway. James drew Steve to one side to ask, "Are you sure we aren't overreacting about how much of a threat this guy is?"

"He set her apartment on fire without a thought for all the other people in the building. They could have all died that night. We may not be taking him seriously enough."

James nodded in thoughtful agreement.

Adam, Alex and Michael were taking the truck and trailer to get a load of firewood, Jeffrey and James went to New Farm and Pat, Lindy and Steve headed for the garden.

Mid-morning, Lindy stepped back from the sink of soapy jars and looked around. Pat was working with quick efficiency, coring and quartering tomatoes; her hands seemed to move without conscious control, never dropping or misplacing anything. Between the colorful tomatoes, stacks of cucumbers, piles of broccoli and cauliflower it looked as though a cornucopia had exploded.

Picking up a broccoli floret, Lindy asked wonderingly, "Do you can these?"

"We could pickle them I suppose, but none of us would care for that. We usually blanch and freeze them."

"How did they keep them before there were freezers?" Lindy asked.

"I imagine they were only eaten while in season. Have you ever watched those documentaries about Victorian walled gardens? No? The brick walls were 16 to 24 feet high. Inside there were potting sheds and heated greenhouses, exotic fruits and vegetables and a small army of gardeners all to feed the wealthy family. It sounds absurd now but, my, they were beautiful. I don't know if it was any sillier than us shipping fruits halfway around the world. Can't you imagine Steve as a head gardener?"

Lindy chuckled, "It would fit him perfectly. How do you watch shows like that without a TV?"

"Oh, I have a little TV in my room with most of my favorites on DVD. I never have time for that in the summer though. You could watch it on the computer in the study if you wanted."

"It's funny, but I haven't missed watching television at all here. There's too much going on."

"The boys felt very deprived without it growing up and it's the first thing they each bought when they moved out."

At that moment Steve came in with a basket of zucchinis. "Steve, how long were you interested in watching television after you moved away?"

"Two months, maybe? At first it was like a glimpse into another world, but then you realize it's all fake, scripted or twisted. Watching the other guys soaking it up was hard; that's when I felt like I was the one from another world."

"I was just telling Lindy about the gardening documentaries."

"Ah, the exception. Speaking of exceptions, Mom, I've been thinking of getting one of those solar setups that could power my laptop."

"But you wouldn't have internet without power."

"No, but I could watch a DVD or run my garden design program. Anyway, solar power is neat." He looked a bit sheepish, but Pat couldn't think of any reason why he shouldn't get one if he wanted it.

"There might have been something like that in the camping section at the hardware store. I really wasn't paying attention, but you could check there."

"Okay, maybe I'll see if the canning lids are still on sale," he said with a wink as he grabbed an empty basket and headed back outside.

Things weren't going so well with the firewood. Even stacked neatly, they couldn't fit two full cords into the truck and trailer. They were hot, sweaty and frustrated at the thought of having to make seven more trips. Not wanting to lose a good sale, the farmer offered them another option. His grain truck would hold close to three cords and he could use the front-end loader on his tractor to fill it. For an extra hundred they could rent the truck for the day.

Adam went into negotiation mode and counter-offered to buy the rest of his split, dry wood if he waived the rental fee. The chance to sell another six cords of his highest priced product and not have to deliver was too good to pass up and they agreed.

"Um, Adam? Twenty cords of wood?" Alex had to ask.

"I figure we can put eight cords of split wood in the garage at New Farm. The new wood shed should hold about seven and we can all work on splitting to fill that. The other five unsplit we can store in the lean-to for now. Just imagine if Mom is right about an historic bad winter. We won't regret having the extra." Adam could be very persuasive and they suspected their mom would be on his side, so they accepted his argument. He stayed to drive the grain truck and Alex and Michael headed for home.

At New Farm, Jeffrey was working on his list of needed supplies; having most of the addition built by the contractors was simplifying things wonderfully, but he still needed extra siding, drywall and trim. At the top of the list he put a toilet seat for the outhouse.

James had just finished hanging the outhouse door when one of the construction workers asked to use it. That encounter reminded James to call Michael and have him ask about buying sawdust. He then had Jeffrey add hand sanitizer to the shopping list.

"I'm wondering if we should buy more lumber as well," James was thinking out loud.

"You too? I was thinking about building our own shelves in the pantry. And don't forget the wardrobes you have to make."

"Ha, ha. Hey! All the workers are leaving. Is it lunchtime already?"

The ambulance crew and emergency room staff had been professional and efficient in their care for the young man who was now hooked up to a daunting array of life support machines. In their eyes he was simply another traffic accident victim; they had no idea that his actions would be changing all their lives.

As he slipped into a coma, even he didn't grasp the incredible irony that his life was now dependent on the very machines that his program was designed to take down.

"It's barely eleven. Wilson doesn't run a very tight ship. I suppose I could go to town and get my orders in," Jeffrey said. James had volunteered his car for running around in while the truck was in use.

"Let me grab my tools and you can drop me at home," James said over his shoulder as he jogged away.

Jeffrey expected to let James out at the driveway and keep going to town but found Steve there waiting for him. "Hope you don't mind my doing some shopping with you."

"How did you know I was going?"

"Did you both forget his radio was on?" Steve laughed. "That was some colorful language broadcast during the door hanging."

"Whoops."

"James, do you mind staying here until I get back?" asked Steve.

"No problem." He swung his tool belt over his shoulder and sauntered up the drive.

At the DIY center, Jeffrey placed his order then tracked Steve down in the camping section. Looking over his shoulder at the solar charging kits, Jeffrey exclaimed, "$500! I can find the same or better for $300 online."

Steve looked dubious. "Are you sure?"

"Have I ever let you down?"

"Well, there was that time you were supposed to pick me up after the game…"

"Yeah, yeah. Come on. I told James I'd make his outhouse pretty. Let's grab some t.p. and sanitizer."

"Humph. Can someone explain how a town this size can have a DIY center but not a Costco or Sam's?"

"Ha! Just be thankful you don't have to eat fast food. They've got plenty of that."

"Let's check the canning section. A few hundred lids would be about right as a welcome to the family gift, right?"

They kept up the easy banter through the rest of the shopping. Although their personalities were nothing alike, they had been close growing up and that shared history kept them good friends now.

Adam dropped off his first truckload of wood in front of the New Farm garage and headed back for another. Meanwhile, Michael and Alex were unloading the pickup and trailer near the spot where the wood shed would be built. Michael was working with a near constant low grumble; this was not an activity that he enjoyed on any level. Finally Alex reached the end of his patience. "Why don't you go make lunch and I'll finish this?" He was wishing once again that they had more than one truck in the family.

Soon after Michael disappeared inside, James came out pulling on gloves and smiling. He struck a pose and began singing 'I'm a Lumberjack.' By the end of the song Alex was laughing so hard he had trouble catching his breath. Cheerful mood restored, they continued heaving the wood out of the trailer.

Everyone made it back for lunch and while they were eating the phone rang. Pat took the call and when she returned announced, "That was Greg. The baling is going well; he's finished the rounds and will do the squares this afternoon. He wants to move the bales tomorrow unless we had plans for the Fourth." Nobody minded working on a holiday so that was settled.

The conversation turned to adoption. When asked about searching for their biological families the expressions turned grim. "We might have done if we hadn't almost lost James," said Michael. "He was five when the state came and took him away because his birth mother had changed her mind."

"We had no warning," said Pat. "The sheriff pulled up with a social worker and court order and he was gone. Matt didn't even get to say goodbye."

"What happened?" gasped Lindy. "How did you get to come back?"

"I was picked up on the highway two weeks later. I had had enough and wanted to go home so I started walking. The deputy found my 'mother' passed out drunk and brought me straight here. Looking back, he probably broke a lot of rules but they never bothered me again." His mouth drawn down and voice rough, he continued, "Those two weeks were terrifying. She was either ignoring me or screaming and hitting me the entire time. I didn't know if I would ever feel really safe again." Looking up at Pat, he asked, "How long was it before I stopped wetting the bed?"

She shook her head; that clearly wasn't important. "Your arm was broken. Matt had a lawyer threaten to sue the social worker for putting you in a dangerous environment if they tried anything again."

"Oh! Was that how that happened? I don't remember." James looked surprised.

Michael spoke again, "That's why none of ever went looking. Birth families were a danger. I had nightmares for months that they were coming to take me away."

"So did I."

"Me too."

Adam said, "We were too young to remember any of that but they told us about it later."

"Of course, we already knew about our parents," Alex added. "So there was no mystery to solve for us. What about you, Lindy? How does it feel to be adopted as an adult?"

"Safe. Wanted. Wonderful." She paused thoughtfully. "I love my parents but having children was never a conscious choice for them. We just happened and they were responsible for raising us. It wasn't a bad way to grow up, but it didn't feel like this. I don't know how to explain but they would never feel jealous of my being here instead of there."

It had been an emotional meal, but they still had work to do and didn't linger. Jeffrey returned to New Farm to watch the foundation going in and begin moving firewood into the garage. Adam may have been regretting his negotiation as he still had four more trips to make with the big truck. Michael decided he had had enough of the outdoors and chose to can with Pat. Steve and Alex headed outside to begin building the wood shed; basically, it would be a shallow, three-sided pole barn.

James was about to walk back to New Farm where the chimney sweep was expected soon when Lindy called him into her room.

"Look!" Lindy exclaimed. "Their eyes are open. Aren't they precious?" She cuddled a little ball of fluff against her cheek; it appeared to be all round stomach at this stage but the tiny blue eyes were open.

"Aw, hello cutie. Have you named them?"

"No, we need to wait to see their personalities first. I suppose I'll have to be careful with my clothes if they're going to be moving around and exploring."

James gazed around the room that did look like an explosion of fabric had happened. "Well, you should have a few days yet, but they will be into everything."

She blushed as she realized her inner slob was revealed, "I'll start hanging things up now. Are you going to call before bringing the chimney guy over?"

"Yes, I'll make sure you have time to get away to your gun lesson. I had better get going now. You'll be careful and listen to Steve?"

"I will. Can you leave your radio on again?"

He chuckled, "Any special requests?"

"Surprise me." She knelt to return the kitten to its mother then began picking up clothes.

Through the radio she heard the front door close before James' voice came through, "For Lindy, this is Believe in the Boogie." Intuition drew Lindy to the living room window where she could see James dancing down the driveway. Laughing, she watched until the curve put him out of sight then went back to cleaning her room.

At New Farm, James went through the house with the chimney expert. He learned that each appliance would need a separate chimney for safety. The best position for the kitchen stove would put its chimney through the central hall upstairs, but there was ample room. James explained that they wanted to use the fireplace chimney for a wood stove and asked about the best way to do so. After examining what was there, it was decided that the chimney needed new lining, but otherwise was in good shape and James could come to the store next week to choose a stove. This wasn't a busy time of year for them so they would be able to schedule the work quickly.

When asked about the furnace, James assured him that it was vented outside. Lindy had looked it over earlier and verified that the plumbing was in good shape and had probably been updated when the Andersons had to replace the boiler. Since the propane tank was now in place and hooked up, it was a relief not to have to worry about that part.

By the time they finished inside, the construction crew had completed their work for the day and left. Adam had been through with the big truck and left a pile of unsplit wood by the barn lean-to and Jeffrey had made a good start on shifting his pile into the garage. As James and the chimney sweep left, a truck pulled in with two large dumpsters. Jeffrey waved it over and told the driver to put them in the empty space on the other side of the house.

Back home, Steve received the call from James and rounded up his students. Michael stayed behind in the kitchen while Alex, Lindy and Pat headed over the hill. Alex carried his AR-15 while Lindy and Pat each held a shotgun. Steve followed with the bag and a .22 rifle. This time he set them up farther back from the target area.

After quizzing Lindy to see what she remembered from the previous lessons, he demonstrated how to work a shotgun. After shooting the 12 gauge, she looked discouraged and rubbed her sore shoulder. "I won't be much use with that."

"This should be easier for you." He handed a 20 gauge over.

Gingerly raising it to her shoulder, she was tense until after the shot. "It didn't hurt!"

"Keep going." When she had finished, Alex jogged down to change out the targets and brought hers back to explain about the shot pattern while Pat took a turn.

Steve let Alex demonstrate the AR-15 for Lindy. Pat had shot one before and didn't care for it. Lindy was willing to try, but ended up struggling with the weight. "Don't worry," Steve reassured her. "Your upper body strength will improve quickly with all the work you've been doing. Let's finish with the .22. I think you'll like it."

He was right. Lindy enjoyed the little rifle so much that she didn't want to stop. She felt like cheering every time the shot went where she aimed. When they finished, she and Pat sat to the side and watched Steve and Alex take turns with the AR-15. Their proficiency spoke of many hours of practice and was fascinating to witness.

"Maybe we can come back tomorrow evening so Adam can join us," suggested Lindy.

"Possibly," replied Steve. "But moving bales is exhausting, so we'll have to wait and see."

When they returned to the house, James was happy to report that the chimney had been swept and the stove passed inspection without any problems. Michael had been working like a trooper and the piles of produce had all been processed and put away. Delectable smells were wafting from the oven and he received the much deserved praise graciously.

12 FRIDAY

The ringing cell phone shattered the peaceful silence of the night. Lindy was so startled that her flailing arm knocked the phone onto the floor and she had to scramble for it under the bed.

"Hello?"

"Lindy? Are you okay? This is Mom. Nothing has happened to you?" The voice sounded frantic.

"I'm fine. Why? What's wrong?" Fear and panic were threatening to overwhelm her and her own voice was high-pitched.

"We're fine. Do you hear me? Your dad and I are fine. We had a scare and I was afraid for you."

"What do you mean? What kind of scare?" Lindy stayed on the floor where she had landed but shifted into a more comfortable position. Her bedroom door opened and Pat peeked in before shuffling inside in slippers and a bathrobe. She sat on the bed and waited in case she was needed.

"The neighbor's dog woke us up. You know the one your dad is always griping about. He got up and was threatening to go wake the neighbor and I got up to try to calm him down. That's when we smelled smoke. The back of the house was burning but we got out in plenty of time.

"Then I started worrying about you. Anyway, your dad is talking to the firefighters now. We'll go to a hotel and see how it looks in the morning." There was the sound of a shaky breath being drawn. "I think your dad wants to buy a steak for that damn dog. Ha!"

"Okay, Mom. I'll talk to you tomorrow. Love you." Lindy ended the call. "Wow. Another fire. That could have been…" Suddenly her whole body started shaking and she was sobbing uncontrollably.

"Shh, now. It will be okay. Breathe. That's right." Pat held her and gently stroked her hair. Mellow chose that moment to make her presence known by whining and pressing her nose onto Lindy's neck.

"Ack!" gurgled Lindy and she wrapped her arms around the old dog for a hug.

"Come on. Back in bed, dear." Pat tucked her in and slipped out of the room.

Morning came all too quickly as Mellow scratched on the door to be let out of Lindy's room. Mama Cass shook off her kittens and followed the dog out. It took Lindy a few more minutes to get ready to face the day and the circles under her eyes testified to the disturbed night.

The men ate quickly and everyone was outside waiting when a pickup drove in pulling a large flatbed trailer. Pat waved at the driver, then spotted the figure sitting on the end of the trailer. "Why, how nice! It's Katherine."

"Kat's back!" exclaimed Adam and he and Alex ran over and hopped onto the trailer on either side of her. The other men were slower but they all paused to greet her before climbing on board. Lindy waved as they pulled away, but nobody noticed and she felt a pang of jealousy.

"Who is she?" Lindy asked Pat as they went to do chores.

"Katherine? She's Greg Davis' daughter. He rents our fields. She always worked for him in the summers. Then she left, oh, it must have been four or five years ago. I think this is the first time she's been back."

"Where did she go? College?"

"Why, I don't know. I have a hard time imagining her at college though." Pat smiled at Lindy. "You're getting along well with the chickens, I see."

Lindy had to laugh. It was a colorful carpet of feathers around her legs. Reaching down, she picked up Grace and tucked her under her arm while she shuffled through the flock. Grace was quite content to be carried and clucked happily.

Out in the hayfield the work quickly settled into a routine. Kat, Steve and Michael stacked the bales that the others threw up onto the slow-moving trailer. At first the twins tried to impress their neighbor by running with the bales, but even they couldn't keep up that pace and slowed down. When the bales were stacked so high that they couldn't throw them up from the ground, everyone was ready for a break and Greg turned back to the farm. He stopped the trailer at the base of a hay elevator that was already in place leading up to the barn loft and everyone went inside for a cold drink before unloading.

Lindy got a surprise when she was introduced to Kat; she had always considered herself to be of average height at 5'7" but Kat was easily 6'3" and Lindy felt dwarfed. Glancing over at James' amused expression, she felt her sense of humor return and was able to greet Kat in a friendly manner. When he dealt with that sort of height difference daily, how could she let it bother her?

Kat wore her hair in a single, shoulder-length braid and had pale blue eyes. Lindy decided her name fit well because she moved with an easy grace that reminded her of a mountain lion. She seemed aloof, not exactly cold, but more like indifferent and spoke as little as possible.

Lindy tagged along when they headed back outside and started up the elevator. Half of the workers went up into the loft to stack and the others hauled the bales off the trailer and onto the elevator. As soon as it was empty they piled back onto the trailer and drove out to gather another load. Back and forth they worked all day until the last square bale had been tucked away into the barn. The big round bales would be loaded with a tractor and lined up along the fence line where they would serve as an additional windbreak.

The men were all dragging their feet after the last load and groaned loudly when they sat down that evening. That's when Lindy produced her surprise of homemade ice cream. They were happy but she noticed more than a couple were having trouble keeping their eyes open.

They were heading up for an early night when James paused and asked Lindy if she had heard from her parents.

"Yes, it was arson and the police are looking for a connection to John. They've decided to go visit my sister in California while repairs are being made."

After he tottered off to bed, Lindy sat out on the porch and listened to the distant sound of the Fourth being celebrated. Pat joined her after a few minutes.

"They didn't ask how your date went."

"Some of them probably forgot and the others didn't want to think about it." Pat smiled complacently.

"Did you have a good time?"

"Yes, we're going out again next week."

13 SATURDAY

Breakfast was a cheerfully exuberant meal. The family had decided not to do the farmer's market this weekend so they could all take part in the haystack building and enjoy the last days they were together. James finished eating first and announced that he would meet them at the hay meadow in about half an hour.

"What do you think he's up to?" asked Jeffrey.

Nobody had an answer so they scattered to get ready for the day. Steve took the truck to pick up the hay wagon they were borrowing. The twins cleared breakfast and Michael put a roast in the oven. Jeffrey and Lindy went to the barn to gather the pitchforks and Pat prepared a cooler of cold drinks. When Steve drove back in, everyone piled onto the wagon for the short ride to the meadow. Biff was in heaven running to each person in between barking spurts.

"So, are we supposed to wait for him?" asked Adam.

"Let's just get started. There's plenty to be done," Steve decided.

They had pitched enough to cover the floor of the wagon when James pulled up. He had passengers in his car and jumped out to assist them. Three very elderly men were soon moving slowly towards where Lindy and Pat were standing. The short, round man with a cane and a very tall, but stooped man with a walker were both wearing feed store hats while the man with a rather large nose leaning on another walker had on a dapper fedora.

"Goodness! He looks like an ancient Ian McKellen!" Lindy whispered.

As they gathered around, James made the introductions. "Gentlemen, this is my mother, Pat Stevenson. Mom, meet Mr. Yeager, Mr. Limmer, and Mr. Baumgarten; our hay-making experts." He stood grinning happily for a moment before running for his pitchfork to help his brothers.

Lindy felt a little shy, but Pat was equal to the situation and soon was engaged in a riveting conversation with two of the guests on topics ranging from the weather to deep sea drilling. There are few things old farmers enjoy more than a robust argument and these two even seemed to switch sides in mid-flow to counter their own statements.

The dapper Mr. Limmer turned his charm on for Lindy and attempted to draw her out in conversation. It turned out to be fascinating as he spun tales from his childhood on a nearby farm to his life as a bachelor travelling the globe. The discussions were so interesting that they didn't even notice when the brothers finished their work and the hay wagon creaked past. James had to step in and begin herding his guests back to his car for the short ride to the barn.

On disembarking, James explained to Lindy that they wanted to build a haystack like the pioneers would have; one that would shed rain and not rot like some of their previous attempts. His reasoning behind bringing in three retired farmers was that what one forgot, the others might recall. It was a good plan in theory but in practice fell short. Very soon, Mr. Yeager and Mr. Baumgarten were standing toe to toe shouting at each other while Mr. Limmer shrugged helplessly. "I'm sorry. I remember the stacks looking like giant loaves of bread with straight sides and taller than the loft door, but how they were made…"

Steve and Jeffrey listened to the shouting match then stepped back to compare what they got out of it. Finally, Steve interrupted the argument, "So the main difference between your methods is one uses a center pole and three supports and the other doesn't, right?"

When they nodded agreement, he said, "Okay, we'll try both and make one stack on each side of the hay wagon. Jeffrey will handle the stack with a pole and I'll do the other. The twins will pitch hay down off the wagon, Michael helps Jeffrey and James helps me. You two start thinking about what we need to do so the tops shed rain. Let's get to work!"

Jeffrey headed for the barn to find a pole and supports while the twins climbed the sides of the wagon. They began pitching hay down to Steve and he and James immediately began spreading it out into a circle and stomping it flat. It took Jeffrey longer to get set up, but he and Michael were soon building their own stack. By mid-morning the wagon was empty and the men went back to the meadow for another load. Pat invited their guests to the house to take a break and they were soon relaxing on the porch with tea and lemonade. That's when the stories really began to flow; some funny, some tragic, all interesting.

All three of them had served in WWII. Mr. Yeager was Navy and fought in the Pacific. Mr. Limmer was a pilot and sent to work with the RAF. Mr. Baumgarten had been part of D-Day at Normandy. When it came to talking about the war, none of them were inclined to argue. Lindy sat on the floor with her arms wrapped around her legs and listened. Her grandfathers had been too young so she had never been exposed to real-life accounts to this part of history. Even when the young men returned and began unloading hay again, nobody shifted or interrupted the tales. Mr. Yeager was describing the time his ship was torpedoed when the brothers joined them on the porch. Lindy reluctantly rose and went with Michael to get lunch on the table. First they added the extension leaves so there would be room for everyone, then she set it while he got the food.

The guests were delighted with a meal so delicious and tender that it was easy on even the most troublesome of dentures. They volunteered to return and 'help' every Saturday and Pat replied, "We would be honored if you did. Of course, Michael won't be cooking but I hope you will come often anyway."

After the meal, all the men returned to the haystacks where they were ready to work on the tops while Pat and Lindy cleared up. Then, Pat asked Lindy to help her with the milk run and they loaded eggs into the Tank. On the drive Pat recalled stories her mother had told her about being a child during the war and promised to dig out the Life magazines they had saved from those years.

The milk run seemed fairly routine except that Mr. Hansen had a pile of boxes of jars waiting for them. Apparently, when he had spread the word the response was strong. Many people didn't want to throw away perfectly good jars but didn't can themselves and couldn't be bothered with selling them.

"Most were happy to get rid of them. You bring me some of that zucchini bread next time and we'll call it even. By the way, I heard tell your boys bought a kitchen stove. You make sure they replace the gasket before they try using it." He gave a firm nod and went inside.

Pat looked at the stack of boxes and sighed. "I guess we're loading these by ourselves." The back seat, the floor around Lindy's feet and the space between her and Pat were filled to capacity but they got them all in.

When they returned to the farm they found all the men standing around admiring the haystacks. They certainly looked good with fairly straight sides and tops so neat they looked combed.

Although the younger men encouraged the elderly gents to stay longer, they demurred and were obviously tired so everyone shook hands and James loaded them back into his car.

Pat passed on the message about the stove gasket to Jeffrey who said he would look up the process online. A brief discussion revealed that none of them were in the mood to work on the wood shed and they all really wanted to rest. The men headed upstairs to shower off the hay dust and sweat while Pat and Lindy went looking for the old magazines in the study. When the men came back downstairs, they found them on the sofa reading snippets of 70 year old news to each other.

"How different it was then!" exclaimed Lindy. "Every day the war news was the most important thing they heard. Now, you have to go looking for information.

"I wonder if it was easier or harder to bear if you had loved ones fighting and you heard about it constantly."

Pat looked thoughtful, "I imagine it depended greatly on your own personality. Your views probably changed as the war went on too."

"How lucky that our three made it back in one piece."

"Mr. Limmer had a prosthetic leg," Steve said bluntly. Then he shrugged. "You get so you can spot them."

"Are you ready to go with Michael tomorrow, Lindy?" asked Pat, changing the topic to something less distressing.

"Yes, I'm packed. It's strange, I'm looking forward to it, but I also don't want to leave here."

"The best trips are when you're happy to come home again." Pat smiled. "So, James will drive up Tuesday for his meeting and you can come home with him Wednesday or stay longer if you're having too much fun."

At this moment James bounced through the front door. "Well? Did you like my surprise? Weren't they great?"

Everyone agreed that it had been a good idea and the day was a success. Lindy asked, "How did you find them?"

"The social director at their nursing home was a friend in high school. We got to talking at our ten year reunion about how some of her residents were founts of knowledge and when this idea hit me, I called and asked to borrow some of them."

"Did they really want to come back? I'd love to talk to them again."

"Yes, I arranged to get them in two weeks. I hope that's okay with everyone." He looked anxious until they all agreed. "Now for the not so good news. I heard the weather forecast on the radio. It's supposed to start raining Sunday night and not stop for most of the week. I'm going over to New Farm and work on moving more of the wood into the garage."

After a chorus of groans, they all stood to go with him. "Wait. Why don't some of you work on finishing the wood shed here? Any more than four people are just going to get in each other's way over there. I'll take the twins and Lindy. And I'm voting for Michael to cook something incredible for dinner instead of throwing logs around."

Working as a team, they were able to move and stack most of the pile inside the garage before being summoned home for dinner. Walking back up the driveway they saw that Steve and Jeffrey had finished the wood shed and lined the floor with sturdy pallets.

"Nice," said Alex. "We can get all the split wood put away in the morning and start splitting the rest in the afternoon." Lindy didn't say anything, already feeling a little sad at leaving the following day.

Nobody could be down during dinner though. Michael had outdone himself with experimental dishes, conversation was lively and everyone was determined to enjoy the last evening as a complete family. After eating, they settled back down in the living room and talked about how labor intensive life in the country used to be. Everyone froze as Mellow walked through the room carrying a kitten by the nape of its neck. Alex jumped up and gently released it, checking it carefully before returning it to its mother. Pat shook her head. "We're going to have to keep an eye on her if she's getting overly maternal again. Remember the year she kept trying to adopt the chicks?"

Adam joined the old dog on the floor and reassured her that they weren't angry. When Alex returned he suggested they put a gate across Lindy's door to keep the kittens inside and Mellow out. And on that note they all headed for bed.

14 SUNDAY

Morning found Lindy outside wandering around; first she did the chicken chores, then visited Susie and the piglets and finally made her way to the garden. That's where Pat found her. "You know you don't have to go, right? We could probably get what you need online."

Lindy smiled. "I know. Staying would be easy, but I feel like I need to go or I'll turn into a coward and hide for the rest of my life." Chuckling, she added, "I have to admit I'm glad I don't have to go by myself, but I wish you were coming too for the shopping part."

Pat sighed wistfully, "That would be fun. Too bad there won't be room in Michael's car. We'll have to go up this winter when it slows down here."

"Can we? Shopping, go to the theatre, eat out…"

"All of the above. Come inside now and have some breakfast." And the two women linked arms and headed back to the house, thinking happily of the future.

After breakfast Michael drove his car out of the pole barn where it had been parked under a canvas sheet. Lindy blinked in surprise at the low-slung, dark purple sports car that pulled to a stop in front of the house.

Michael climbed out, already explaining, "I know, it's not practical. We bought it to celebrate my becoming head chef." He grinned foolishly, "It's a lot of fun though."

Shaking her head, Lindy went back to her room and repacked into a small bag the bare minimum she would need before she went shopping. Now she understood why he had mentioned keeping an entire wardrobe at the farm; he could hardly carry enough luggage back and forth. Outside again, she found him packing the tiny trunk with fresh vegetables and eggs. When he finished, every spare inch of space in the car was full except where they would be sitting.

By 9:30 they were ready to go. Everyone gathered around for hugs and to see them off. Lindy waved until the curve hid them from view and she turned to face the next adventure.

It was just after 1:00 when they reached the outskirts of the city. Michael had a tendency to flip back and forth between obscure heavy metal bands and classical music; unfortunately, it was all played at a very loud volume leading to Lindy having a pounding headache. As they moved into the city though, he turned the music off so he could concentrate on the increasingly heavy traffic. After forty-five minutes of cautious driving they were deep downtown and Lindy was craning her neck to see the skyscrapers. Heading down a one-way street, Michael pulled into an entrance to underground parking. Swiping a keycard raised the barricade and he drove down the ramp and through the dim interior until reaching his space.

"Wait here a moment," he said before jogging away. A few minutes later he returned pushing a shopping cart. As Michael loaded the produce he explained that the building kept several carts for the residents' use and that they were tagged with alarms in case they were removed from the building. He had to swipe his keycard again at the elevator but his apartment was accessed with a normal key.

Lindy gazed around with interest. The door opened directly into a large open space that held living, dining and kitchen areas without any demarcation between each. The walls and floor were a very pale cream color and most of the furniture was black. The exceptions were a startling deep purple and looking closer, Lindy realized the dining table she had thought was black was actually the darkest purple. The overall effect was striking but would have felt harsh if there weren't an abundance of large, vibrant tropical plants throughout.

Michael showed her the small hallway with doors to his room, a study, the bathroom and the guestroom. Entering, she nearly tripped over a stack of cardboard boxes. "What the...?" exclaimed Michael as he read the note 'Please ship home'. Glaring at the dusty room and unmade beds, he stalked out muttering about the twins. He soon returned with an armload of clean linen and helped Lindy make the beds. Then, while she dusted, he sealed and labeled the boxes before loading them onto the cart and taking them down to the lobby for shipping.

Michael soon returned and whipped up a stir-fry while Lindy enjoyed the view from the tall windows. She was relieved when her headache faded after eating and asked what he would do next. "I don't have to be at the restaurant until 6:00 so why don't we walk over to the nearest shopping center? It's only a couple blocks away."

"You have to work tonight?"

"Yes, and I've booked you a table so let's find something dressy for you to wear."

Lindy was a little annoyed to have her evening prearranged without her input, but swallowed her ire since she was a guest. Her sense of humor quickly returned as she recognized the signs of an autocratic big brother in action.

Emerging from the elevator into the front lobby, Michael led her to the desk where a large, stern man in uniform was monitoring a bank of camera views. Upon introduction, Lindy soon found herself the possessor of her own keycard and a sheet of instructions on her responsibilities as a temporary resident. Michael verified that the twins had turned in their keycards and they walked outside. As they made their way, Lindy was grateful to have Michael by her side; even on a Sunday afternoon the downtown streets were thronged with people, most of whom seemed to be in rush to get somewhere.

Entering the mall was a relief as there were far fewer people inside, but soon Lindy felt a different anxiety as she saw all the shops were the expensive types of boutiques that she normally wouldn't go near. Michael smiled in understanding, "Don't worry, this is just for one outfit so you can shine tonight. You'll do most of your shopping in one of the suburban malls. As they approached one shop the door was flung open, "Mr. Stevenson! What a pleasant surprise to see you again! It has been too long." The thin, elegant woman held her hand out for him to take which he did briefly.

"I'm happy to be back, Ms Driscolli. This is my sister, Lindy. I'd like to find something special for her to wear."

"Hmm." The saleswoman's appraising gaze made Lindy feel awkward. "Formal?"

"Semi."

"I have several that would suit." And so began a whirlwind hour that concluded with Lindy owning a robin-eggshell blue sheath dress that cost more than a week's salary at her old job. Michael was just beginning and whisked her around for shoes, a manicure and a quick haircut. They just had time to go home, change and catch a taxi to the restaurant.

Soon, Lindy found herself seated near a flowing waterfall where she felt both on display and secluded. Michael promised to check on her as much as possible before dashing away. She expected to spend most of the evening alone, but was joined by the owner of the restaurant, a wickedly funny man who asked after the twins with his hand on his heart and batting his eyelashes furiously. "Seriously, though, is the family well? Is Michael happy? I was afraid we would lose him after the accident. I forced him into grief counselling but you never know if it will help."

"He is terribly missed when he leaves. Could you move your restaurant closer to home?"

"Alas! The customers are fickle creatures and would not follow. On the other hand, the junior chefs are developing nicely; perhaps we can arrange for more time off for Michael. And you? How are you enjoying the city?"

"It's a little like stepping through a mirror. Just this morning I was feeding the chickens and now I'm Eliza Doolittle."

Michael's boss threw his head back and laughed. "And which side of the mirror do you prefer?"

"Oh, home! This is a fine adventure but I want to go home to the farm."

"Michael mentioned you were here for shopping. Would you enjoy it more with some company? Let's see if you and my assistant are compatible." He sent a message with his phone and shortly a young woman with masses of red hair approached. "Addie, this is Michael's sister, Lindy. Please keep her company while I'm busy."

Addie slipped into his chair and set her tablet on the table. Leaning forward eagerly she asked, "What's he up to? Most people he would abandon heartlessly so he either really likes you or..."

Lindy smiled back, "I think it's more about keeping Michael happy. He probably isn't looking forward to following me around the mall tomorrow."

"Very likely," nodded Addie. "Keeping the talent happy is one of Philip's main goals in life and Michael is his top talent. Does that mean I get to go shopping with you? What do you want?"

"It's more what I need." Lindy proceeded to explain about her entire wardrobe being destroyed in the fire. "But it won't be fancy clothes. I need practical things like a winter coat and sweaters."

"But this will be fun!" cried Addie. "I love shopping and can help you find things that will suit you and last. The key is not to be distracted by what's in fashion now. You want clothes that will still look good years from now."

The girls settled in for a good chat; occasionally Michael or Philip would stop by briefly, but mostly they were left alone. By the time Michael came to get Lindy, Addie had arranged to pick her up the following morning. As the taxi carried them back to the apartment, Lindy's thoughts turned to the farm and wondered what they were doing.

James paused to stretch and gauge their progress. There were only three splitting axes on the farm so they had been taking turns rotating between using them and stacking wood into the shed. Then Jeffrey had been distracted at a crucial moment and came close to giving himself a serious injury. The glancing blow to his calf had bled profusely and reduced him to a spectator. The others had taken this safety reminder to heart and were staying focused on the task at hand.

Near the barn a line of large, round hay bales was being formed next to the fence. Kat and her father had been busy all morning moving bales. Of course, this was a scene that was being recreated on farms all across the region. Getting ready for the next winter was not something prudent people left to chance.

As noon approached, Steve strode over to where Kat had parked while Greg unloaded more bales with his tractor. "Hi, Kat. Will you two join us for lunch? Mom's cooking today."

"I wouldn't mind. I'll have to ask Dad what he wants to do."

"That's fine." Steve leaned back against the side of the truck in companionable silence. It never even occurred to him to make small talk and he appreciated Kat's natural reticence. She would no more pry into his business than she would answer someone else questioning hers. When her father joined them, she repeated the invitation.

"Humph. More of Michael's fancy food?" Greg asked.

"No, he's gone. From the garlic smell I'd guess spaghetti."

"Ah, Pat's cooking? Sounds good."

Normally Kat would ignore her dad's rudeness, but today it bothered her so she began talking to Steve as they walked to the house. "How are your tomatoes? We've got a touch of blight in ours already."

"No blight yet, but some of my early producers are showing signs of blossom end rot. I think it's from the very wet spring we had."

"Give and take. I'm not seeing many grasshoppers."

"True, I think most of the buggers drowned in their egg holes. Something has to make up for the mosquitoes," Steve grumbled.

"Would you like some guineas? I know someone who is tired of them and Dad won't have any at our place."

Steve brightened up, "Guineas, hmm. I might be interested, but I'd better make sure they wouldn't drive Mom mad."

Over lunch the conversation centered on hay and the weather; specifically on if they were likely to get enough rain in the coming weeks for a second cutting or if they should turn the cattle onto those fields. It was decided that they would, as usual, have to wait and see. Then Greg turned his attention on Jeffrey's injury. "Haven't you got any old leather chaps? That would have saved you the worst of the damage."

"I don't think we do." Jeffrey turned to Pat.

"No," she said. "Matt never expected to need chaps. Does the farm supply store carry them?"

"I'm going in tomorrow to pick up wormer for the pigs," Steve said. "I can check then."

After lunch, Greg and Kat went back to hauling bales; Pat reminding him to stop back when they finished and they could go over the accounts. Instead of paying him for haying, she deducted that fee from the land rent he paid.

As Steve, James and the twins returned to the woodpile, Pat arranged a lounge chair with a cushion and put Jeffrey to work snapping beans. Deciding that he looked a bit lonely surrounding by buckets, James slipped into the chicken pen and scooped up Grace; stroking her back he carried her to Jeffrey and settled her on his legs. "Did you think I needed a babysitter?" Jeffrey asked sardonically. His calf was throbbing and he felt like a fool for hurting himself.

James squatted and looked him in the eye. "I think we all need friends. And today your friend is Grace." As he returned to his work, Jeffrey frowned at the hen who cocked her head quizzically back. At that moment a grasshopper landed on the chair and Grace snatched it up. Suddenly he was transported back in time and could see his brothers racing around the yard, knobby knees and bare feet flashing as they chased grasshoppers. His breath caught in his throat as he remembered his father standing on the porch in worn overalls and heavy work boots; looking stern as Jeffrey ran up to show off a particularly fine grasshopper, then breaking into a smile and crouching down to admire the catch. Even years after his passing, Jeffrey missed him.

The hours passed and dark, heavy clouds began to build on the horizon. Kat parked the hay trailer and walked over to where the men were still working on the wood. Jeffrey watched as Adam held out his axe and she stepped up to the round he had set up. Her every move showing grace and power, she swung the axe down with a loud 'Thwack!' and the round split neatly in two. All other movement stopped as they watched her efficiently chop the halves into thirds. Without a word she calmly handed the axe back and walked over to where Jeffrey was chuckling. "I can't figure out if you do things just to torment the twins or not."

"Humph." Stooping beside his leg, she gingerly eased up the bandage and studied his wound. Now frowning, she asked, "Did you apply an antibiotic cream after you cleaned this?"

"No, there wasn't any in the medicine cabinet."

"Where's your first aid kit?"

"We took it over to New Farm. That seemed like the more dangerous environment." Jeffrey was flushed with fresh embarrassment.

Stalking away, Kat went to her truck and took the first aid kit out from behind the seat. Setting it up beside his leg, she began by cutting off the bandage and re-cleaning the wound. Face pale and hands gripping the edges of the seat, Jeffrey asked, "How does it look?"

"I've seen worse." She calmly flushed out the gash.

"Damn, Kat! Where have you been?"

That question brought her eyes up to meet his for an instant before she looked down again. "I can't tell you that, but I am competent at first aid." Shield firmly in place, her tone said the conversation was over. The fresh bandages she applied were certainly neater than those she had removed and he had no reason to doubt her qualifications, but she hadn't been overly gentle and sweat dotted his forehead.

Distracting himself by watching the play of muscles under her skin as she cleaned up the equipment, Jeffrey wondered what her body fat percentage was and didn't realize he spoke out loud until she answered, "Sixteen percent."

"Sorry, I didn't mean…"

"It doesn't matter." Setting the kit aside, she strode into the house without another word.

"Shit!" Grace looked up then went back to preening her feathers.

In a few minutes Kat and Greg walked out the door and headed for their vehicles. Jeffrey had been so distracted by the bandaging that he hadn't even noticed Greg go inside.

Pat came out and started gathering the last of the snapped beans.

"Mom, do we have any painkillers?" Jeffrey asked in a subdued voice.

"Of course, dear. I'll get you some." She then called out, "James! Come get Grace and do the chores."

James jogged over, picked up the hen and began cooing to her, "Who's a good girl then? Did you have a good day?" Just then a cool breeze swept in ahead of the clouds and Grace began scolding. "Okay, calm down. I'm taking you back now."

They could see lightning slashing across the clouds and each stepped up their pace. Adam fetched the canvas tarp that had covered Michael's car and hooked it over the wood shed opening using carabiners. Alex began moving vehicles into the pole barn in case of hail and Steve ran up to the garden to strip nearly ripe tomatoes off the plants. Pat let the dogs out for a last run around and helped Jeffrey into the house. The weather radio in the kitchen was blaring out alerts and warnings. A tornado had touched down in the county south of theirs. Strong winds and large hail were associated with the storm.

James and Adam ran out to chivy Steve back to the house and help carry the buckets he had filled already. An eerie gloom descended and the first fat raindrops fell as the lights flickered and went out. This was normal and Pat had already placed and lit an oil lamp on the table. "Who wants to play cards?" quipped James.

Jeffrey shook his head grimly, "I just want to go to bed."

"No, dear. You'll have to sleep on the couch in case we have to go down to the cellar. Or you could use Lindy's room," Pat offered.

"The couch is fine," he growled and limped away.

The rest of the family sat around the table, listening to the updates and soothing a frightened Biff.

15 MONDAY

Alex was the first up in the morning and stood on the porch surveying the damage. He flinched at the sight of a maple tree uprooted and hung up on the trees on the opposite side of the driveway. That was going to be difficult to clear but would have to be one of their first priorities.

The pole barn was missing at least two of its roof panels. He couldn't see from his current vantage point if it had sustained any other damage. The other buildings seemed to be fine but he decided to check all around while he did chores. A lowing noise alerted him to the arrival of the cattle, looking wet but unscathed.

Pat gazed out the kitchen window as she cooked breakfast. With the power still out she had to light the burner with a match but that was a minor inconvenience. More worrisome was the food in the fridge and freezer. She decided that after the garden slowed down she would work on canning meat from the freezer, especially now that they had such an abundance of empty jars. She wasn't really worried; the power company was generally good about getting the lines back up and running.

Steve stood in the tattered garden and mentally tallied up what was lost, what could be coaxed back and what had survived. The sunflowers had snapped and it looked like something had been dragged across the peas. The sweet corn was laid flat and the lettuce was pressed into the mud. All the root vegetables seemed fine and the cabbages hadn't budged. Any branches of tomato that had grown above the cages were broken, but the peppers didn't look bad. Turning away, he began thinking about what could be planted this late in the season.

When he joined the others at the breakfast table, Alex told them about the roof damage. He went on to say, "I could see more trees either uprooted or with broken limbs in the shelter belt. I think I should take the truck and ride the fences in case any fell across them."

Pat nodded. "I'll ride along." A lifetime on farms had given her plenty of fencing experience.

"I suppose the rest of us should get to work on that tree," Adam said.

"Carefully," added Jeffrey. "And make sure your radios are on. This storm has me convinced that Steve has a good idea with the solar battery charger. If the power lines were down for any length of time, at least we could keep the radios charged." Seeing his brother's expression lighten for the first time since the storm rolled in he added, "I ordered your kit Saturday and it should arrive this week. Now, you guys get out there and do some work. I'll call Lindy and Michael. Then I'm going to do something exciting...like peel potatoes."

With a slightly more cheerful mood, the family set to work. James began moving the cars out of the pole barn so he could reach the tractor. Alex and Pat started by applying liberal amounts of bug repellent before loading the truck with fencing materials, tools and a chainsaw. Adam dragged out the heavy chains while Steve prepped the other chainsaws. As the truck headed out into the pasture, James came chugging out on the 1955 Allis Chalmers. The orange-red paint was faded, but the steady growl spoke of a well-maintained machine. Normally it was used to move hay for the cattle, but today they would attempt to pull the tree away from the branches holding it up. The entire root ball had popped up, so Adam fastened the chain around the base and to the back of the tractor. With a slow, steady pressure James drove forward. At first it seemed like this wouldn't work until a loud crack signaled a branch giving way and the maple came crashing down. The men discussed pulling the tree farther but decided there was no real benefit and they got down to the work of cutting it up.

Pat was feeling immensely grateful as they listened to the radio discussion of storm damages. Not only had they come through the storm in good shape, but she had most of her family around her. They didn't get far before finding a cottonwood branch down on the fence and naturally, it was in a marshy area so the mosquitoes rose up in clouds around them. Luckily, it was a small limb and hadn't damaged the fence so they soon had it cut and continued their rounds. In the far pasture they found a tree had snapped and taken the fence out completely. Pat radioed Jeffrey to let him know where they were and that it would be a few hours before they finished.

It was almost three hours later when they had finished stretching the last strand of barbed wire into place. Alex moved to help his mom cross the fence to the truck when her foot slipped on the wet grass and she fell back into the ditch. Flailing for balance, she landed hard and felt a dizzying wave of pain as her arm snapped.

"Mom!" Alex shouted and leapt down into the muddy water. Easing her up gently, he checked her for other injuries, then helped her to stand. Looking at the truck and considering the slow, bumpy ride back to the farm, Alex quickly decided to call for a ride to pick them up from the road.

"Jeffrey! Is the driveway open?"

Jeffrey startled at the urgent tone coming from his radio. "Yes, they're just clearing up the mess now. What's wrong?"

"Mom has a broken arm and we need a ride to the hospital. Send someone to the east side of the far pasture to pick us up."

"Got it." Hobbling onto the porch, Jeffrey could see that no one else heard the radio over the chainsaw noise. He was about to go himself when he spotted Kat's truck moving past the remains of the tree and coming towards the house. Hurrying as best he could, he met her in the yard and asked for her help. Nodding briskly, she ran back to her truck and left much faster than she had arrived.

Kat found them sitting on the side of the road. A miserable looking Pat huddled under Alex's arm, both wet and muddy. Jumping out, Kat grabbed a blanket from behind the seat and hurried to drape it over Pat's shoulders. "Thank you, dear." Pat's voice was hoarse and shaky.

The hospital was so busy that it was four hours before Kat brought Pat and Alex home again. She came inside to help the exhausted Pat get cleaned up and in bed before quietly leaving. James slipped into his mom's room and sat on the end of the bed. "What do you need? Food? Kittens? Something to read?"

"I'm famished," Pat replied gratefully. "Then I'd like to hear what happened here today."

"I'll be right back."

James returned carrying a bed tray with a simple meal and a vase full of daisies. Pat's eyes lit up. "Oh! How pretty. Where did those come from?"

"There's a card." He smiled at her reaction.

"Pete...how sweet. But how did he find out already?"

"Steve called him about the pole barn roof. When he asked about you..."

"I see. Well, tell me the rest of the news." She began to eat while listening.

"We finished clearing away the tree. Yay! More wood to split. Then Steve dropped me off out by the truck so I could bring it in when he went to town. Adam and I drove around the nearby roads clearing branches off. Steve didn't find any chaps at the farm supply but he was told to check out the flea market. Apparently they resell stuff from farm auctions. He found two pairs of old chaps there plus some tools. He said something about splitting mauls and wedges. This afternoon we helped him in the garden.

"Now, do you want me to cancel my meeting and stay here to help? I hate leaving."

Pat smiled, "No, James. I want you to go and bring Lindy home."

"Then that's what I'll do." He moved the vase to her bedside table, kissed the top of her head and took away the empty tray.

As Pat shifted around to find a comfortable position for her cast she murmured to herself, "At least it's my left arm."

Meanwhile, that morning in the city, Lindy waited on the sidewalk for Addie to pick her up. Knowing how heavy a bag can get when doing serious shopping, she had her driver's license, debit card and the key to Michael's apartment in one pocket and the cell phone in the other. She patted the phone pocket and smiled, remembering Jeffrey's call earlier. It was like a breath of fresh air to hear from home.

A blue SUV with tinted windows pulled up in front of her. The window hummed down and Addie shouted 'Good morning!'; Lindy climbed in and they were off. Once back in traffic, Addie never took her eyes off the street and the mirrors; at the same time her mouth moved constantly. "I've got the day all planned out. We'll start with the big important stuff and save the little accessories for last in case you lose the will to continue. First stop will be my favorite outdoor store. I'm big into snowmobiling and ice climbing so I can steer you towards the quality, durable gear. Just be warned it won't be pretty, girly stuff. You'll be able to work through a blizzard if needed, but it's going to cost.

"After that we're going to my secret source for sweaters. I'll tell you about them now so you know what to expect. They're three retired sisters who decided to move back to their family home when they each found themselves living alone. One of them was my favorite high school teacher, Mrs. Wright, who always wore the prettiest clothes. She tried to show me how to knit, but I'm hopeless. Anyway, they're all mad about yarn and produce more than they could possibly wear, so they sell some to their friends. I arranged for you to look at what they've got on hand. Ah! Here's our first stop."

It appeared to be a typical sporting goods store; in other words, a place Lindy would never have shopped at before. Grabbing a cart, Addie steered directly for the winter coat section. "We can waste a lot of time trying on different coats, but this is what I have and I put a lot of research in before buying one."

"Rab? I've never heard of that." Lindy ran her hand down the line of puffy coats, lingering on the blue and purple colors. She slipped a size 10 purple off the hanger and pulled it on. "Why is the hood so big?"

"That's so it fits over a helmet and it's marketed for cold-weather sports enthusiasts, so if you haven't spent much time with that…"

Lindy finally looked at the price tag. "$400! Are you crazy?"

"Were you serious about working outside all winter or not? Because I can take you to Wally's World and you can buy a $30 crap coat but you won't last five minutes when you need to."

Lindy remembered the misery of a snowstorm with a flat tire and said, "No, let's do this right." The cart was quickly filled with boots, hats, mittens, gloves and long underwear. When Lindy winced at the total, Addie patted her arm and said, "Trust me. This was the worst."

Next, Addie drove to an older residential area and pulled over in front of a charming two-story house with a riot of flowers in the front yard. They were clearly expected because the front door opened before they were even out of the SUV.

"Come in, come in!" called the older woman. "Addie, you're looking well. And you must be Lindy. A pleasure to meet you. I'm Mavis. My sisters are both out this morning, but they helped me pick out a selection for you to look at." They followed her into what would have been a library in most homes. The floor to ceiling shelves were full of a rainbow of yarns.

"How beautiful!" exclaimed Lindy in delight.

Mavis smiled complacently. "Do you knit?"

"No, but I've just begun learning."

"Well, let's see if we have anything that works for you." Mavis led them to a table piled with hats, scarves, gloves and all sorts of sweaters. The young women dove in happily. Lindy was worried about how to pay, but Mavis had an app on her phone that processed the debit card. Leaving with bags full of lovely items, Addie chuckled, "I can't go there without buying something. It's addictive."

"That blanket you got is gorgeous. I've never seen anything like it before," Lindy said.

"It's like an explosion of color and texture, isn't it? Exactly right for my personality. Mrs. Wright knew I've been wanting one since I saw the last one they made. They use up leftover bits of yarns in them."

Once behind the wheel again Addie asked, "How about some lunch? Do you like Chinese?"

Over their meal they shared stories of their families, jobs and relationships. The friendship blossomed and Lindy invited Addie to come stay at the farm sometime.

"Thanks, but it doesn't sound like my type of adventure. I've got my winter vacation already booked. We're doing a two week glacier trek. It's going to be amazing!" Addie's waving arms nearly knocked over a waiter and she humbly apologized. Blushing, she said, "Maybe we should go."

This time they walked to the other end of the strip mall where a trendy looking shop sat. Lindy looked askance at Addie, "I thought we were done with expensive stuff."

"We are, this is a second-hand store. The beauty of it is this is where the wealthier people sell things from last season or that they've outgrown. The higher-end name brands tend to be well made so are even more of a bargain."

For three solid hours Lindy stayed in the changing room trying on the armloads of clothes that Addie brought. She was wilting by the end and longing to put her feet up and never think about clothes again. In contrast, Addie was still bounding with energy. "This is how I keep going at my job. Thank goodness Michael is back! The other chefs argue constantly. You look about done in. Ready to call it a day?"

"Oh, yes!" Lindy texted Michael to let him know they were heading back and when Addie pulled up in front of the apartment building he was waiting. Lindy hugged and thanked her friend while he unloaded and moved her purchases into the lobby.

"You've got my phone number and email so keep in touch!" Addie called as she climbed back into the SUV and drove away.

Michael hurried Lindy upstairs, quickly explained the meal he had left ready for her to heat up and left for work. Within ten minutes Lindy was fast asleep on the sofa.

16 TUESDAY

James was up and away with the rising sun. His mind was awhirl with conflicting emotions: guilt at leaving, anxiety at the bombshell he was about to drop on his publisher and pleasure to see Lindy again. He wasn't looking forward to telling Michael about their mom's injury though. Michael tended to take his role as the eldest son very seriously and, even recognizing that this was partially compensation for guilt at being away so much, it could be hard to deal with at times.

Switching on one of Mark Owen's solo CDs, James began singing as he drove to the city.

At the farm, another busy day was in full swing. Adam's radio crackled to life as Jeffrey's voice asked where he was. Adam answered, "I'm in the barn inventorying what we have in the livestock first aid cabinet."

"Okay, Mom finished her list of feeds to get."

"I'll be done here in a few minutes." Adam hooked the radio back onto his belt and turned back to the chicken medicines. They didn't use much on any of their animals, believing that fresh air, ample space and good food were the best preventatives; but he liked to have proper supplies on hand just in case.

When he finished, Adam closed the cabinet and hooked the padlock through the handle. It wasn't that there was anything particularly valuable, but some of the medicines would be poisonous for humans and people had a tendency to be incredibly stupid sometimes.

In the yard he saw that Alex had the trailer hooked to the truck and was waiting for him. "Do you know where Steve went?" Adam asked as he climbed into the cab.

"I saw Kat pick him up earlier. The power has started to flicker back on so I suppose he will be back on his computer full time when he gets back."

Steve grunted as he swung the cage down out of the Davis' barn loft. "What were these built to hold? And aren't they a bit overkill for guineas?"

"Not what, when. Built to last by my great-grandmother who did nothing by halves if the stories are true." Kat caught the cage with her own grunt of effort. After all three cages were safely on the ground, she heard mumbling as Steve moved away from the loft edge. Curious, she scaled the ladder and saw him moving behind a stack of bales. Following, she was taken by surprise when he circled behind and wrapped his arm around her throat. Instinctive reaction had her shifting and twisting in a move that sent him over her shoulder; a less-trained assailant would have landed flat on his back, but Steve turned it into a roll and rose back to a standing position. He was grinning in appreciation as they circled, both watching for an opening. In a bizarre parody of dance, they closed the distance between them in a flurry of motion. Clouds of dust billowed into the air as their bodies thumped the loft floor or slammed against the support pillars. Sudden stillness struck when Steve caught Kat in a hold that would have dislocated her shoulder if she had fought it. Realizing the futility, she tapped out and they sprang apart again.

With a glare of determination, she said, "Again."

This round ended with her leg around his throat. When his vision began to fade from lack of oxygen, he slapped the floor. Released, as he laid on his back and gasped for air, Kat's face slid into view from above. Hair that had escaped her braid was plastered across her face with sweat and a little blood. There was a scrape across her cheek and dust everywhere, yet he was certain he had never seen anyone as beautiful.

"Klingons," he breathed. For the first time, she smiled. Then she kissed him.

Adam heaved the last bag of pig feed onto the stack in the feed room. He had never seen this room full before and now it would have been difficult to find room for any more. Frowning, he couldn't ease the nagging feeling that they were overlooking something.

In the city, Lindy stepped back from the piles of clothes she had been attempting to arrange into some semblance of order. Finally, she called out to Michael and asked if he had more cardboard boxes.

"Why?" Michael poked his head into her room. "Oh. I'll get some downstairs. You want to ship some of this back to the farm?"

"Yes, please!" That was a relief; she had dreaded trying to fit all this plus the bulk foods Michael was buying today into James' car. No longer worried, she could enjoy the rest of her visit.

It was late morning when James arrived. He had to park in a public ramp a few blocks away; on-street parking had been eliminated years ago to facilitate traffic flow. After a warm welcome he was comfortably seated on the sofa explaining all that had happened in the short time since they had left the farm. Michael was visibly upset about the broken arm, but restrained his reaction for Lindy's sake. She was distressed and even more eager to return so she could help Pat.

"So what's the plan for today?" asked James. "My appointment is at 2:00."

"If I can borrow your car, I'll go pick up the bulk food that I ordered," Michael replied.

"I'll tag along with Michael," added Lindy.

"So I get to use your car? Yeah!" At Michael's look of dismay James started laughing. "Just kidding. I'll take a taxi."

While their host went to whip up a quick lunch, Lindy and James put their heads together about plans for the evening. "There are lots of options: gallery shows, an opera, night clubs, concerts, the theatre, an evening riverboat cruise."

Lindy's eyes sparkled with interest. "Do you know what's at the theatre?"

"There's a big production of The King and I. Others are showing Oklahoma and Who's Afraid of Virginia Woolf. Of course, there are also amateur shows."

"Do you think we can get tickets for The King and I? I love the movie."

Michael spoke up from the kitchen area, "I can get you tickets. Give me half an hour."

James lowered his voice dramatically and said, "He's the man."

Late that afternoon James leaned against the wall in front of the elevator, massaging his temples. That had been an intense and uncomfortable meeting. Losing an author with a solid fan-base was a blow to the publisher; learning that he wanted to switch pen-names and genres didn't help. Cajoling, threatening and begging didn't change his mind, but he did agree to a compromise; if they would offer him a reasonable contract for his next three books, he would sign over all future rights to the story arc and pen-name he was leaving behind. This would allow them to hire a ghostwriter and continue the series, with the added benefit that they would keep all future profits.

With a deep breath, James released his tension and by the time the elevator arrived he was scribbling story ideas into his notebook. The idea that he was free to write anything was enough to make him giddy.

Michael had called in his order for bulk foods and all they had to do was drive out to a warehouse district and pick it up. Lindy's eyes widened in surprise at the stack of fifty pound bags that needed to fit into the car. Michael ticked items off his list as the car was loaded. "Two rice, one sugar, one salt, one powdered milk, one wheat flour, two white flour, one beans, case of olive oil, case of coconut oil, case of cooking wine, raisins, walnuts, almonds. Okay, I think that's it."

Seeing her frown, he said, "Next time someone comes up to visit I can get more. I was limited mostly by car space so aimed for the most useful items."

"What about at your place? If the winter knocks out power and deliveries here and you're stuck in your apartment, do you have supplies?"

"Hmm, well as long as gas is available, I can cook at home and the fireplace runs on gas too. It wouldn't hurt to have extra. I know, I'll place the same order and keep it in the guest room so I'll be covered for emergencies and have it ready to send home with the next visitor."

Lindy nodded thoughtfully, "But how will you get all this back to your place?"

"I'll ask Addie if I can borrow her SUV. I've used it before to pick up plants. She will probably rope me in to cook something for one of her dinner parties again." Michael chuckled tolerantly. He clearly didn't mind the exchange of favors.

On the drive downtown, Lindy's mind was still thinking of possibilities. Suddenly she asked, "What about water? I mean, if the pipes froze or something."

"Ha! I learned my lesson on that one a few years ago. Some kind of contaminant got into the city water system and everyone was on a boil order for two weeks. What a pain. I keep these stackable water containers in the backs of closets and under the beds. I'll show you when we get back."

This time Michael put James' car in a secured parking garage for the night. There was no way to hide the supplies in the back seat. It was only a block from the apartment building and they were soon back inside. Sitting on the sofa, he brought up a new subject. "I know you want to go straight home tomorrow and I'm grateful you will be there to help Mom. I'd like you to come back sometime for a longer visit though. I could arrange for time off and we could do more fun stuff. Also, the university offers a Master Gardener course that you would probably enjoy. So I want you to consider this an extension of your home. You are welcome anytime for as long as you like."

Tearing up with gratitude, Lindy reached over for a big hug. At that moment, James walked in and did a double take. "Uh oh. Private time?"

Laughing, Lindy grinned over Michael's shoulder. "I've just been offered dual citizenship for the city and the countryside. I don't have to regret leaving now because I know I can always come back.

"How did your meeting go?" she asked as she settled back in her corner of the sofa.

"Still in the negotiation stage. Wait and see." James dropped into an armchair. "Did you want to go to Michael's restaurant for dinner tonight?"

"No, I'm going to wear the same dress so someplace different please."

"Suggestions, oh master of all things culinary?" James teased.

"Ethnic?"

"Oh!" Lindy sat up straight. "I haven't had good Vietnamese in years."

"I know just the place. It's not fancy, but the food is exceptionally good. And it's walking distance from your show."

After dinner, James tucked Lindy's hand in his arm as they strolled down the sidewalk. Pausing occasionally to admire or laugh at an extravagant window display they both enjoyed a carefree evening, knowing that their problems and responsibilities would feel lighter for having had a break. Smiling with mutual anticipation, they turned into the grand entrance to the theater.

Back at the farm, Jeffrey stretched his leg out on the footstool and flexed his foot. It was healing nicely and didn't hurt nearly as much as yesterday. Kat had checked the wound when she had stopped to pick Steve up and given an approving grunt. Tomorrow he should be back to almost normal mobility, yet he felt depressed; maybe it was how empty the house seemed. With Steve hard at work in his room, Adam and Pat upstairs already and James, Michael and Lindy away, that left just him and Alex in the living room this evening.

"Say, Jeffrey." Alex's voice suddenly interrupted his gloomy thoughts. "Would you mind helping me set up my schedule for Fall classes? Trying to balance locations, times and preferred instructors is getting convoluted."

"Sure. I always liked being an advisor." The reminder that there were still two students in the house was timely. If he missed teaching too much he could look into tutoring high school students.

Upstairs, Pat tried to find a comfortable position for her arm. The constant throbbing ache was distressing, but the pain pills made her feel woozy and nauseous. In the end, her body was exhausted and she retreated to her bed early; now, if only she could stop her thoughts from whirling around inside her head.

A tapping on her door was followed by Adam peering in. "Are you up for a chat, Mom?"

"Yes, that sounds nice. I would like some company."

"I've got an idea that you might be able to help sort out. Remember when you mentioned that really bad winter Grandma told you about? Could you tell me as much of the story that you recall?" Adam settled into her rocking chair with a hopeful expression.

Smiling, Pat reminisced, "I should remember it well, Mom told me the story every winter. How much was accurate, I don't know.

"First, the background: your great grandmother was having a difficult pregnancy so they sent your grandmother to stay with relatives in South Dakota. She was seven years old and had never even met these cousins before so was very homesick. Her mother asked her to keep a journal while she was away so she could tell her all about it. That's how she could remember so much of the experience.

"The year was 1951, and December 6 was the first day of storms that lasted four months. There were thirty-one days of blizzards that winter. You need to know the frequency of the storms to understand the impact. After that first storm, the next hit three days later and lasted two days. Then, after four more days, another storm; three days, another storm; two days, another storm and so on. For those first two months, they never went more than a week without a blizzard. The plows had trouble keeping the main roads clear and it was difficult for families to get to town for supplies. Most made it at least once in December to stock up.

"In mid-January, there was an ice storm which layered a hard sheet of ice over the snow drifts, making road work even harder. A week later, the worst storm hit. It started as a clear Monday morning, so children were in school, people were on the road and cattle were outside in the fields. It came on so suddenly that after the radio put out the warning, parents drove two and a half miles to school then were stranded there because of zero visibility.

"Your grandmother had been kept home because of a cold and she remembered the wind hitting the house so hard it shuddered. It was like the lights had been turned off. Her aunt kept pacing from the door to the window even though it was impossible to see out. The three cousins were at school and her uncle had driven to town that morning. As it happened, his car stalled out on the road just a mile from home, but it took him over two hours to make it back, pulling himself along the fence and fighting the wind every step. They were frantic about the children, but had no telephone and the radio was full of static and no help. It was thirty long, sleepless hours before those parents learned from a neighbor that all the schoolchildren had taken shelter at a nearby farm. Imagine how crowded that house must have been!

"Those were the lucky ones. So many died of exposure trying to walk to shelter or froze waiting it out in their cars. Entire herds of livestock lost; even the wildlife was hit hard, hundreds of dead pheasants were found.

"It was Wednesday before Mom could see outside again and the view was completely transformed. They had to dig down through eight feet of snow just to find the roof of the chicken coop, but the entire flock survived. Some of the cattle had wandered and died out in the open and it was a struggle to keep the rest fed and watered."

Pat shook her head. "I could tell you more about the rest of that winter and the spring floods that followed, but I'm not sure what you're hoping to learn."

Adam tilted his head back and studied the ceiling thoughtfully before answering, "I'm not certain myself. Something's been bothering me, but just at the edge of my awareness. Okay, random questions. If county water was interrupted, how would we get water in the house?"

"The windmill would still work and we could haul it by bucket. We would have to break the ice on the cattle's water if the electric heater didn't work. Although I seem to recall there used to be a wood-burning heater that was in the tank. I wonder what happened to that thing."

"What about at New Farm?"

"All of these farms had their own wells at one time. Where it is or what shape it's in, I have no idea."

"Okay, thanks Mom. I wish I could pin down this worry, but it will have to wait. You look wiped out. Do you need anything?"

"I could use an extra pillow or cushion for this arm, please."

"Coming right up. Think happy thoughts; Lindy comes home tomorrow."

17 WEDNESDAY

Lindy jumped out of bed full of energy; today she was going home. First she decided to leave the guest room in pristine condition so Michael wouldn't have reason to regret the visit. Washing the sheets, a quick dusting and cleaning the bathroom seemed like a small way to thank him for his hospitality, but she suspected it would matter to him. Humming to herself as she packed the few things left to take with her, it was difficult not to sing out loud. The show had been fantastic and she thought about how much Pat would have enjoyed it. Suddenly Lindy remembered that she still hadn't bought the apple peeler and pulling her notebook out, she jotted down a reminder. Maybe if she spotted a kitchen gadget type store James would be willing to stop.

Balancing the bundle of sheets and towels, Lindy slipped into the laundry nook and started the load washing. She didn't hear anything over the machine noise, but the wafting scent of bacon cooking drew her towards the kitchen.

"Good morning," she greeted Michael quietly, having noted James' snores still sounding from the sofa.

"Morning." He gave her hair a friendly tousle and slid a cup of coffee her way. "How was the show?"

"Fabulous! The costumes and music were amazing. And we had great seats. Thank you so much."

Michael just smiled. It was his boss who had the theatre connections and had been happy to help.

She continued, "I don't want to impose, but I'd really like to bring Pat for a visit this winter. What do you think?"

"I think it's a great idea. If anyone could coax her away from the farm, it's you. And I'll call in a couple weeks to see if anyone wants to come for a few days. Maybe Jeffrey since Steve is tied to the garden." Michael turned his attention back to the stove top and deftly folded over a perfect omelet. "Want to wake up your driver so he can eat while it's hot?"

With a mischievous grin, Lindy tiptoed over to the sofa and knelt next to his head; resting her chin on the cushion, she stared at his face until that subtle awareness of being watched disturbed his sleep. Cracking open one eye, he mumbled something that sounded like "Mornin, dollface."

"Hungry?"

"Famished!" One spine-cracking stretch later and he was sitting up and deciding if he was awake enough to reach the coffee.

Shortly after Lindy finished tidying the guest room they were in his car and heading out of the downtown area. Michael had enjoyed the company, but was happy to get back to his routine and the gym was first on his agenda.

It took very little cajoling to convince James to combine stopping for gas with a quick detour into a suburban mall on their way out of the city. After filling up the car, they were hiking through the sprawling shopping center when they found the kitchen gadget store she had been hoping for. While she was buying the hand-cranked peeler, James was drawn to a display of specialty rolling pins and on a whim picked out one designed for biscuits and another for egg noodles. On the way back to the exit they detoured to use the restrooms. Lindy balanced her purse on the edge of the sink and made faces at herself in the mirror while washing her hands.

Suddenly, the lights went out, eliciting groans and exclamations from the women in the stalls. The emergency lighting kicked in with a rather ominous red glow before flickering and failing. One young woman announced that she could access the light app on her phone and cursed angrily when nothing happened. Vague rustling noises led to a dull orange glow appearing a few feet from Lindy. A rather frazzled looking woman explained how she had bought glow sticks for her kids on the Fourth and had kept the extra. Everyone drew closer, like moths to a flame; it was such a relief to have any light. Lindy grabbed her purse and left the room.

The hallway was gloomy, but enough light filtered through from the skylights in the main shopping area to make it navigable. James practically leapt forward when he spotted Lindy emerging from the doorway. Glued to her side, they quickly worked their way through the clumps of people.

"James," Lindy began before he interrupted.

"Wait until we're in the car." His voice was tense and her concern ratcheted up another notch. She couldn't see any cause for him to worry. A group of teens were whining and swearing about their phones, but everyone else seemed calm enough. Back in the car, James drove immediately for the entrance to the interstate. It took extra time to reach with the traffic lights out, but most drivers were behaving civilly and taking turns. It wasn't until they were well on their way that he eased up on gripping the steering wheel so tightly and spoke, "Would you mind checking the radio for news please?"

As she spun the dial unsuccessfully, the worry lines in his forehead deepened. "What's going on, James? Is your phone dead too?"

"Yes, and I don't know. The power outage could be caused by any number of things, but the phones and radio are harder to explain. I just wish we were home already."

Giving up on the radio, Lindy switched back to the CD, hoping the familiar music would be soothing for James. Watching the countryside pass, she found herself thinking of all the conversations that had been cut off in an instant: the emergency calls, arguments beginning and ending, business and personal. A cold shiver ran down her spine as the thought whispered in the back of her mind 'what if the phones don't come back?' She tried to imagine what that would be like and failed; instant communication was always available.

"It's a good thing Michael made those snacks for the drive, our lunch options are pretty limited with everything shut down." James glanced over with an apologetic smile. "Sorry for getting upset."

"That's okay," Lindy replied. "I'm still not sure if I should be really worried or not."

"Hopefully, I overreacted and we can laugh about it tonight."

Back in the city, Michael had just stepped off the elevator when the lights went out. Spinning around, he grabbed the closing doors and forced them open again. "Everyone get off quick!"

The other passengers suddenly grasped what was happening and hustled off. The young couple with a baby stroller were effusively grateful, but an older man in a suit grumbled at the inconvenience of having to take the stairs.

Inside his apartment, Michael headed straight for the shower, hoping to get cleaned up while there was still hot water. He kept it short and had to leave the door open so he could see but it was still a relief to wash off the workout sweat. Soon he was stretched out on the sofa with the newspaper, unconcerned with what was most likely a temporary power outage. It wasn't long before he dozed off.

On the farm, the power loss was causing more immediate inconveniences. "Damn!" Steve slumped back in his chair as the monitor went blank. He had been in the middle of sending an update to his team and they were all going to be waiting for him to connect again.

Gazing blankly out the window, it slowly filtered in that it was a beautiful day and he might as well enjoy it. Downstairs, the house was empty and he stepped outside to see where everyone was. Pat and Jeffrey were relaxing on the porch watching the guineas explore; when Steve opened the door the birds let out a cacophony of alarm calls. He was relieved to see that Pat was clearly amused by their antics.

"We've lost power again," he said glumly.

"Ha! You think it was another drunk driver taking out a pole?" asked Jeffrey.

Pat took it more seriously. "It may be just another glitch, but this is the last straw for me. We're going to start canning the meat from the freezer today."

Steve straightened from his slouch as a thought hit him. "I've got the plans for a DIY smokehouse on my computer. If I print them out, will you look it over and see if it's something you can build, Jeffrey?"

"How can you use your computer?" Pat looked confused for a moment, then remembered, "Oh! Your solar charger, how nice."

"I'll go set it up now and put this sunshine to work. Where are the twins?"

"Adam is helping the vet today because he was short-handed. Alex is finishing the trim on the barn." Pat stood and spoke to Jeffrey, "Will you help me move some meat out of the freezer? It can help keep the fridge cool while thawing."

"Sure. Looking on the bright side, this is a good excuse to grill steaks tonight."

Steve chuckled and said, "I'll be back down in a little while to help with the canning."

Both James and Lindy released involuntary sighs of relief when they pulled into the farm yard and found everything looking normal. Their eyes met and they laughed at their nervousness. As soon as the car stopped moving, Lindy was out of her seat and racing for the door. She stood inside for a moment, eyes darting around looking for changes and resting briefly on the sleeping dogs and sunbathing cat before turning to the kitchen which rang out with clattering noises and voices. Stepping through, she soaked up the busy scene before her: Jeffrey carefully slicing fat off meat, Alex carrying a pressure canner out the back door, Steve with his hands plunged into a steaming sink of water and Pat loading filled jars into another canner on the stove.

Alex was the first to spot her as he came back in and shouted, "Lindy!"

Every head snapped around and broad smiles beamed at her. Pat was the first to reach her for a hug all the while telling her how happy she was to have her safely home again. Lindy couldn't stop the tears that streamed down as she absorbed the welcoming warmth. When the initial hubbub had settled and she had moved away from the door so James could join them, Lindy spoke, "I hope you weren't too worried this morning. We didn't have any problems."

The others exchanged puzzled glances and Pat asked, "Worried about what, dear? Did something happen?"

"Oh! Well, maybe James should explain, I'm still a bit confused myself." Lindy looked uncomfortable and flustered. James sat at the kitchen table and explained the sequence of events they had witnessed. The first thing everyone did was to pull out their cell phones and confirm they were dead. Then Alex picked up the house phone and hung it up again, shaking his head. Steve took down a battery-operated radio from the top of the fridge and spun the dials. All that came through was a static-filled hiss.

"There's no way to check the internet without the phone." Jeffrey looked at Lindy. "We thought it was just a localized power outage. That's why we weren't worried."

The wind-up timer on the counter began to beep and Pat reached over to tap it. "Well, this discussion will have to wait. We can't stop in the middle of our work." Even while saying that she was pulling James into a hug.

Lindy announced that she would be right back to help as soon as she got changed and the kitchen was again filled with the bustle of business.

Three hundred miles away from the farm, Michael woke to a sharp knocking on his door. This was unusual because in his building the residents generally avoided even making eye contact let alone come calling and security kept unannounced visitors out. Looking through the peephole he saw Addie from the restaurant.

"Hello, what brings you downtown?" he asked as he let her in.

"Philip sent me. He didn't want you coming all the way to work to find it closed." Addie perched on a barstool and ran her hands through her riot of hair. Michael noticed that she didn't look her normal, competent self and wondered what had gotten to someone who could handle the wildly varying restaurant crises with aplomb. He automatically moved around to the kitchen and began throwing together a light lunch.

"I give up. Why didn't he just call?"

Addie's mouth dropped open in surprise. "Because the phones don't work? How could you not know that?"

Michael snorted, "Because I'm not hooked into mine like you are. Anyway, how could they not work? Don't the towers have backup power? They shouldn't all have failed."

"It's not lack of signal, the phones themselves are dead. Check yours."

Looking skeptical, he retrieved his phone and attempted to turn it on. "Hmm, all phones? Even older flip models? What about land lines?"

"Ha! Do you know anyone with a flip phone still? And the land line at the restaurant was dead. Your security guard didn't have a dial tone either."

Michael chuckled, "Half my family still uses flip phones. How did you get past him anyway?"

"It wasn't easy! And he knows who I am. He made me leave my driver's license as insurance that I wouldn't run through the building defacing the decor or murdering your neighbors."

With a smile, Michael slid a plate in front of her. "So, what's Philip's plan?"

"Mmm," pausing to swallow, she continued, "He sent Tony to find a generator that can keep the cooler running. Then he was going to try to get an announcement out on the radio about the closure and he said something about trying to track down the A-listers who were booked tonight and tomorrow."

"Tomorrow!" Michael stared at her in consternation. "You must know something else that you haven't told me."

"Nothing official, really. But you know how Philip has connections; well, he heard something that makes him suspect the power isn't coming on anytime soon." Addie held his gaze as she finished, "Maybe not for weeks."

"Huh." He looked shell shocked now. When Addie opened her mouth to speak, he held up his hand and said, "Wait, please. Let me think."

Michael began to pace, his expression deeply concerned. After a few minutes he spun around and asked, "What are you supposed to do next?"

"Nothing. Go home, I guess. Philip said he would contact me when I was needed again." When he resumed his pacing she added, "One other thing, the radio stations are off the air. I noticed on the drive over."

"But..." Michael shook his head. "I just can't make sense of this." He stepped out onto the balcony and stared down at the street. Watching from inside, Addie could tell when he made a decision; his shoulders squared and his head came up. Striding in, he took the stool next to hers and looked her in the eye. "Did Philip tell you to come here last?"

"Yes."

"I think he knew what I would do. How many times has he said he would never have been such a success without us?"

"Once a week at least." The thought brought a brief smile to her face.

Nodding, he said, "And he hoped you would be safe with me. I know the city can handle a few days without power, but after a week or more and in the hottest months of the year? No refrigeration, not even any fans, none of the things to do that normally fill the hours...some people will cope well, but what about the many who won't?"

"Michael, what if they can't keep the water running?"

His expression turned bleak. "It would turn into a hellhole. That's why I think you should come to the farm with me. You don't have to stay there, of course, but at least come for a few days and see how events shake out. I know Lindy will be happy to see you again. What do you think?"

"I'm relieved you asked! You can imagine I'd be climbing the walls with nothing to do at my place. I've never been able to handle inactivity. Do you want me to swing back and pick you up after I go home and pack?"

"Honestly, I'd rather not be separated since we can't communicate. Let's load up here first and I'll come with you."

This startled Addie, but she agreed readily enough. Michael continued, "I'm going to gather up a cooler full of perishables. Can you swing around to the front and wait for me?"

While she headed down, he quickly took a cooler out of the closet and filled it from the fridge. Then, mindful of the effort of carrying it down six flights of stairs, he chose items to fill a backpack. The few boxes of ammo for his handgun, extra bottles of water, a folder of important papers, a most precious photo album, all the cash he had on hand and a change of clothes filled the pack without weighing it down excessively. It was with relief that he thought about the complete wardrobe already at the farm; one less hassle for today.

Finally reaching the lobby, he speared the cooler with a glare. It had been an incredibly awkward container to haul down the stairs. Pausing only to run his hand across his sweaty pate, he picked it up again and stepped outside to where Addie waited with her SUV. As he slid his things into the back he asked how she was set for gas.

"Nearly full, I topped it off yesterday when the price dropped five cents." She shook her head, "Five cents doesn't seem so important today."

He smiled in approval. "But a full tank could be priceless now. I'm going to check on something. I'll be right back."

When Michael returned he was followed by the security guard and they each carried two cardboard boxes. After loading them in, he shook hands with the guard and handed him a generous tip. As he climbed into the passenger seat Addie asked, "What was that about?"

"Those are the spoils of your shopping trip with Lindy. We arranged to have them shipped to the farm, but they hadn't been picked up yet."

"Oh! That is lucky. Imagine if they had gotten lost in delivery limbo." Addie fell into a pensive silence. Glancing over, Michael noticed her chewing on her lower lip and wondered in what direction her thoughts had gone. Finally she burst into speech again, "Am I being stupid to even think about taking my winter gear? I mean, there's no way this can stay messed up for months, right?"

Keeping his voice low and calm, he answered, "My thoughts are that if the rioting is as bad as I suspect could happen, there's a good chance nothing in my apartment will still be there when I return. I took what mattered the most. Your winter kit is important to you; if there's room, take it. Which would you regret more: leaving and losing it or having to haul it all back upstairs in a couple weeks?"

Addie heaved a sigh before saying, "I'm taking it."

Michael may have had second thoughts about his advice after his third trip down to the parking lot. Fortunately, Addie's apartment was only on the second floor; even so, he planned on finding out just why one person would need three sets of skis. Inside the apartment he found Addie loading quantities of fresh fruit into a cooler. Curiosity led him to peek into the cabinets which turned out to be nearly empty. She laughed at his expression.

"I eat most meals at the restaurant and pretty much survive on fruit the rest of the time." Closing the cooler, she straightened up and looked around. "Okay, you bring this and I'll grab the suitcases. I'm finished here."

Crossing the parking lot, Michael spotted two young men checking out the SUV. Just as he was about to say something, Addie's voice cut sharply across the lot, "Joey! Whatever you're doing, knock it off."

"What are you going to do? Call the cops?" A sneer marred the cocky youth's face.

"Oh, much worse than that." Addie's voice dropped dramatically. "I'll tell your grandmother."

His eyes cut nervously up to an apartment window before he shot back with, "Whatever. I wouldn't want any of your crap anyway." Then he and his friend swaggered away.

Addie shook her head, "Scavengers. But the whole neighborhood is terrified of his grandmother. Anyway, let's get this loaded; I'm not worried about him, but there are worse around."

As she pulled out of the lot, Addie asked, "Do you think we'd be better off taking the bypass around? I know it's longer, but I'm worried about trying to get through the city center now."

"You're probably right. It's nearly four and most businesses will have given up on the power coming back on today and sent everyone home. Without traffic lights it's going to be a mess." Even after acknowledging the logic of her decision, part of him wished they could take the shortest route. It felt wrong to drive further away.

After a cautious half hour spent making their way out of the city proper, Addie spoke suddenly and a little too loudly, "So what can I do at your farm to help out? You know it's completely foreign to me, right?" There was a plaintive note in her voice that spoke volumes about how uneasy the thought of farm life made her.

At first, all Michael could think of were the ways she wouldn't be a help; then he turned it around and considered her strengths and the answer was obvious. "How would you feel about doing a comprehensive inventory of the farm? Everything from food and goods to sorting through all the forgotten, but possibly useful items tucked away in the attic and sheds?"

Addie pursed her mouth thoughtfully, "Hmmm, it would all have to be done on paper. Challenging."

Both were occupied by their own thoughts as they drove on through the afternoon. Michael watched for potential problems ahead of them while Addie deftly steered around the worst of the traffic. There were a few times progress slowed to a crawl, but they made it around the city and were eventually back on the same route James and Lindy had travelled that morning.

"Does it seem strange to you that everything looks completely normal? Look, there's a highway patrol car and the semis are still going just like any other day." Addie gestured at the busy interstate.

"Is your satnav working?" Michael watched the patrol car pass and pull ahead of them.

"I don't have one. I got a good deal on this used so I didn't mind that it lacked a few bells and whistles. Why?"

"Just wondering what is still running. If we had a better idea of how extensive the problem is, maybe we could figure out what caused it. Are the cop's radios functional? That would make a huge difference in the next weeks. What about geographically? This could be only affecting one state or just the Midwest."

Addie wrinkled her forehead. "But does it really matter? I mean, it would be great to know, but is there anything that we can do to fix something this big?"

"Probably not." Michael looked back out his window at the fields flowing past and sighed, "I just want to know."

After two hours on the interstate, Michael directed Addie to an exit ramp. She eyed the truck stop and asked, "How much farther? I'd like to stretch my legs. Hey! It looks like the pumps are working. Should we stop?"

"Sure. Maybe there's been some news."

Addie pulled into the line of cars waiting for fuel and shrugged at Michael's quizzical expression. "Might as well top it off while we can."

"Okay, I'll go inside and see what I can find out." Leaving her tapping her hands on the steering wheel, Michael walked toward the dark building. He could hear the muted roar of a generator running, which explained the pumps.

When he stepped inside the man behind the counter said, "Cash only."

With a nod Michael replied, "Okay. Has there been any news? All I know about is the power and phones being out."

The attendant ran his hand over his head wearily. "We were just talking about that." He nodded towards the men and women scattered around the small shopping area. "CBs are still working fine and the truckers are passing along what they know. We haven't heard of anyone with power yet. No word from south of the border yet, but it sounds like Canada is out too. Where are you coming from?"

"Up from the city," Michael said. "You might want to pass along a warning that the traffic was already messed up when we left so it's probably a nightmare now."

The discussion turned to ways to get around potential bottlenecks and Michael let his mind wander as he kept an eye on Addie's progress to the pump. Suddenly a throat clearing beside him brought his attention back inside. An older woman stood there, peering at him suspiciously. She looked tough as nails with tattoo sleeves enveloping lean, ropy muscles. When she spoke, her voice rasped like a long time smoker. "You're Michael Stevenson, aren't you?"

At his cautious nod, she thrust out her hand and said, "I've got your cookbooks. I always wanted to stop by your restaurant, but never got a chance. My family used to complain about how boring chicken was until I started following your recipes. Now they love it! There's just one thing I can't get to turn out right..."

When Addie parked near the door and came looking for Michael, she found him deep in conversation and overheard, "I'm almost certain uneven heating is to blame. Timing is essential so if the pan is flawed or the burner isn't working properly the whole dish will be off."

Then he wrote on a business card and handed it over. "Come in after things are back to normal and I'll give you a demonstration if you like. Show this card and you can skip the reservations. The meal is on me."

Back on the road, Addie murmured, "Normal sounds good."

Michael pointed back to the interstate. "Let's keep on this way, it's not as interesting but will cut some time off the drive compared to taking the highways. Hearing how widespread this is makes me want to get home faster. I'm still hoping Philip hit the panic button for no real reason, but I can't help but worry that he was right."

It was nearly nine when Michael pulled into the driveway; he had taken the wheel when they finally left the interstate behind, but the last hour had been uneventful. Hopping out, he entered the combination into the padlock and swung the gate open. The process of driving through and closing the gate again reminded him of a long ago visit to a ranch where those motions had been repeated many times every day.

Then they were pulling up in front of the house and watching as the front door opened and his family came spilling out to greet them.

18 THURSDAY

Pat sipped a cup of tea as she watched James walk down the driveway; he was going to check on New Farm. The family had stayed up late the night before discussing the situation and what their options were. Soon enough Pat would get back to work canning meat, but for this moment she would enjoy the fresh morning and the contentment of having all her brood safely home. A fat bumblebee bumped its way among the hollyhock blossoms that waved to her along the porch. Biff loped down the steps and flung himself into the grass, wriggling blissfully onto his back. This was one of those moments that Pat wished she could bottle and open up to enjoy in the middle of winter.

Lindy strode up swinging a bucket while behind her the chickens spread out across the yard. Hopping onto the railing, she spoke while watching their antics, "Steve said to let them out, but what do we do if the hawk comes back?"

Pat sighed, "Hawks are protected so there's nothing we can do except run around and shout. Don't get me wrong, they are important to keep the rodent population down; it's just hard when they target your flock instead. Now raccoons! Well, you can shoot or run over every one of those buggers and I'll cheer you on. Nasty brutes.

"Are you and Addie going to be okay sharing a room? Maybe you can help her get her winter things stored in the attic today."

Lindy laughed happily, "And my winter clothes too. Wasn't that wonderful of Michael to think of looking for them when he must have had so much on his mind? Yes, Addie and I will do fine together. Although I suspect she is much neater than I am, so hopefully I don't drive her mad."

Glancing back at the flock, she continued, "Do they ever bother the garden?"

"Rarely," Pat answered. "A couple times we've had to run a temporary fence across to keep some persistent troublemakers out, but they're normally content with their other options."

They continued chatting as the others joined them and soon ideas were being tossed around about what should have priority on the to-do list and what could or would have to wait.

"Mangels." Everyone stopped talking and turned to look at Steve. "We should try to supplement the livestock feed and everything can eat mangels. If we can get the seed and get the garden space at New Farm tilled and planted, we have a chance at a crop still this year."

Alex was nodding thoughtfully. "We'll have to be lucky with a late frost but where can we find the seeds? Anyone who ordered them would have planted back in the spring."

Pat leaned forward suddenly. "Mrs. Bucket! Her husband was always planting root crops for his pigs."

"Was?" asked Jeffrey. "What happened to him?"

"Oh, he ran off with the librarian back in March or April. His wife sold the pigs, but probably hasn't done anything with the seeds he would have bought already, unless he was planning on leaving and didn't buy any. Anyway, Alex and I can go talk to her later." Pat settled back in her chair, pleased with a potential solution.

Just then, a red truck pulled into the yard. James hopped out of the passenger side while Pete Wilson climbed out more slowly from behind the wheel.

"Hey, everyone," James called out. As they drew near, he continued, "Mr. Wilson needs to talk to us about the addition and I thought we should tell him what we've heard."

Pete nodded to the others, but his focus was on Pat as he explained that only two of his workers had showed up that morning. "A couple of the others may have had family problems that kept them away, but I'm afraid the rest are likely to be sleeping off a binge. It won't even occur to them that we run on a generator on the job site anyway. What I was hoping for would be to draft a few of you into working with us. Enough hands and we should get it done in three or four days. What do you say?"

Jeffrey exchanged looks with the others before speaking, "There's something you should know before we make any decisions."

After telling him what they knew and what they had heard, Jeffrey waited for a response. Pete stood silent; first looking at his feet, then up at Pat, around all the others and back to Pat. He had a methodical mind and it slowly churned through the implications. This house already held nine adults and there was no way Pat would consent to moving away from her home and family to his place twenty miles away. While it was too soon to propose, he didn't want to wait for years more. Easing the population crush here would help so finishing the addition and working to make New Farm habitable was his best hope. Clearing his throat, he finally responded, "Sounds like we had better get to work then. Pat, is there anything you need?"

Knowing that when he asked a question like that, he expected a real answer, she took her time to think first. "Hmm, if I had a wish list the top item would be an outdoor oven away from the house. Other than that I need to keep enough help here to continue canning out the freezer."

"I'll see what I can do about the oven, but I know I can give you some more time on the freezer. I have a spare generator you can use. It's not very powerful though, the freezer will be all it can handle."

"Oh!" Pat said gratefully. "That will take so much of the pressure off if I'm not in a race against time. Having to wear this for the next five weeks is hard enough." She pointed to the cast on her arm.

"We'll try to make things as easy as possible for you," Michael assured her. "I'll help can and do the cooking. Who else is staying?"

"I'll stay," offered Alex. "If we have time, Mom and I can go see Mrs. Bucket later."

"If Lindy wouldn't mind taking over the garden today, I'd like to help on the building." Steve looked at her questioningly.

"Sure, I've missed playing in the dirt." Staying at home suited Lindy's mood perfectly.

It was quickly decided that James, Jeffrey and Adam would join Steve at New Farm. Pete looked pleased with the arrangement and promised to get the generator as soon as he had everyone sorted out on site.

After turning the recruits over to his foreman and verifying that they were on the same page regarding the goals for the day, Pete drove into town and to the building where he kept his work equipment and supplies. Pausing only to hook up the flatbed trailer, he moved on to the DIY center. There, as expected, most of the activity centered around the generator aisle where voices rose in complaint. Obviously, they had sold out and customers were demanding to know when more would arrive. With typical blinkered views, they refused to accept that the store had no way to communicate with their suppliers.

The counter that catered to construction projects and contractors was located back by the lumber section. One of the regulars working there nodded at Pete and pulled out an order form. Since he had made some decisions on the drive in, he was able to dictate a list of materials to be delivered to his business site. Then he placed a second order to be loaded onto his trailer. Charges approved to his account, they leaned on the counter and chatted about the recent storm, baseball and the latest antics of the county commissioners.

As he was leaving, Pete asked where he could learn about outdoor ovens and was directed to the aisle of books and magazines. Most of what was there seemed to be aimed at people with lots of money wanting to impress their friends, but he found a couple books for back-to-earthers which looked potentially useful. At the checkout he watched the cashier looking up prices in a binder; when she couldn't find something, she called on her walkie-talkie for a price check. She then tallied up the total on a calculator and the customer wrote a check. After paying cash for the books, Pete drove around and helped load up his order in the lumberyard. Finally, he was able to go home and retrieve the spare generator from his garage. It wasn't something he would have felt comfortable about leaving in the back of the truck while shopping.

Meanwhile, as the water was heating, Michael and Addie prepped meat for canning and Alex and Pat went on their search for seeds. Pulling into the Bucket farm, they looked at each other for encouragement. It was an awkward situation when a couple that seemed happy together on the surface split up; especially if one half had no idea it was coming.

The woman who answered the door looked drawn and tense. She focused on Pat and listened silently to their request. "I don't know. I guess we can look in the barn."

The barn smelled stale and dusty when she swung the door open. Sleek farm cats switched from twining around their ankles to hunter mode when they sensed the mice inside. Another door led to the feed room where stacks of seed bags showed the inroads the rodents had made.

"Huh. Well, there isn't as much left as there would have been, but I'll sell it. Two hundred."

Pat looked to Alex for confirmation and he nodded, although he didn't look happy. While Pat counted out the money, he moved the truck over and began carrying out bags, trying not to lose any more seed than he could help.

"Okay," Pat asked when they were heading home. "What was wrong?"

"The feed room was damp and smelled moldy. So the seed was stored in a hot, humid environment. If it only started leaking recently, it won't be too bad, but if it has been like that for months..."

Pat sighed, "I felt sorry for her."

"Yeah, me too." Alex shook his head.

Arriving home, they both waved at Lindy in the garden. Pat fretted, "I hope she isn't overdoing out in the sun."

Alex replied soothingly, "If she looks too hot when she comes in for lunch ask her to help you this afternoon."

As Pat lowered herself out of the cab, she paused and looked at Alex. "You're growing up."

A pleased smile flitted across his face as he eased the truck back into gear and drove to the barn. There, he set to work sorting the seed into bins; while the majority was mangel and turnip seed, there were smaller amounts of rutabagas and beets.

Inside the kitchen it was the normal steamy mess of a major canning project. Michael wasn't bothered since this was his usual environment, but Addie looked flustered and had sweaty curls plastered to her forehead. With Pat's return, he asked Addie to take the scrap bucket out for the pigs. Her first reaction was alarm but she dutifully took the bucket and walked outside. Reaching the pig pen, she stood as far back from the fence as she could and gingerly tipped the bucket out.

"Bleah!" she said, watching the enthusiastic response to the food.

Alex paused while walking past, taking in her expression of fascinated horror. "You going to be okay?"

"They're...ugh. Yuck." Pulling her eyes away from the animals, she focused on the plastic trays in his hands. "What are you doing?"

"Germination testing." Addie trailed along as he strode to the house and went in the back door. In the laundry room he spread the four trays out on the table and covered them with clear plastic. Peering closer she noted that each tray had a neat label taped to one end.

"What will this tell you? Aren't you going to plant the seeds anyway?"

"Yes, but I don't know how quickly we can get it ready over there and in about five days we should start seeing growth here. Each tray has twenty seeds, so this will tell me how heavy to plant depending on how many sprout. If the germination is really bad, we won't be growing for feed but to save seeds from next year."

Addie tensed up. "You don't think you will be able to buy seeds next year." Her voice sounded hollow and far away to her own ears.

Deliberately keeping his response casual, Alex replied, "Oh, Steve always tries to save his own seeds every year. We've just never grown feed crops before."

"Oh, okay." Addie shook off her fears and looked around the bright room that seemed to be all windows. "This is nice but won't the plants get in the way? Why don't you have a greenhouse?"

Alex laughed. "This is nothing. In the spring it's solid seedlings in here. We did try a greenhouse once. Dad bought a kit and we all helped put it together. It lasted about two weeks before a wind spread the panels all over and turned the frame into a twisted pile of junk."

Alex's radio chirped and Michael's voice asked if he knew where the old pull along wagon was. Instead of answering, they walked through to the kitchen where Michael was making sandwiches. Nodding to them he said, "I'd like to send lunch over to New Farm with a couple jugs of lemonade and thought the wagon would work well."

"I think I know where it is. Be right back." Alex left and Addie stepped forward to take over where Pat was cautiously adding jars of meat to the pressure canner.

"Oh, thank you! This cast makes even the simplest job seem harder." Pat sat down and began filling more jars.

Alex returned pulling a child's red wagon as Pete drove in and the next few minutes were a bustle of activity. When everything calmed down, the generator was purring behind the house and a thick extension cord ran down to the freezer in the basement. Addie had volunteered to pull the wagon to New Farm after seeing how far Alex had to stoop over to reach the handle.

"Tall people think they've got the best advantage, but there are times when it pays to be closer to the ground." Addie had gotten to know the twins fairly well while they were staying with Michael and wasn't above teasing.

"Oh, I don't know," responded Alex with an innocent expression. "You're the one doing all the work." Her exaggerated look of outrage gave way to laughter.

The crew at New Farm cheered their arrival and descended upon the lunch. Addie looked around at the makeshift seating they were using, the front steps, sawhorses and tailgates. "Picnic tables would make this more efficient. Can you buy some?"

"With the lumber we have on hand, we could build them easily enough." Jeffrey waved his sandwich vaguely. "A couple here and at home would be nice."

The foreman nudged his co-worker. "Juan, didn't you build one?"

"Three years ago. It hasn't fallen apart yet so I could show you how if Mr. Wilson says it's okay." This met with everyone's approval and the conversations became general again.

Brushing away crumbs, James stood and asked Addie if she wanted to see what they were working on. He explained the purpose of the addition and the trench to run a water line for a summer kitchen. "At first it will just be a sink and grill, but eventually we'll have a stove out here. The sides will be open and with a roof for shade, hopefully it will be cooler to work in than inside the house. The other benefit is it won't be heating up the house."

"What about bugs?" Addie waved at a persistent fly.

"Oh. You think we should screen it in?"

"My first rule is to keep the chef happy and I'm fairly certain Michael wouldn't want flies in his food. Of course, if you and Jeffrey don't mind..."

"Well, it may end up being more than just the two of us. That was the plan when we thought the twins would be going back to school and Michael settled in the city. Now, though, huh. I'll just say that tempers get short in the friendliest of families during the winter months. Shifting four of us over here would relieve that pressure but still be close enough to see each other often." Looking over, James saw that Addie had wrapped her arms around herself and looked miserable. "Addie?"

She stared down at her feet and shook her head before speaking. "You really think this is how it's going to be. I don't understand! The power just went out yesterday but you're planning like it's Little House on the Prairie again. Normal people are just getting annoyed that their beer isn't cold enough and the kids are bugging them about the TV not working.

"If Philip hadn't sent me to Michael, I'd think you were all bonkers. I hope you are. I want my life back to normal. I want to take a hot shower. I want to go to the store and buy mangos and green bananas and, and...pineapples! I miss my IPad. I hate being on a farm. This isn't how it's supposed to be." Her voice had risen to a shout but sank to a whisper at the end.

Alex had run around the corner of the house, but stopped and waved the others back when he saw James gripping Addie's shoulders and speaking in low, calm tones. As he drew nearer he overheard, "This is how we deal with the unknown. We ask ourselves what if this happens or that goes wrong, what would we need? Most of the time, nothing happens and life just goes on. It's like taking out life insurance. You don't want to need it, but it's good to have."

Meeting Alex's eye, James continued, "Are you going to be okay walking back? Michael and Mom could probably use your help again."

Addie smeared the tears from her face and straightened her shoulders. "Yes, I'm ready to get back to work."

As they walked down the road between the two farms, Alex spoke thoughtfully, "You know, there's something James didn't tell you."

"What?"

"Your nose gets really red when you cry. Ow!" Addie had dropped the wagon handle spun around and kicked Alex in the rear. "Damn, woman! Where'd you learn to kick like that?"

"Macy's Fight Gym." Calmly taking up the handle again, Addie walked ahead. They couldn't see each other's faces, but both wore smiles.

Pete had stayed for lunch and afterwards he and Pat looked through the books at oven plans. Lindy had offered to spell Pat in the kitchen and the chatter of the four younger people drifted out to the living room. After much studying and comparisons, they agreed on the design for a double-walled brick oven.

Pete looked thoughtful. "I know I have the mortar for this but no bricks."

"There was a pile behind the shed from an old chimney, would that work?" Pat asked.

"Maybe, I'll check it out. I had better get back to the addition now." A quick kiss and fond smile were his farewell. Pat eased back into the cushions and dozed off for a much needed nap.

Lindy gazed blankly out the window as she washed more jars. Then she blinked and her eyes focused on the empty clothesline. "Laundry. Oh no." She spun around and stared at the others.

"What's wrong, Lindy?" asked Michael.

"Laundry. How are we going to do the laundry?"

Michael shrugged. "We'll figure something out. Maybe Mom will have an idea. That's not the only thing we need to adjust to; we're going to be doing a lot more seasonal eating."

"What do you mean?"

He reached over and plucked a piece of broccoli out of the basket Lindy had brought in from the garden. "Normally we freeze a lot of broccoli this time of year. Now it has to be used fresh, so expect to see it daily in your meals. I want to talk to Steve about planting more kale. That will last into the cold weather and we will need the nutrients when we don't have access to fresh greens and citrus."

Alex wrinkled his nose at the thought of depending on kale, not one of his favorite flavors. Addie, on the other hand, looked pleased. "Oh, that kale salad you featured last fall was delicious. This could be much worse without our own chef."

Lindy turned back to the window with a small frown of annoyance. As much as she admired Michael, she thought he was wrong to downplay her concerns. Keeping up with the laundry for nine hard-working adults was going to be a major undertaking, especially if they had to do it by hand.

A gentle breeze picked up that evening and Adam hauled out a box of assorted sports equipment.

"Are you kidding? We've been working all day!" groaned James. He was the first to rummage into the box and pull out the Frisbees, though.

Soon, Pat and Pete were the only two left on the porch. Watching the exuberance of the younger generation, Pete said, "You and Matt did a great job bringing up your boys. Every one of them has grown into a fine man."

Pat leaned against him and gave a rueful chuckle. "There were plenty of times I was ready to give up on the job. All those teenagers!" She stopped laughing and continued, "The worst times were seeing them in pain when they had to deal with hardships. I could give them love and support but some demons have to be fought alone."

Her eyes followed Steve as he dove for a Frisbee and rolled back to his feet triumphant. Pete was watching Lindy chase Biff for the disc he had snatched out of the air. "And which one have you chosen for Lindy?"

Pat smiled a bit smugly. "Any of them would make a fine partner for her. I do have a wish though...well, I think she would be good for Steve. He still carries a lot of anger and she's gentle and soothing. He could protect her too."

Pete glanced at her in surprise before realizing she must not know about Steve's lady friend. He wouldn't have known himself if he hadn't spotted them talking near the trees at New Farm. Deciding to play it safe, he changed the subject. "James is the scariest of them. He would have made a fantastic conman. In the short drive back he had me confessing my intentions for you and I'm still not sure how he did it."

"My ugly duckling. He was always small for his age and all his brothers were much better looking; he compensated by learning to cajole and negotiate for always a little more. His gift is that he intuitively knows when to stop talking and listen."

When the sun began to set and the chickens made their way back to the coop, Pete stood to go. "Pete," Pat began. "Would you consider setting up your camper here if it becomes difficult to drive back and forth?"

"Difficult?"

"Dangerous."

He sat back down. "If it would make you feel better, I can bring it over tomorrow and leave it here."

She squeezed his hand gratefully. "Yes, that would be a comfort. Just knowing we have that option." She and Mellow watched him drive away, then went inside while the others locked up for the night.

19 FRIDAY

Addie tapped a pen on the edge of her clipboard as she decided how to proceed. The old smithy was a low-ceilinged square building with small, high windows. To combat the gloom she had swung the double doors wide and the sunlight danced across the dust-filled air. For the moment there was sunshine, at least; the clouds massing to the west promised more rain to come. That limited her options because she wouldn't be able to move things outside as she sorted and catalogued. Giving up any idea of organizing today, she decided to begin with a raw list of items. A quick sketch of the floor-plan divided into quadrants and she dove into her work.

Some time passed and Alex stuck his head in, "There you are! Hasn't anyone given you a radio? Didn't you hear the dinner bell ringing?"

"Hmm? Oh, was that what that noise was? I'm busy." Addie waved one hand distractedly. Alex grabbed the clipboard and flipped through page after page of neat, precise handwriting. "Hey! I'm not finished."

"Well, you're going to stop long enough to eat lunch. Come on. And dust yourself off; you're filthy."

With a glare, Addie ran her fingers through her hair and pulled out some of the cobwebs she had acquired. Alex was already striding back to the house and she had no choice but to follow since he still held her clipboard. As she mounted the porch steps a low rumble announced the arrival of the thunderstorm. Turning, Addie inhaled with pleasure as a gust of cool air swept past and watched a sheet of rain advance across the yard. There was nothing violent or frightening about the storm; instead, it felt cleansing.

After a few minutes of peaceful rain, Pete's truck drove in and pulled up in front of the house. A flurry of movement and slamming doors and the men who had gone over to work at New Farm that morning were dashing up to the porch. Amid the laughter and good-natured shoving, Addie asked Pete about his camper.

"Yes, it's an Airstream that I picked up last year at an auction. I've been thinking about cutting back on work and doing some travelling during the winter months." His expression grew thoughtful, then he shrugged. "At least it will let me stay close by."

Inside they found Michael placing a large platter on the table. "We're out of bread so these are egg salad wraps. I'll be right back with the vegetables."

Catching Pat's eye, Pete said, "I can start on the brick oven tomorrow but have you thought about what you could use in the winter?"

"Hmm," she mused. "There's the old cook stove in the shed, but it's falling to bits and rusted out. We may be stuck with envying Jeffrey's stove and asking him for baked goods." Her laughing eyes clearly showed that she wasn't overly concerned at the moment.

The meal was delicious as only one prepared by a skillful cook working with the freshest ingredients can be. As they finished eating and sat listening to the steady rainfall, thoughts turned to making the most of the afternoon. Pete had sent his workers home when the storm arrived and everything planned for outdoors was hopeless.

"Well, we can get a lot of canning done," said Pat.

James looked over at Jeffrey. "What do you think about going to town and picking out a wood stove for the living room? Our options will be limited with what they have in stock, but maybe we can get them out to install it if we approach them now."

"You might have better luck if you offer cash up front. Considering they won't be able to run credit checks or process credit cards." Steve watched their reactions, then offered, "I can help if you don't have enough cash. One of the benefits of being paranoid."

While this was being discussed, Addie and Lindy were busy whispering to each other. Now Lindy spoke up. "Do you think other stores are open and would take cash too? It would be nice to have some extra shampoo and toilet paper. You know, basics."

"We can try and see. Will you make a list of what you want?" James asked.

"Yes, but I think Addie should go along."

"Okay, let's get cleaned up and presentable first so we don't scare anybody."

Their first stop in town was at the stove and fireplace store. When the salesman heard what they wanted he shook his head dourly. "We just don't carry an inventory. Besides the floor models which aren't for sale, all we've got is a small stove with a broken leg that's being returned and a very large one that the customer misunderstood the size. That's going to go back because it wouldn't fit in the space they had."

"Can we see it? Maybe we could make it work and save you the trouble of shipping it back." Jeffrey wasn't expecting good results but felt it was a worth a shot.

Shortly they stood around what could only be described as a massive stove with a water tank on the back. James and Jeffrey both shook their heads at it. It was much too large for any room at New Farm. As they were walking away Jeffrey suddenly stopped and went back. "James, you know where this would work? The living room at home; we could move Mom's stove to our place and put this one in. A little plumbing and she will have hot water this winter."

At that statement Addie perked up and started showing more interest. While she loved winter, cold showers were a trial to put up with.

James took over the negotiations with the salesman and arranged to have the stove installed along with the chimney lining and the new chimney for their kitchen stove as well. Upon learning that the salesman was also the owner of the store, James pulled out his secret weapon and offered the cash payment of half now and the balance upon completion. Suddenly the schedule opened up and they agreed on the following Monday.

Back in the truck, they discussed where to go next. "If we were in the city I would say Costco or Target, but I doubt they'd be open at all without power. What are the options here?" Addie asked.

"Let's check out the drug stores first," said Jeffrey.

The first one they drove past was obviously closed but the second had a scattering of vehicles in the lot so they went inside. After verifying with the employee at the door that they could make cash purchases, Addie took a shopping cart and headed for the health and beauty section. Loading up on shampoo, deodorant, body wash, toothpaste and feminine hygiene products, she looked wistfully at the pharmacy counter that was locked up with metal mesh. "I'm really going to regret not having allergy pills this fall if things don't get back to normal."

James patted her on the back. "Let's find Jeffrey."

Surprisingly, they located him in the baby section looking at a package of washable diapers. He looked a little sheepish when they joined him. "I just noticed that one of the few shelves that had emptied other than food items was the disposable diapers, but nobody is buying these."

James leaned closer to look at the price tag. "Whew! I can see why; that's outrageous." His eyebrows shot up when he realized his brother was considering buying them. "Why? What are you thinking?"

Jeffrey's face flushed and he shook his head, but stubbornly grabbed two packages in different sizes and placed them in the cart. James and Addie exchanged glances and shrugged before she said, "That reminds me..." and headed back to the health section where she grabbed boxes of condoms.

James was chuckling helplessly but straightened up enough to pick up extra disposable razors and a few other odds and ends that caught his eye. Then, while the other two headed for the checkout, he went searching for the store manager. When he came outside he directed Jeffrey to drive around to the delivery door in back. There, the manager was waiting with a forklift and a pallet of toilet paper. James handed the man a wad of cash and they drove away.

"How did you manage that?" asked Jeffrey.

"I offered him a bribe. The other option would be driving to every store we could find and buying as much as possible. I hoped this would get us out of town faster and draw less attention. I guess there was another option of running out and figuring out how to live without but, well, yuck."

Addie leaned over and kissed him on the cheek. "You are a prince among men. Will it be alright back there in the rain?"

"It should be fine. It's well wrapped in plastic. We can park in the shed and figure out where to store it all later."

Returning home they saw that Pete's camper had been parked behind the woodshed. James said, "I like him. More importantly, Mom likes him. Did you know he served in the Gulf War?"

"Does he have family?" Jeffrey asked.

"Divorced, no kids. I think he was originally from farther north; one of those tiny towns in the middle of nowhere." They had paused in the door of the pole barn while talking. James flashed his grin. "Ready to make a run for it?" And they raced for the house, arriving damp but laughing.

Inside, they found the kitchen to be the center of activity again. Pete was patiently slicing his way through a pile of carrots while Alex washed jars and Michael and Lindy worked around the stove. Lindy greeted them with a smile and an update. "Mom is upstairs resting. Steve went over to talk to Greg about working up the garden at New Farm and the vet stopped by and asked Adam to help him out this afternoon. How did the shopping trip go?"

Once they heard the story the discussion turned to where to store the toilet paper. When the decision was made to clear a section of the attic for it, Lindy volunteered to help move things around and Addie decided it was as good a time as any to begin the attic inventory.

"Sounds like we're on kitchen duty." Jeffrey said to James.

Over at Greg's farm, Steve leaned against the combine while watching Kat work her way across a tractor with a grease gun. Over the patter of the gentle rain and cooing of the pigeons in the rafters came the occasional grunt as she stretched to reach an awkward place or hit her elbow. When she finished and put away the grease gun, she joined him. Propped against the tire, she gazed out at the rain and spoke, "I'm going to stay here and help Dad for a year or two. His hired hand quit and he needs someone." She stole a glance at Steve's face before continuing in her calm, low voice, "I could use some quiet time to regroup too."

He had seen the strain in her eyes and recognized the signs of someone who had been living on the edge for too long. Moving over, he slid between her and the tire and wrapped his arms around her; they stood together watching the rain.

That evening everyone was gathering for supper when Adam walked in wearing his underwear and a t-shirt.

"Sorry, I left my jeans on the porch; they're pretty bad." Even his t-shirt was splattered with mud and manure. "I'm going to clean up."

They listened to his heavy steps plod up the stairs before sitting down at the table. Their mood was subdued but the stew with dumplings smelled too good to ignore. Once Adam came back down and had eaten a bowlful, even he perked up.

"We were working Tillet's herds. His whole operation is feedlots so it's pure muck when it rains."

Pat looked thoughtful. "I always feel sorry for cattle that never get to graze on grass."

"Will you have to do that job on your cattle?" Addie asked.

Alex nodded, "We wait until we wean the calves, usually in late fall. And our herd is much smaller so it's not such a massive undertaking."

"You don't seem to have to do much with them normally," Lindy observed.

"True. You came right after we turned the bulls out with the herd. We keep them separate so there's no danger of calves arriving in the dead of winter. We're lucky that it's such a hardy breed that calving in early spring works well.

"You noticed their horns? Once I saw a pack of dogs chasing a calf; the cow charged into them swinging her horns. One dog was flipped into the air and another trampled; she held them off long enough for Dad to get out there with his gun."

"Where did the dogs come from?" asked Lindy.

"It's not an uncommon problem around here. People decide they have to have hunting dogs but can't be bothered taking proper care of them. The dogs are neglected and bored so they start running in packs. Once they start chasing livestock it takes a very determined person to train them not to; exactly the sort of owner they don't have."

Adam leaned forward. "Tell them what else they can do with their horns."

"Okay. When the snow is deep and has buried the hay, the cattle dig their horns under the snow and flip the hay up on top. You'll get to see them in action this winter. They wouldn't do well in a hot climate, but are perfect here."

The conversation wandered onto other topics and the evening passed quietly. They had already fallen into the habit of going to bed with the sun so when it dipped below the horizon Pete went out to his camper and the others said goodnight.

Lindy woke during the night and got up to use the bathroom. The rain had stopped and the tattered clouds teased with glimpses of the full moon. In this half-light she was heading back to her room when she heard the soft tones of a guitar through the open front door. Peering out she saw a slight figure sitting on the steps, his back curved over the guitar while moonlight turned his hair copper bright.

Easing through the screen door, Lindy curled up on the other end of the steps and wrapped her arms around her legs.

"I didn't mean to wake you," he murmured.

"You didn't. I didn't know you played."

"Not terribly well. I've never had lessons, but I find it soothing."

"Hmm." An easy silence fell between them as he gently plucked a melody and sent the notes drifting into the night air.

It was while she was sitting there, watching him, that the realization of how much she loved him flooded through her.

20 SATURDAY

"Earth to Lindy. Come in, Lindy." Addie sounded exasperated.

"Oh... what?"

"You were a million miles away. What's going on?"

"Just thinking. Sorry." Lindy focused on her friend. "What did I miss?"

"I was trying to tell you about an idea I had for the laundry. Why don't we unplug the freezer long enough to do a couple loads every day until we catch up? We can check with Pete, but I think the generator should be able to handle it without any trouble. A clothes dryer is usually the power hog but they don't even have one here."

"Pat thinks they're too hard on the clothes. Anyway, your idea is brilliant! Let's ask him now." Lindy began weaving her way out of the smithy. She and Addie had discovered that they worked well as a team when sorting in the attic the previous day. Then they had chatted non-stop, but today Lindy tended to get lost in her own thoughts.

They found Pete laying bricks for the base of the oven he was building for Pat. When Addie repeated her idea, he readily approved it. While Lindy went to get the first load going, Addie stayed to talk. At first she kept the conversation neutral, discussing the work at New Farm and the oven, then she broached the subject on her mind.

"What do you think is happening in the rest of the country?"

Pete's hands paused in the process of laying the next brick while he considered the question. "I expect it's mostly like around here at the moment. People trying to carry on as normal the best they can or else treating it like an extra-long holiday weekend. Of course, there will always be a few who will demand their mayor or sheriff fix things right now. They're the ones who complain the loudest and tend to cause panic in others.

"As for what happens next, a lot will depend on what went wrong and if they know how to fix it. Then, if they can let everyone know what to expect and that someone is working on it; well, that would help a lot. Otherwise, things are going to start unravelling in the next couple weeks."

"What do you mean?" Addie asked.

"Most people can't do their jobs without electricity. Even my team won't work indefinitely without getting paid, which means I need access to the bank. Another example is the post office. It relies on machines to sort the mail. Are they going to suddenly sort millions of pieces of mail by hand? And how will they be paid?

"It's all connected. Push over the power and communication then the economy starts to wobble. When the economy goes, commerce follows. It won't be long before the entire structure falls down."

Addie was staring at Pete in horror. Deep down she had been certain that Michael's family was paranoid and that an outsider would have a saner perspective; instead, she heard an insightful, clear analysis of the situation that indicated the family might not be paranoid enough. "But what are you going to do? What should I do?"

Pete calmly took another brick from the wheelbarrow and tapped it into place. "I'm going to do my best to look after Pat and shelter her from the worst of it." He gazed at her over the top of his glasses. "You're intelligent and a problem solver. The laundry idea proves that. I hope you will keep helping out. We're going to need you."

"Oh." Addie looked startled, then thoughtful. Part of her inability to accept what was happening was due to feeling out of place and superfluous. Being needed, having a role to fill gave her an anchor and balance to control her fears. "Thank you."

Back in the smithy Addie found Lindy poking around in the corner they had just reached before the laundry sidetracked them. "Could this be the forge they used? It looks a little like a combination fireplace and fire pit."

Addie crouched down to look closer. "I think you're right. I wonder if any of the guys know anything about blacksmithing. I'd love to see this being used.

"That barrel of stuff must be the tools. I saw some hammers and tongs in there."

Lindy pulled a piece of canvas back and started coughing in the cloud of dust. "I found the anvil...no, I found three anvils! Funny, each one is a different size and shape."

Addie lifted the lid on a large wooden box. "What is...oh, I think it's coal." She let the lid drop, turned and perched on the edge while her eyes scanned the rest of the building. "Damn."

Lindy joined her on the coal box. "Yeah. Where are we going to put all this junk so we can use the forge?"

They shared a look before bursting into happy laughter. Addie recovered first and wiped the tears from her face. "It's crazy, I know; but I really, really want to try. Why is this suddenly so irresistible to me?"

"The history? Or because it feels like something more real than modern life? For you, maybe because it doesn't involve animals or grubbing in the dirt? I don't know. I don't think I'm quite as drawn to it as you seem to be, but even I'm longing to try." A satisfied smile appeared on Lindy's face. "And I think I know what to do about the storage problem. After the work is done on New Farm all that material stacked in the barn will be gone. They're not planning on having livestock, there aren't even any fences now so the barn will be empty."

A little reluctantly, they resumed work on the inventory and the hours trudged past. Late in the afternoon the conversation turned whimsical.

"Imagine," said Addie. "If all the brothers had wives and were dropped in an empty place. They would build homes and farms and within a generation there would be an entire village and everyone in it would have the same last name."

"And other than the twins, all would be unrelated so the cousins could safely marry. The Stevenson clan." A shadow passed over Lindy's face. "It wouldn't be fair if one of the couples couldn't have babies."

Addie said firmly, "In the proper tradition of this family, they would have adopted a bunch of babies before being relocated."

Lindy shot her friend a grateful look. But then Addie continued, "Lindy, who would be the father of all those adoptees?"

Her face flushed bright red, Lindy was looking around in a panic for an escape when Adam poked his head in the door. "Adam! What are you doing back already?"

Taking that as a welcome, he came inside. "We've finished the addition. Well, the part we were all working on at least. James is going to tackle the wiring next before we do the drywall. Anyway, right now Pete has gone over and is talking with his crew about the situation and sounding them on what they want to do.

"You get a pretty good feel for people when you work with them. I think Rick will try to get to Arizona and check on his folks. He doesn't have any family left here. But Juan has a wife and three kids. He will probably want to keep working. Jeffrey told Pete to offer payment in food if he's interested. Either way, we're going to start replacing the windows tomorrow." He looked around the crowded space. "How are you two doing?"

Addie answered, "We're almost finished the raw inventory in here. Do you know anything about the forge? When was it last used and why is it even here on the farm?"

"No, not really. I know where you won't find any information though: the county museum. I had to do a report on local history in high school and I went there for research. There was a very nice display on military history and a good section of antique furniture. The practical side was a bit sketchy and the equipment was just a mess. Most of the farm stuff wasn't even labeled, let alone properly displayed. I think there was about two square feet of floor space dedicated to blacksmithing." He shook his head in disgust. Then he smiled at Addie. "I heard about your laundry idea. Thank you. I wasn't looking forward to washing my jeans by hand."

"No worries. I think we should have a backup plan though in case anything happens to the generator. I've got an idea about that. Which of you is the most mechanically inclined?"

"Probably Alex with Jeffrey as a close second. Although all of us can do any basic work needed. They're the two that enjoy it the most."

"Okay, I'll have a chat with them later." She turned and gestured at the wall behind Lindy. "All we've got left is the stuff on this rack. I think we can push and get it done before supper."

Lindy reached for the first item on the top shelf. "One coffee percolator, some rust spots."

Adam took the hint and left them to it.

After supper, the family spread themselves around the living room and caught up on the day's events. Alex started with a report on the milk run, "Hansen was pretty upset. He's got no working equipment and is spending all his time milking by hand, then having to dump it. He doesn't have any pigs or chickens that he can feed the excess to. Ten cows doesn't sound like a lot but when it's one old man milking them twice a day...well, he already looked worn out. I offered to bring Addie over tomorrow to look around and see if she had any suggestions. Sorry, Addie, I know I should have asked you first."

Addie looked startled. "No, that's okay, but what do you think I can help him with? I know nothing about a dairy operation."

"But you're good at organizing. I thought you might have a fresh outlook without the preconceptions the rest of us have." Alex looked so hopeful that she didn't have the heart to say no.

Michael updated them on the canning. "We'll be finished with the freezer tomorrow. That will free up the generator for the laundry and any emergencies we might need it for. I already talked to Pete about using it long-term to run the freezer and that's not going to work."

"That's right. It's a decent little generator, but it wasn't designed to run 24/7 even if we had a limitless supply of gas. Just running a couple hours every few days will extend its life quite a bit." Pete had his arm around Pat's shoulders on the couch and they both seemed to radiate a quiet contentment. "By the way, I paid my crew up in cash today. Rick has decided to go check on his parents. Juan is willing to keep working with the understanding that I'll pay him when I can and, in the meantime, we will send food home with him for his family. From now on he's going to be driving out on one of those little moped things to save gas."

After the discussion, everyone split off in different directions. Steve and Lindy went up to the garden, James and Jeffrey moved closer to the couch to talk about New Farm, Michael took Biff out for a run, Adam and Alex started cleaning up the kitchen and Addie spread her notes across the dining table and began to organize her lists.

When the sun headed for the horizon, Addie tidied up her mess and went to take her turn for a cold shower. Afterwards, as she towel dried her hair she thought about Lindy's preoccupation and speculated on what, or possibly who, could be distracting her. Out of respect for her friend's recent troubles, she decided not to tease.

As Lindy settled down in bed that night she breathed a sigh of relief when it was obvious that Addie wasn't going to ask her that awkward question again.

21 SUNDAY

"Can you hire someone to help?" Addie held onto her temper with an effort. Bob Hansen was not a friendly person at the best of times and he obviously didn't expect her to give him any useful advice.

"Humph. And who would I get? How would I pay them?" He spat off to the side in disgust.

"Who lives across the road there?"

"Charlie Hogge. He's got his own farm to run. Doesn't even have any boys to help him."

"He has daughters? How old?"

"I don't know and I don't care. What does it matter?"

"It matters, Mr. Hansen, because if any of them are old enough to milk cattle then they are your most promising source of labor. Your other options are to add chickens or pigs to use the extra milk which would make more work for you or to start making daily milk deliveries to your neighbors or get rid of some of your cows." Addie turned to Alex who was having a hard time not laughing and said, "I'm going over to talk to the neighbors. You have a look at that old wagon and see if it's usable."

Addie looked around the neighboring farmyard with interest. She didn't have the frame of reference to recognize what was a typical small family farm that was struggling to make ends meet. She saw pigs and chickens by the barn and in the yard a tall girl was hanging laundry on the clothesline. "Hello. I'm Addie. Is your mom around?"

The girl nodded and led the way into the farmhouse. "Mom! There's someone here to see you."

A slightly overweight woman holding a toddler appeared, followed by three more girls. Her face wore a pleasant smile which was at odds with the worry lines in her forehead. When Addie had explained the situation the woman frowned. "Oh, I don't know. Krista is only twelve and has never done anything like that before."

The tall girl folded her arms across her chest. "You need me here. I could do it, but there's too much work for you alone."

Addie spoke up, "I'm afraid he couldn't pay you, but you could have fresh milk every day and cheese. There might even be a butter churn somewhere over there."

Krista scowled fiercely but had seen the look in her mother's eyes at the mention of milk. "Okay, I'll do it. But how are you going to manage here?"

Her mother smiled proudly at her eldest and said, "Anna will help more with your chores and the little ones will do as much as they can. Julie can pick up, right?"

The little girl who couldn't be more than six stuck her chin out and said, "Yes, and when I'm big I can milk cows too."

A few minutes later, Addie was introducing Krista to Mr. Hansen. He looked incredulous that they expected a girl to be any help and Addie felt guilty for putting a child in such an unpleasant environment. Krista looked unimpressed by his attitude and everything else until she saw the cows. "Oh! They're lovely!"

Addie couldn't see the appeal herself and stayed well back while the old man thawed under the girl's unabashed admiration of his herd. He pointed out each cow and told her their names and personalities.

Alex smiled happily. "I was right about you being able to help him. The wagon would work for him to make deliveries if he chooses to; he knows someone with horses. And I bought two cows for the farm."

Addie swung around and stared at him. "You did what?"

"I'll come back this afternoon with the trailer to get a lesson in milking and pick them up. He didn't want to part with them, but he knows they'll be well cared for with us. Even with Krista's help, it's going to be difficult for him to keep up. So, are you ready to go home?"

Pat relaxed on the porch, calmly petting Mama Cass. Michael had sent her away to take a break and, honestly, she had needed it. The ache in her arm was steadily decreasing but she still seemed to run out of energy faster than normal. Her thoughts turned to Pete and she sighed contentedly. He was kind and understanding. He wasn't jealous of her memories of Matt. Pat wondered at her fortune to have had two good men in her life.

While she watched, Alex and Addie rode in on his motorcycle. As they dismounted and pulled off their helmets she observed that they seemed to be arguing again. Suddenly, Alex grabbed Addie's arms and kissed her. Addie jerked back and slapped him hard before spinning and stalking away down the driveway. He stared after her for a moment before marching into the barn and slamming the door behind him.

"Well!" exclaimed Pat to herself before an indignant meow reminded her that she was supposed to be petting the cat.

Addie spent the rest of the day at New Farm; first collecting nails that fell out when the old windows were pulled out, then following James and handing him his tools as he ran wire through the addition. She would ask questions about why he did things a certain way but didn't listen to the answers.

Finally, she interrupted him to ask, "Do you think people can change who they are?"

James set down the wire bracket he was placing and turned his attention to Addie. Her eyes were troubled as she met his gaze earnestly. "I think anything is possible if that person wants it badly enough. How likely it is, well, that's harder to say. Are we talking about behavior or character?"

"I think...I think maybe some of both."

"Hmm. Behavior or habits just takes self-discipline. Learning to put the toilet seat down or clean up after yourself is easy enough; but I suppose you're asking about more important changes. Addictions, it's scary how difficult it is for a person to break free and make it last. Then there are those who are just wired wrong; people who can't comprehend the difference between right and wrong." James peered at Addie's sad face. "I wish I could help you more. I can tell you this truth: you can't change someone else. You can be supportive of improvement, but you must be careful not to compromise your principles and any real changes will take time.

"Was that any use at all?"

"Not terribly," she replied with a wry twist of her lips. Then her expression sobered and she said, "I either know him too well or not well enough, but I don't trust him." With that she levered herself up off the floor and walked away.

"Well, hell." James had a cold sinking feeling in the pit of his stomach that he had handled the discussion badly.

At the supper table that evening the source of her concerns was obvious. The glances Alex shot in her direction seemed to alternate between hurt and resentment. When he left to check on the new cows, James followed.

Leaning on a stall in the barn, James asked, "Which of you is real? The farmer or the playboy?"

"Huh, what?"

"It's just that I've known you your entire life and even I don't know the answer. What chance is there for someone who has just met you?"

"I'm both. When I'm here I'm a farmer to my bones. Away from here I have fun and party. What's wrong with that?"

"Nothing. The problem is when someone else has seen both sides. They can see someone admirable in the farmer but can't reconcile that with the playboy."

Alex's temper flared. "You expect me to change who I am? Not going to happen!"

James gave him a look that was equal parts frustration and sympathy. "You don't have to change. Just stop putting pressure on Addie. Do you want to make her so uncomfortable and miserable that she leaves?"

Alex seemed to deflate. "No, not that. But I don't know how to act around her anymore. Tell me what to do, Jimmy."

"You really can't just be her friend?"

"I tried. It's not enough."

"Then fall back on Dad's rule."

Comprehension dawned on Alex's face. "She's my sister while she lives here. Right."

James shook his head as he watched his brother walk away confidently. Oddly enough, he knew it would be okay now. The old rule provided boundaries that were familiar and solid. He was relieved that a crisis was averted but saddened that Alex was missing out on a life partner who would have been a good match; her strength would have bolstered his weakness and his calm would have steadied her volatility.

Musing on the problem, he decided it must be a case where genetics overruled environment. Both the twins had an inherent weakness. Proof seemed to be Jeffrey who was almost their equal in attractiveness and had countless students with crushes on him, yet had never let temptation get the best of him.

When he got back to the house, Pat caught his eye and nodded. He knew then that she understood what was happening and approved of the solution. He paused and hugged her. It was a comfort to have her support.

22 MONDAY

Alex was up at 4:30 a.m. to do the morning milking. It hadn't been easy to force himself out of bed but he expected it would become habit soon enough and then he would no longer need to borrow Steve's windup alarm clock. He planned on turning the new cows out into the small paddock behind the barn today; that would keep them close while they adjusted to their new home. The main herd didn't have access to it so the grass was still tall and it had its own water tank.

Talking in a low murmur, he set his stool next to Clarabelle. She was the more placid of the two and seemed safer for a novice to begin on. Carefully following the process Hansen had shown him, Alex cleaned the udder before beginning. He felt awkward and clumsy at first but slowly found the rhythm. Finishing with her, he covered the bucket and set it aside before taking a clean, empty bucket into Annabelle's stall. She shifted away from him nervously and lifted her rear hoof, ready to lash out. Alex kept his tone gentle and soothing until she settled and he could begin. In the quiet, repetitive motions his thoughts went back to the previous day and he couldn't escape the conclusion that there was something he still had to do. Resting his forehead against the cow's side, Alex sighed and attempted to imagine himself in Addie's position. He needed to get the words right so she wouldn't feel obligated to respond; this had to be something he gave to her, not asking anything in return.

The sun was just lightening the eastern sky as he finished. After leading the cows out into the paddock he carried the milk buckets up to the kitchen. As he was placing them on the counter, Addie walked in and froze. She immediately began backing out again.

"Addie, I owe you an apology. I was out of line yesterday. I'm sorry. It won't happen again." He looked her straight in the eyes as he spoke, then turned and walked out. He kept walking until he reached the top of the hill behind the house. There, he sat on a rock and let the wind blow the scattered thoughts and regrets out of his mind.

Addie retreated to her bed where she curled up and told Lindy everything.

"How do you feel?" Lindy asked when the tale was told.

"Mmm, I guess I'm relieved that he didn't make me talk to him right then. And if he really does back off, then maybe we can go back to the way it was before."

"Do you like him?"

Addie shot her a sharp look before sighing. "I could have liked him if things were different. God, he's so arrogant. He just assumed I'd be happy to have a roll in the hay with him." A mischievous smile danced across her face. "And maybe I would have if I hadn't seen them operate in the city first. He and Adam swept through the restaurant like magnets pulling every female under the age of fifty after them."

"But not you." Lindy looked curiously at her friend.

"No, I had just caught my ex cheating so I was immune to charming men when they showed up."

"Ah, and you think Alex would cheat too."

"Of course he would. They both admit they've never been in a real relationship. They've never even tried dating just one girl at a time."

Lindy sighed now, "It seems a shame..."

Addie threw her pillow and laughed. "You just want me in your Stevenson village."

Lindy ducked and blushed, "Well, you can't blame me for wishing. Come on. It must be time to eat and Pete said he wanted to talk to everyone this morning."

Pete waited until everyone had filled their plates and sat down before he began speaking, "I'd like to ramp up the work at New Farm now that you've emptied the freezer and aren't overwhelmed. This is how I'd like to arrange things: James, you and Addie finish off the wiring in the addition then start on the drywall. I'm going to have you hold off on rewiring the rest of the house until we see how things settle. Lindy, I'm assigning Michael to be your muscle. Get all the old plumbing ripped out first while you have him. When he has to go back to his own work I'll pull someone else to assist you. Alex and Adam will begin tearing off the old siding. The rest of us will continue with the windows."

Pat's eyebrows rose in surprise. "Are you leaving me here alone?"

Pete reached over and squeezed her hand. "You're going to sit in the shade and supervise. Don't think I haven't noticed how exhausted you are each evening. It won't do you any harm to take it easy for a few days. Please?"

"Alright, we can try it your way."

"Okay, while the inside teams get their areas started we will finish the windows, wrap the house and put up new siding. Have I forgotten anything?"

Lindy waved her hand. "Aren't the stove people coming today? We still need to move the living room stove from here to New Farm."

"Umph. You're right. Michael and the twins do that first, then go to your assignments. Pat and I will stay here until they've installed the new stove. Any other issues?"

Everyone shook their heads and scattered to get ready.

Pat stood and frowned down at the new stove. It hadn't taken long to install since the pipe was already in place; they had set it on a larger hearth pad and the bulky stove made the living room feel smaller. Maybe it was the water tank mounted to the back that made it look wrong. With a sigh she turned away; there wasn't anything she could do about it.

"Are you sure you don't want to ride over?" Pete asked when she joined him outside.

"I'm sure. It's a nice day to walk." Pat took his arm and they headed down the driveway. "When can we try out the oven? I'm already missing fresh bread."

Pete smiled at her. "Tomorrow. Michael said he's going to start some dough rising tonight."

Steve and Jeffrey worked together to pull the old window out of an upstairs bedroom. While Jeffrey hauled it down to the dumpster, Steve began prying off the rotten outside trim. Returning, Jeffrey paused to study his brother's preoccupied expression. "You're quiet this morning."

Steve continued working for a few minutes until the pry bar slipped and he gouged the back of his hand on a nail. "Damn!"

Seeing Jeffrey's concern, he scrubbed his hands across his face and heaved a sigh. "I tried using my computer last night. It's the first chance I've had to use it since everything got so busy and I've been meaning to print out the instructions to build a smokehouse. It wouldn't power on and at first I thought maybe something had happened when the power went out because I was using it then. So I went downstairs and got the other computer to try. Same problem. I checked the solar battery and it was fully charged. I don't get it. It has to be related to whatever shut down the phones, but I can't figure out what."

"We can try my laptop tonight, but I doubt it will be any different. Hmm, some sort of power surge? But if it hit the phones it couldn't be limited to wire transmission. Do you suppose there could have been a massive solar storm we didn't hear about?"

"You're thinking EMP? I wondered about that last night but I had a feeling it didn't quite fit. Maybe...let's find James. I want to ask him something."

They found James and Addie beginning on the drywall in the addition. Steve asked, "James, you were on the road when the power went out, weren't you? Did you see any vehicles stall or people pulled over?"

"Not exactly, we were inside the mall but were driving within five minutes. I don't recall seeing anyone with car troubles, but I was distracted."

Lindy poked her head out from under the kitchen sink. "I didn't see anything like that either. Why?"

Steve had turned back to Jeffrey. "You see it, right?"

"Yes, if a pulse powerful enough to cause all this happened, there should have been quite a few cars that stalled out and caused accidents. Some may not have started again. We can probably rule out any kind of EMP." He shot a piercing look at Steve's face, evaluating the worry lines and indications of lack of sleep. "So, what else is bothering you? It's still the same mystery as yesterday."

"Well, I'm pissed at losing all my gardening files for one." This earned him some chuckles from the others. "But mostly it's the ramifications for getting things running again. If all the computers are toast, what about backup systems? If it's all lost, or even just a significant amount of the data, how long does it take to rewrite all that software? My team has been working on our project for seven months. If the company network was wiped out we didn't just lose seven months of work, we may have lost years of programs."

"Aren't you a dour looking bunch." Michael nudged his way into the kitchen. "Lindy, are you ready for me to take the sink out yet?"

"Oh! Just a couple more minutes." She grabbed a wrench and scooted back under the sink.

The rest of the group split up and returned to their work, each following their own train of thoughts about what Steve had said.

By noon the chimney lining was in place in the old fireplace and the installers had the wood stove attached to the pipe coming down from the blocking plate. That was an important feature to stop heat loss. James was admiring the effect the sturdy stove had on the look of the living room when Jeffrey joined him. "I wish we had been able to refinish the floor first, but at least we got the old carpet out in time. It's going to be cozy, isn't it?"

Jeffrey smiled at his enthusiasm and looked around. "I kind of like the rough, lived-in look of the floor. Which is probably a good thing because renting a floor sander might be tough now."

"Ouch! Everything seems to come back around to what's changed." Changing the subject, James asked, "Are they gone for lunch?"

"No, the boss wants them to push through and finish the job. He's glad to make use of Pete's generator too. In fact, I got the feeling he was a little too interested in it. I wonder if we should haul it home tonight."

"Let's mention it to Steve and get his opinion."

Outside, everyone who hadn't been working at New Farm recently commented on the new picnic tables before tucking into lunch. After a few minutes of serious eating, Addie asked Juan how things were in town.

"Not too bad. We live in a quiet neighborhood and haven't had any trouble. My wife works at the nursing home and they've had to make some changes. The patients that need machines were moved up to the hospital on the first day; but they always do that if the power is out more than twelve hours. She said some of the families have been taking their relatives home to stay with them because they're worried the care levels will drop.

"I was talking to one of my neighbors last night. He works at the supermarket and told me about his manager. On the first day a refrigerated truck was making a delivery and he made the trucker stay so they could put all the frozen foods into it. The driver tried raising a stink but it's a company truck and the manager took full responsibility. Then there were normal deliveries the next two days, but none over the weekend. They don't think there will be any more. Even if the warehouse is still sending them, they probably won't make it to the stores."

Steve leaned forward, "It might be best if you don't let on that you're coming home with a backpack full of food every day."

Juan nodded, "I'll be careful. I want to get home in one piece."

Suddenly, there was the sound of a sharp yelp followed by frantic yips. Everyone jumped to their feet and, following the noise, ran around the house. They found Biff standing awkwardly with one leg pulled down as if in a trap. With each yip, he pulled back frantically. When Adam saw the dog was caught in some rotten wood he moved forward cautiously, testing each step in the tall grass and brush. Gently easing Biff's leg free, Adam carried him away to examine for any possible injury.

While the others gathered around the dog, Pete was pulling grass and broken branches away from the boards. "Good news! Your dog found the old well. I've been worried about the water supply."

"Why?" Addie peered around him at the unimpressive hole that was being revealed. "I thought rural water would be hooked up when Lindy finishes the plumbing."

"They will if it's still running. That can only last as long as the county has fuel for the generators at each pumping station. The boys could walk over and get water from the farm, but that should be a last resort." Pete paused to wipe the sweat out of his eyes and sent one of the younger men to get a piece of plywood for a temporary well cover. "I think we need to make another shopping trip. Since Juan says they've got some stock in the stores and it's still quiet, we should go while we can. I'd like to scrounge around and see if I can find a pump for this."

Addie gave a quick nod, "I'll talk to everyone about what they think we need and make a list."

After she made the rounds, Addie joined Pete where he sat talking to Pat. "Well, I have my doubts about whether we can get all this. Do we even have enough cash?"

"Don't worry about the money. I often get paid in cash. Don't ask why." Pete gave her a forbidding look. "Now, run through the list for us, please."

"If you say so." Addie shrugged. "Michael wants any and all the spices we can get. Also yeast. And he wants us to check the grain elevator and see if we can buy wheat or other grains. Steve will take any seeds that are left over from spring, ammo and batteries. I have my doubts about finding the last two. Jeffrey asked if we could check to see if the picture window might have been delivered early - he's definitely dreaming. He also mentioned baby supplies again; like bottles and stuff. His ex-wife wasn't pregnant, was she?"

Pat looked startled at the idea, then shook her head. "I'm pretty sure he would have mentioned it if there was any chance. I can't imagine what's got him thinking along those lines."

"Anyway, Adam asked for first aid supplies, fabric and thread. Alex wants candles, matches and a boar. For James: a manual typewriter, lots of paper and new winter boots. Lindy suggested vitamins and things we can't grow like canned citrus. How about you, Pat?"

"I've been wishing I had bought those reusable canning lids. Can you look for more lids? I can use regular or wide-mouth. Vinegar and pickling spices; I know we can make our own vinegar, but for now it's nice to have it on hand. Oh, maybe an extra roll of chicken wire."

The low growl of a tractor caught their attention when it turned into the driveway. They watched Steve stride out to meet it and direct the driver to the garden area. Pat strained to see, "Who...oh, it's Katherine. How nice."

Addie turned back to Pete, "Is it okay if James and I come with you?"

"Of course. We'll take my truck."

The afternoon passed quickly the way a busy day can. Steve and Alex planted the root vegetable seeds, the stove people finished and departed, and work progressed on the house. Suppertime came and went without the return of the shoppers; it wasn't until the sun was touching the horizon that the truck pulled in.

Pete looked rightfully proud of the pump in the bed of the truck. Eager hands reached for bags to carry the supplies inside. Soon they were gathered around the dining table while the shoppers ate their very late meal and related the successes and failures of the afternoon.

James leaned back in his chair with a weary sigh and continued his tale, "I knew it was a long shot on the typewriter, so I'll have to make do with pencils; at least we got lots of those. No ammo for sale anywhere and the batteries are gone too. Sorry, Jeffrey, no luck on the window, but we did get the chicken wire and some netting while there. It was a good idea to visit the grain elevator too; we got three bags of wheat and one each of barley, rye and oats. Lots of spices left on the shelves so we bought some at different stores.

"You didn't expect us to find those reusable lids, did you, Mom? I went a bit mad and bought loads of normal lids everywhere I could find them. I'm glad we weren't looking for much canned or processed food; all I got was a few jars of mandarin oranges and some marmalade. Is that something we can make with the fresh citrus we have left?"

"I don't see why not," said Pat. "It's a good way to use the peels."

Steve walked by carrying a shotgun, sleeping bag and flashlight.

"Where is he going?" asked Addie.

"He's keeping an eye on New Farm tonight."

Steve enjoyed the cooler breeze that picked up as the dusk deepened. It was also a relief to be away from his family for a while; the farm was feeling crowded with so many people taking an active interest in each other's lives.

Because they had already removed the cattle grate and locked the gate, Steve approached New Farm through the trees. He moved silently from habit, alert to his surroundings when a rustle in the brush to his left made him pause. Before he could move, an arm slid around his waist.

With a rueful chuckle he murmured, "I used to think I was pretty good at that. You move like a ghost."

Kat didn't reply, just matched her long stride to his.

23 TUESDAY

The morning sunshine flooded the kitchen with a golden light that added to Michael's feeling of satisfaction. His dough had risen beautifully during the night and today he would be experimenting with the brick oven. In the meantime, he skimmed the thick, luscious layer of cream out of the milk bucket and hummed to himself. When the back door opened and Lindy stepped inside with a basket of vegetables, he greeted her cheerfully.

"Good morning to you too! What is that gorgeous smell?" She set the basket next to the sink and started peeking into the pans on the stove.

"Porridge! Glorious porridge served with lashings of fresh cream." Michael poked through the basket. "Do you ever have days that feel like everything is going to be wonderful? The only thing that would make it better would be if the peaches were ripe."

Lindy couldn't help smiling at such a chef-centric view of life.

Steve joined the others for breakfast and reported a quiet night. "I did hear someone drive by slowly very early this morning, but they didn't stop."

Discussing their choices for the day, Pete agreed with Michael's plans to stay home and bake. Because they didn't want anyone alone all day, Addie volunteered to stay and help him.

"I'll need a new plumbing assistant then," said Lindy.

James waved his hand, "I'd like at apply for the position."

"Right." Pete pushed himself away from the table. "The rest of us will see how far we can get on the outside."

Michael straightened his back as he stepped away from the hot oven. The morning had been spent experimenting with the fire and cooking times. Biff lay nearby, perfectly willing to dispose of any more failures. Now though, there were two pizzas baking which would be lunch if all went well. He had already determined that his tools were inadequate for the job and found himself wishing he had the long-handled implements they had seen used in Italy when he and Amelia were honeymooning.

Addie had radioed the crew to come home for lunch and was in the kitchen steaming vegetables. Angling the longest spatulas he had, Michael pulled out the first pizza without burning himself. It looked almost right and smelled very good. After removing the second pizza, Michael spread the fire across the oven floor and set the metal plate they were using for a door across the opening. Not daring to leave the food untended around Biff, he carried both pizzas inside carefully, to be met by cheers and helping hands.

The lunch was declared a complete success and soon after he was back outside preparing the oven for the next stage. First he scooped out the remains of the fire and ashes. Then, using a slightly damp old towel, he wiped off the hot base and placed two large loaves inside. This was the part he was most nervous about. With the door in place he couldn't see the progress, but if he checked too often, he risked losing the heat too fast.

A fluttering movement caught his eye and he turned to see Addie hanging sheets on the clothesline. A stray thought crossed his mind that it would be very inconvenient to dry sheets in the winter which led to wondering how he would bake during the long, cold months. With a grimace, Michael shook his head and focused on what he was doing. Too much thinking like that would distract him and result in burnt bread.

As it turned out, he had a mostly successful day. Biff did get lucky with a couple more pieces, but for the most part the loaves all emerged golden and delicious. The New Farm crew also had a good day; the twins had finished tearing off the old siding. The windows were being installed at a steady pace, although one was found to be the wrong size and they were adjusting the frame to fit. Lindy was done with the kitchen and the downstairs half-bath. Her body ached from the unaccustomed work, but her sense of accomplishment was high.

After an evening meal of spaghetti and garlic bread, the family gathered around the supplies bought the day before and sorted through the bags.

Adam plunged his arm into a paper bag and pulled out a handful of candy bars. "What's with all the chocolate? Who put that on the list?"

Addie jumped up and snatched the bag away. "I did. This is for my sanity."

"Oh!" Pat sat up straight. "Iron rations!"

"What?" her kids exchanged confused looks.

"It was in a book I read ages ago. They tucked away a few luxury items for a special treat when they would need a boost. Months later they brought it out during an emergency and it was exactly what they needed."

"What sort of items?" Addie asked curiously.

"All sorts of things they had used up and couldn't get anymore. Let's see...there was instant coffee, bouillon base, some hard candy, canned meat. Imagine if we couldn't get any other supplies, what would you be most thankful for in the middle of February?"

"Peanut butter." "Chocolate." "Pineapple." "Cinnamon." "Grape jelly." "Cranberry sauce." "Tea." Those and many others were tossed out into the discussion. Addie was trying to catch them all as she made another list. Pat leaned back under Pete's arm happily as she listened to her children take her idea and run with it. By the time they were satisfied with the list and had agreed on how and where to store it, the sun was setting.

Lindy hurried outside to shut up the chicken coop before it got too dark. Without any reflected lights from towns or other farms, the darkness fell fast and deep. As she shut the pen gate behind her and turned to go back to the house, an arm caught her across the neck and a hand clasped over her mouth. Yanked backward, her feet scrabbled for purchase and her heart pounded frantically. She knew she was being pulled behind the buildings, but couldn't do anything other than pull ineffectively on the arm cutting off her air supply.

"Hello, Lindy. Miss me?" John breathed into her ear.

She tried to say no and shake her head but all that came out was a strangled moan. He laughed and kept talking, his breath hot on her cheek and his body pressed against hers in a parody of a lover's embrace. "I've been searching for you for weeks. You thought you were so smart hiding from me, but you got careless and I found you."

Lindy made a questioning sound, hoping to distract him and slow their retreat from the farm.

"How?" John laughed. "Your precious little family invited my informant out and you paraded yourself in front of him. He couldn't wait to tell me where you were and collect his reward."

His voice turned harsh, "All those men. Which one are you sleeping with? Or is it all of them? There's got to be a reason they're protecting you!"

Suddenly, his arm was off her throat, but before she could move it was replaced with a knife. She couldn't help the little whimper of panic that escaped her mouth.

He was breathing hard and radiating anger now. "You have much to make up for, Lindy. You've caused me a lot of trouble. But I must not damage your face. After all, I'm going to be looking at it every day for the rest of your life."

Lindy had a moment of clarity where time seemed to stop and she stepped away from her body and thought of the future. She could imagine being his prisoner, at his mercy and listening to his insane jealousies forever. Despair at the hopelessness of the situation flooded through her before she made her choice. She felt detached and almost relieved that there was another option. Breathing deeply, she closed her eyes and began to lean forward against the knife when the words from his continuing monologue sank in. "Don't worry. I won't forget what they've done to me. I'll see them all burn. Your parents slipped away, but I'll get another chance at them someday. These people, maybe I'll bring you along so you can watch the fire take them. Then you'll know. You belong to me and only me."

Lindy's heart faltered painfully with the realization that he was going to kill the people she loved. Then the radio at her waist crackled to life and James' voice said, "Lindy, where are you?" John's hand jerked at the sudden noise and the knife edge bit into her skin. When she pushed back in reaction, they were both knocked off balance and she felt the knife slice across her shoulder as they fell. Suddenly a deep growl seemed to fill the night and in a confused whirl of movement and noise, an explosion of pain struck Lindy in the temple and she fell into a black abyss.

James rounded the corner of the farrowing house and saw dark shapes in the hay field. Mellow had shot ahead and given him a direction to search, now Biff began barking and ran after her. James' flashlight wasn't strong enough to illuminate what was happening even if it hadn't been bouncing as he ran, but he could tell when Mellow reached the shapes by the shout, movement and yelp as she was flung back. Biff was nearly there and his half-grown bark sounded threatening even to James. Suddenly, one of the figures broke away and ran across the field towards the trees. Biff started to follow, but stopped with a whine and ran back to the still form on the ground.

When the flashlight reflected off an out flung arm, James forced the panic down long enough to radio for help. Dropping the radio and flashlight, he slid on his knees next to Lindy, not even aware of the desperate moan of his voice saying, "Please, please, please." His fingers felt numb as they slid through the blood on her throat searching for a pulse. With a gasp he felt the faint thrub against his fingertips and the soft breath against his cheek undid him. Tears poured down his face as pulled off his shirt and pressed it against the slice on her throat. Only peripherally aware of the arrival of the others with more light, his entire focus was on the pale, unconscious face before him.

Steve pushed himself faster, setting aside the anger at being so far from where he was needed. He was aware of Kat's form running beside him, but kept alertly keyed to their surroundings for other dangers. It only took minutes to reach the others, yet the voices clamoring from the corners of his mind threatened to pull him into a flashback. Forcing himself to concentrate on the now, Steve pulled the twins away from the others and sent them out to search for the intruder. Looking down, he saw Kat had taken the first aid kit from Jeffrey and was examining Lindy's injuries. Crouching down beside them, he tried questioning James but couldn't get anything sensible out of him.

Finally, Kat sat back on her heals and announced that Lindy likely had a concussion from the blows to her head and needed stitches on her shoulder and the back of her head where she had struck a rock, but the cut to her throat was shallow and not dangerous. Michael stepped forward, gently scooped Lindy up into his arms and headed for the house.

For a moment James sat frozen, then Jeffrey helped him up and walked beside him as they brought up the rear of the procession.

Back at the house, Kat took charge and ordered everyone other than Pat out of Lindy's room. Pat had seen a number of farming accidents over the years and wasn't squeamish at the sight of blood. She found her hand shaking slightly as she handed things to Kat, but knew it was reaction to the strong emotions she had felt during the crisis.

When Kat began shaving the hair away from the long gash across the back of Lindy's head, Pat sighed. Kat glanced at her in understanding but said, "It will grow back. I doubt anyone here is so shallow that they would hold a haircut against her."

Pat chuckled weakly, "No, that won't matter at all. You don't think we should have taken her to the emergency room?"

"No, these are really just flesh wounds. The concussion is the only thing that worries me but there wouldn't be anything the hospital could do for that other than keep her in for observation. I believe the care here will be better and she'll recover faster in familiar surroundings." A frown crossed her face. "It would be difficult to guard her adequately there also."

"You think he will try again."

Their eyes met. "Yes."

24 WEDNESDAY

Lindy drifted slowly back towards consciousness; part of her was aware of how much pain awaited once she crossed the threshold and was content to drift. Another part needed to know if she was safe and shoved her across. It was much worse than she expected. With each beat of her heart her head pounded back; her entire body ached but it felt like her shoulder was on fire and something was constricting her throat, making each breath a chore. Her only movement at this point was a tightening of her lips as she fought against moaning.

She couldn't imagine the pain getting worse, but when she cracked open her eyes, the daylight stabbed into them. Closing her eyes as the tears squeezed out, she tried again. Slowly she was able to focus on her room in general, then on the man on a chair next to her bed in particular. He was hunched forward with his head in his hands; the long fingers parting bright red hair that flopped down over his forehead. Lindy longed to reach out and brush the hair back from his face. She whispered, "You need a haircut, love."

Then, just as he lifted his head and turned towards her, the blackness reached out and pulled her back under.

"Kat! She woke up and spoke! But then she slipped away again. Is that normal? Is she going to be okay?"

Kat met James' gaze steadily as he held onto the doorjamb, almost shaking with anxiety. "That's fine. Her body is reserving energy to heal. There will be a lot of pain, so sleep is the best thing for her now. She didn't throw up? Well, she might next time. Be ready."

As his fear eased back a few notches, James noticed the tension between Kat and Steve. "What are you working on?"

"Security plans." Steve had his arms crossed over his chest and wore a forbidding expression.

"Good. What are you fighting about?" Now they were both glaring at him.

"Humph! The level of Kat's involvement in our affairs."

Kat stabbed the table with her finger. "You need me here. You're facing an unstable hostile with unknown resources. If I'm a distraction then you need to improve your discipline. Stuff your pride. Nobody else is going to care that we're lovers."

"Um, actually we're all going to care. We just won't mind." James grinned goofily at the pair now wearing equally fierce expressions. He made a hasty retreat and went in search of the rest of the family.

The second time Lindy woke Jeffrey was sat beside her bed. She tried to lick her lips and asked for water.

"Of course." He reached for a cup with a straw and said, "Try not to move your head. Whoops!"

The slightest movement had triggered a wave of nausea but Jeffrey had excellent reflexes and held a bucket ready. "It's okay," he soothed. "The concussion causes that reaction. You're going to be fine."

Lindy sobbed weakly. The sickness, feebleness and pain were too much and she wanted to escape back into the darkness but it wouldn't come for her this time. In the age-old tradition in times of distress, she called out for her mom. At a loss, Jeffrey radioed his mother for help. When Pat bustled in, he slipped out, waving the bucket as an excuse for his retreat.

Pat washed Lindy's face, then sat and held her hand as she drifted off to sleep again. As she looked at the precious, injured girl, a rueful smile lingered on her face. She remembered her shock that morning at seeing Katherine emerge from Steve's room and knew she had to let go of her previous plans for him and Lindy. Her thoughts turned to the other revelation; she had never seen James affected so deeply before. Did Lindy know how much he cared? She didn't treat him differently from the others. It was so difficult not to meddle!

Glancing around the room, Pat found herself listening; the house felt hushed, almost as if it was holding its breath. This was especially odd because it was full of people. Pete was the only one to go to New Farm and work with Juan today. Everyone else stayed behind to take care of Lindy and make plans.

It was late afternoon when Lindy finally woke and felt steady enough to be propped up with pillows and sip some broth. Kat entered and checked her bandages, then brought Steve in to talk. He asked her to describe her ordeal in as much detail as she could. Lindy was actually thankful that nobody else was with them while she told her story; sympathy would have made her break down but Steve was so matter of fact that she could concentrate on the details he wanted. He proceeded to ask questions to draw more out of her memory. "Did he mention any names? Anything that might have been descriptive?"

Lindy closed her eyes and tried to recall exactly what was said. It was hard because she had zoned out and not listened all the time. "There was something...Si? I think he said Si. Could it have been short for Simon or Silas?"

"Good job. You're doing great. And he's already shown a pattern for arson, so we've got a warning of what to prepare for. Now, do you think your parents are in any danger from him? We could try to get word to them somehow."

"Oh, not really. He's found me so this is where he will be focused. I think he was threatening them to hurt me. Most likely all a warning would do is make them worry more about me."

"Okay." Steve leaned forward to get her full attention. "You should know that we've already implemented changes to our security. Most of them won't affect you while you're recuperating, but there is one iron rule that everybody has to follow: nobody goes anywhere alone, under any circumstances. So if you get a radio message saying Mom is hurt and needs help immediately, you still have to wait for an escort. Panic or reacting without thinking is the worst thing anyone could do. Do you understand?"

"You think he will try to draw off any protection I have." Lindy couldn't quell the slight tremor in her voice.

"Yes, I could see him setting the barn on fire and hoping the house will empty to fight it. Then he would try to reach you alone in here or in the confusion outside. But we're going to anticipate any trouble we can imagine and be flexible enough to react to the unexpected."

"I'm afraid I'll do the wrong thing." Lindy's fingers twitched spastically where she had them twisted in the bedding.

"I have things I need to do now, but Kat has offered to help you and Addie understand what you can do to stay safe. Is that okay with you?"

Lindy looked over at the silently standing figure. It was impossible for her to imagine a less vulnerable female and she longed to be strong like that. "Yes. I want to learn."

As Steve left, Addie came in and perched on her bed while Kat took the chair. She began immediately, "There will be a two person patrol around the farm and one person on guard inside the house all night. The twins have volunteered to adjust their sleep times and take night duties continuously and the third person will rotate in on a schedule. Everyone else is paired up and will make their own arrangements on how they team up during an alarm. My job is to come here to you." Her eyes sparkled with unexpected amusement. "If you tend to sleep naked, now might be a good time to change that habit."

Addie spoke up, "I want to help with guard duties, is that possible?"

"Do you have any training? Can you handle a gun?"

"I've been kickboxing for four years and have done some competitions. Guns, well, I've done a little skeet shooting but that's about all."

"What about you, Lindy?"

"I've only begun shooting since I moved here and I took an afternoon self-defense class once. Fat lot of good I did with that." Her mouth twisted with self-derision.

"I can teach you. It will be hard work, but Steve and I will be training everyone else also so you won't be alone." Kat studied Lindy's face. "You look tired. Do you have any more questions right now?"

"What about using the bathroom at night? Do I need to wake Addie?"

Kat was pleased that Lindy was taking the instructions seriously. "No, as long as you go straight there and back. Don't wander around the house and absolutely don't go outside."

"Okay. One other thing, I want to cut the rest of my hair off."

Eyes wide at this unexpected request, Kat asked, "Are you sure? I tried to leave as much as possible so you could cover up the wound while it heals."

"I know. It's just going to be so hard to keep clean and it feels horrible. I can't move it out of my face at night because I have to lie on my good arm. I just want it all off so it can all grow out together."

Later that evening, Lindy sat in her bed trying to read by the light of an oil lamp. Honestly, she was too anxious to concentrate on the pages. Soon James would be bringing her supper tray in and his reaction to her newly shorn head outweighed all the other issues.

With a bumping noise James backed into the room. As he turned his eyes met hers with a smile before he looked at her hair. "Wow! Your eyes look enormous now."

He placed the tray across her lap and sat on the edge of her bed. He wanted to tell her how beautiful she looked with the lamplight accentuating her cheekbones but didn't dare push her after her recent trauma. "I like it but it makes me look like a shaggy beast now."

James impatiently pushed his hair off his forehead. Then, with a disarming smile asked, "May I touch it?"

With a blush she hoped the low light would hide, Lindy nodded and leaned forward. He gently ran his hands over the top and sides of her head. Chuckling with surprised delight he said, "That's amazing! It's so soft. Don't let the others know or they're going to want to pet you constantly."

Leaning back, he asked if there was anything else she needed.

"Can you keep me company while I eat? Tell me everything that happened today." And he did.

25 THURSDAY

Pat stopped in the doorway to the dining room. "What are you talking about? Of course we're going to report the attack. What if he went after someone else and we hadn't told the police he was around? This is not open to debate."

Her sons exchanged glances as she sat down but none were willing to challenge her decision. Alex walked in smothering a yawn. "I just checked the germination on the root vegetables. The beets had the poorest showing at under a fourth sprouting but the others were over half, so we should get some usable produce."

"What will you do with the seedlings in the trays now?" Addie asked.

"I'll let Steve transplant them into his garden. If they turn out to be healthy plants he might save them for seeds next year. Where's Adam?"

"He's already eaten and gone to bed."

"Smart move. I'm about out on my feet." Grabbing more bacon, he stood and gulped the last of his coffee. "I'll set the alarm for 4:30. Later."

"So," James began thoughtfully. "If someone is going to talk to the police today, I'd like to stop by the nursing home and check on our friends. See if they're still coming out Saturday with all that's happened."

"I think we should talk to both the sheriff and the town police. The police are still handling the arson case for Lindy's apartment but the sheriff will have to be notified about the attack." Jeffrey nodded to James, "Why don't we take care of the town run this morning?"

Pat spoke up suddenly, "There's someone I want to talk to in town also."

Judging by her thinly compressed lips, she had no intention of saying anything more, so Jeffrey nodded. "Okay, let's get ready to go then."

Parked in front of the rather grim-looking brick building that housed the sheriff's office, Jeffrey awkwardly angled his legs out of James' back seat. It wasn't the most comfortable ride, but it did get great gas mileage and they had all agreed to conserve fuel as much as possible. Inside, the receptionist took notes while they told the sheriff and a deputy as much information as they could.

The sheriff nodded soberly, "I heard about the arson. The police are pretty good about sharing information. We've got him posted on our board already. I wish we knew who tipped him off; being charged as an accessory to kidnapping and attempted murder has a tendency to loosen tongues."

James walked over to the board of wanted posters and studied the face of the man he hated. It was clearly an enlarged driver's license photo and looked nothing like he would have expected. There was no sign of a crazed, jealous stalker in the bored expression shown. Tuning back in on the conversation he heard the deputy say, "Maybe 'Si' was referring to the Grease Pit? Some folks still call it Si's from the old owner."

"True. Good thinking. That would be a good place to hide out with fellow lowlifes...but not for long." The sheriff turned a forbidding look onto the brothers. "This would not be a good time to go vigilante. The Grease Pit is going to be subject to a series of raids starting tonight and I don't want to have to bring any of your lot in. Understand?"

Accepting their nods, he continued, "I hope you will do your best to keep yours safe at home. Any rabid skunks that wander in should be disposed of promptly and without frightening others. Have a good day."

As they left James asked, "Did he mean...?"

"Hush, James! It's time to go." Pat pushed him towards the car.

"But..."

"Drive. Now."

James obediently drove but his head was spinning with the implications. "Do we still need to go to the police station?"

"No, the sheriff will take care of that. In fact, I've changed my mind about my errand now. Let's go straight to the nursing home." Pat had planned on paying a visit to the owners of the company she had worked at before they let Lindy go. They should be made aware of just what their cousin was capable of, but she didn't want to inadvertently interfere with the sheriff's plans.

When they had parked in front of the nursing home James said, "Wait. Mom, did the sheriff mean what I think he did? And how did you know what he was talking about?"

Pat settled back into the passenger seat. "Yes, he said if trouble comes to us again we should deal with it and end the matter. I understood because I grew up in a time when people were more likely to take care of trouble themselves instead of going to the police. Justice was often dealt out in a timely manner; sometimes bending or even breaking rules in the process."

Looking at her son's face, she knew he needed more. "I told Lindy a story this morning because she was feeling guilty for leading danger to us. Maybe you need to hear it too.

"When I was a girl there was a boy who wouldn't leave me alone. He'd follow me and hang around our farm at night, looking in the windows. Once he grabbed my arm and left bruises. I don't know if he would have really hurt me, but I was frightened and told my dad. He caught him that night and beat him senseless. Then Dad took him home and told his parents everything. His father shipped him off to the army and I never saw him again.

"My point for Lindy was that stalkers aren't new and families deal with danger when it arises. It wasn't my fault then and it's not her fault now. But do you see how different things were then?"

James face was pale. "If Grandpa had done that now he would have been charged and probably sued."

"Exactly. Justice was dealt on the spot and I felt safe again. Nowadays, there would be lawyers and psychologists, months of court dates and accusations. I'm not saying things were always better then, but they weren't always worse. Our sheriff has seen both ways and is allowing us to protect ourselves without consequences. He did not give us a free pass on hunting anyone down or starting a vendetta.

"Now, are we going to sit here all day or go inside?" Without waiting for a reply, Pat climbed out of the car and bustled into the building. "Oh dear."

Even with all the doors and windows open, the smell of stale urine and soiled bed linens hit them like a hammer. James turned them back, "Why don't you wait outside and I'll see what I can find out."

Forty minutes later James emerged again carrying a small suitcase and guiding a haggard-looking Mr. Limmer. "Mom, this turned into a rescue mission. Whatever I need to do to make it work, we're not leaving him here."

"Mr. Limmer, you are most welcome to come stay with us, but has James explained that it may not be safe at our farm?"

"Oh, yes, he did. That poor, dear girl. But I will take danger over rotting in here any day."

"Where are the others?"

"Both Mr. Yeager and Mr. Baumgarten were picked up by their families," answered James.

"Well then, shall we head home and get you settled in?" Pat smiled at Mr. Limmer.

Pete and Juan walked over from New Farm for lunch. On hearing about their trip that morning, Juan looked dejected. "Susan told me things were getting bad there. She doesn't know what to do; many of the staff don't come to work and they have no way to do laundry. If they close the doors it becomes too hot and the smell is even worse, but that means someone has to watch constantly for the residents who wander."

"Juan, I didn't know it was that bad. Let's take the work generator in this afternoon and get those washing machines going again. We can use the little generator here to recharge tools," Pete offered.

"And if you pay a visit to Doreen Sampson, she will probably round up some volunteers to help out. She is very difficult to say 'No' to," Pat said with a smile. "Now, where is the best place for Mr. Limmer to sleep? I'd prefer to keep him on the ground level."

"Please call me Frank. And you're right, I don't do so well with stairs these days."

"Would you mind sharing my camper with me?" asked Pete. "There's an extra bed and it's only a couple steps to get inside."

"I would be delighted. Thank you so much. Now, is there anything I can do to help? I don't want to be more of a burden than I must."

Addie leaned forward, "Lindy is hoping you might talk to her some. She has headaches still and can't read for long."

A natural storyteller, Frank Limmer was happy to find someone who wanted to listen.

Suddenly, the peaceful calm of a hot, July afternoon was split by the raucous screeching of the guineas. Peering out the window, the family saw a pretty bay mare pulling a small wagon. Addie recognized the people first, "It's Krista and Mr. Hansen!"

Krista had already hopped down and was patting the horse when Addie reached her. "Hullo, Krista. How are you doing?"

She received a cheerful smile before the young girl pulled her back to see the wagon. "See how we fixed it up? Mr. Hansen had some old paint cans but it was my idea to make it colorful. The shade was a lot harder to put on, but it's important for dairy products to be protected from the sun. He must save everything 'cause he had the awnings in his garage."

Addie freely admired the wagon, which was certainly colorful painted blue, green and white. Two blue and white awnings had been mounted on poles over the wagon bed which was full of coolers. "Too bad the awnings weren't longer so you could ride in the shade."

"It's okay," replied Krista. "We do our milk run in the morning before it gets so hot. I wanted to come show you today; that's why we're out in the afternoon. See, we drive around a bunch of farms and sell them milk, butter and cheese. I made the butter and I'm learning about cheese. Mr. Hansen lets me sell our eggs too."

"Are you paid with money?"

"Sometimes. Others like to trade. He took shares in a pig from one farmer. A nice lady gives us bread. Mr. Hansen is going to get wheat for her so she can keep baking."

"So everything is working out well?" Addie was thrilled that her advice hadn't flopped and been a hardship for Krista.

"Wheest! It's hard work and I have to be very, very clean all the time. And my dad keeps calling me a milkmaid even though I told him I'm a dairy farmer." Scorn dripped from her tone, then her face softened. "The cows are lovely and my sisters needed the milk. I think I could do the milk deliveries by myself, but Mr. Hansen says it's not safe. He's got a shotgun under the seat."

A gruff voice broke into the monologue, "If you're done nattering, go check on the Belles already."

Addie shot him a sharp glance but saw amusement in his expression, not annoyance. Michael came out with some zucchini bread to trade for cheese while Jeffrey brought a bucket of water over for the horse. A few minutes later, they waved goodbye to the bright, little wagon and the unlikely business partners.

Late that afternoon, after the cows had been milked and the eggs collected, everyone gathered in the front yard for their first lesson in self-defense. Lindy sat with Mr. Limmer, Pat and Pete in lawn chairs to observe. After an hour learning basic holds and moves, Adam asked Steve and Kat if they would spar. He flung himself onto the grass next to Lindy's chair, wiped the sweat from his face and grinned at her. "This is going to be good."

Lindy had assumed it would be more of the same, but something in the combatants altered and alerted her. They looked the same outwardly, but their stances shifted slightly and a sense of heightened awareness came over them. Without warning, they sprang towards each other and Lindy gasped at the violence of their meeting. Just as suddenly, they leapt apart and circled around. This time Steve moved first but Kat rolled under his charge and caught him before he could turn completely.

Lindy looked around the other spectators as the clash continued. Pat looked horrified by the display but the others watched with a variety of expressions of interest and admiration. Her attention was pulled back by a pained grunt and halt in movement as Steve's left shoulder dislocated with an audible pop. Lindy had to turn away as Kat moved to pull it back into place. She was startled by the wistful look on Adam's face.

"You have to wonder about the saying 'opposites attract' when you see a pair so closely matched, don't you?" he murmured.

Lindy glanced back at the couple and saw Steve holding Kat close with his right arm around her waist. "Two minutes ago it was like they were trying to kill each other, now they look...happy."

Adam turned his attention to her and studied her face for a moment before speaking, "You know, you were really pretty with long hair, but you're beautiful without it."

He rose gracefully to his feet and leaned over to kiss her lightly on the cheek before joining the others talking about the sparring. Lindy was grateful to be alone for a moment to regain her composure and wipe the tears from her eyes.

26 FRIDAY

Alex and Adam sauntered up from the barn after checking over the pigs and cattle. They weren't nearly as tired after another night of guard duty since they had slept well the day before. Even so, breakfast and bed sounded good.

"Hold on," said Alex, nodding towards the smithy where Addie was wrestling to pull something out. Adam looked inside while Alex helped haul out an old reel mower.

"Where's your pair?" asked Adam.

"Huh?"

"Who is supposed to be out here with you? Because we don't go anywhere alone, remember?"

"Oh, no, I forgot." Addie shrugged and turned back to the mower.

Alex's temper flared, "Do you want to end up like Lindy or worse? How do you think I would feel if I found you like James did her?"

Addie whirled around and fired back, "Why is this about you? Ha! If you had half the feelings for me that James does for Lindy..."

"What? How does that sentence end? Is it a threat or a promise?"

"I'll tell you! If you loved me like he loves her, I'd marry you and be a farmer's wife. But we both know you only love yourself!" She spat the last words out and ran for the house, blinded by tears and regretting her hasty tongue.

Alex stood frozen in shock, staggered by what he had just heard.

"Come on, old boy," Adam said kindly.

"She said she'd marry me." Alex sounded stunned.

"Um, yeah. Mixed in with some other stuff." Adam looked at his twin in concern. "Good lord, do you actually love her?"

"What, love? Don't be ridiculous." But as he trailed after Adam a small smile teased at the corners of his mouth and he breathed out, "Wow."

Addie didn't reappear until well after the twins should have been sleeping. Stepping out onto the porch, she found Mr. Limmer sat peacefully watching the chickens wander across the yard. "Say, Mr. Limmer."

"Frank."

"Frank, could I ask a favor? If I bring some items up that I can't identify, would you look at them and see if you recognize anything?"

"Of course. Although it's been a very long time since I lived on a farm."

"Thanks! I have to find someone to go along first. I'll be right back."

Soon, she and Jeffrey were walking down to the smithy. He paused by the reel mower. "Did you find this? Do you want me to sharpen the blades?"

"Would you? I wanted to mow around the house for Pat. She's been so kind to me."

"Sure. Even sharpened, I'm afraid you're going to find it a hard task though. How about we take turns working on it? One could weed the flower beds while the other mows."

"You wouldn't mind? Thanks. Okay, I'm going to hand some things out for you to stack in the wagon." When the wagon was full of odd bits and pieces, Addie pulled it up to the porch. A few items had to go back to the wagon unknown, but others were turned over in Frank's hands until enlightenment came and he described their purpose.

"Oh, we had one of these. It's for making toast in the fireplace. We had to watch it like hawks or all we got was burnt toast." Addie took the wire contraption back and entered a note onto her inventory.

"Well, that's the last thing I had for now. Say, do you want to change back into your own clothes? They should be dry."

"No, I'm fine. Pete's spares are quite comfortable. It is a relief just to put on something clean. Now don't you worry about me; I'm quite content to relax here and enjoy the fresh air. You kids go ahead with what you need to do."

Addie patted his hand and followed Jeffrey back down to the mower. It took quite a bit of persuading to get the blades off so he could work on them and by the time it was assembled again the bell was being rung for lunch.

After the lively discussion during the meal wound down, Pete asked if he could have some help for the afternoon to install the well pump.

Michael asked, "Do you need any special skill sets?"

"A strong back would be an asset. Are you volunteering?"

"Yes, I'm not baking today and if someone will boil the potatoes I'll be free."

"Addie and I already have plans for this afternoon. Sorry," apologized Jeffrey.

Steve frowned, "Kat will be resting for the night shift so I should stay."

"That leaves me," James offered. "I'd rather not have to go down into a well but I'm willing to do whatever you need."

"Juan, did your wife get any more help at the nursing home?" Pat asked.

"Oh, yes! She was so relieved. Your Mrs. Sampson showed up with a group of women all wearing purple hats. Susan said they were just a little bossy, but they work so hard that who could complain? They're using the clotheslines we hung from the trees and all the bad smells are gone. And the police found out about Mr. Wilson's generator and they have an officer guarding it day and night."

"Oh! That's very good news. Thank you for telling us. Frank, we will understand if you want to go back and be with your friends, but I hope you will stay with us at least until you get your strength back. Lindy told me how chatting with you made the time go faster."

As if to emphasize her point, Mellow chose that moment to put her head in Frank's lap and gaze at him soulfully. Laughing, he admitted that he was in no hurry to return and would prefer to stay on with them. When the others went to their various jobs, he made his way to Lindy's room.

Later, propped up by pillows in her bed, Lindy wiped away the tear that traced down her cheek; Frank had just told her about losing a dearly loved friend in the eighties. "How old are you, Frank?"

"94 last month. My mother was born in 1898. It's been a restless sort of life. If I got bored someplace, I packed my bag and moved on. That's why I've been all over the world. A few places I had to make a run for it which wasn't always easy with the old peg leg. And everywhere I traveled, there were interesting people; not always nice, but interesting. It's a pleasure to end up here with those who are both interesting and kind."

"Did you come back here after the war?"

"No." He frowned at an unhappy memory. "When you don't fit somewhere, it doesn't just hurt you, it hurts your family too. It was better to be far away. I only came back for my parents' funerals."

"Why did you come back in the end? There must have been so many beautiful places you could have chosen."

"Oh, yes, but I was drawn back. I needed to come back to the beginning. Fortunately, even here mindsets have evolved in the last few decades. I'm glad I returned."

"So am I."

Again the family gathered for a lesson in defense late in the day. While Steve waved away the suggestion for another demonstration,

Kat offered to spar with any of the other brothers. Not even Adam was daring enough to take her up on it.

When they were told to practice different methods of breaking out of a hold, Addie found herself paired with Alex. Calmly she asked if she could work with James so she would be starting with someone closer to her own height.

After an hour of practice, Kat and Steve exchanged a glance. They could only hope that any danger didn't arrive in the near future. She murmured to him, "You couldn't have taught them anything?"

"I couldn't even interest them after the power went out. Until Lindy was actually attacked...it wasn't real to them. How much has your dad learned?"

"Ha! Point taken."

While his students rested, Steve went into lecture mode and explained basic tactics they might need, including ways to conserve ammunition and setting up an ambush.

As evening descended, James settled onto the porch steps with his guitar. While he listened to his family turning in for the night and softly played to himself, he wished serenading under Lindy's window wouldn't seem hopelessly corny. With a soft chuckle, he promised himself to do it someday.

27 SATURDAY

Alex intercepted James as he descended the stairs. "Another quiet night. Do you think the sheriff would tell us if he caught him?"

"I'm sure he would. That's why I don't think he has," James replied glumly. "Excuse me. I need coffee."

"Wait. I want to talk to you. Can we go somewhere private?"

James groaned. "Can't it wait until after breakfast?"

"I've already eaten and by the time you finish I'll be asleep. Come on, Jimmy. You know you want to know what I want."

"No, I really don't," James growled as he turned around and plodded back up the stairs. In his room with the door closed he asked, "What's this about?"

"I need to know how to win over a girl."

"You're asking me?" James barked an incredulous laugh.

Alex impatiently slashed his hand through the air. "Not how to get her into bed. How to make her want to spend the rest of her life with me. Or at least talk about it without crying."

"Oh." James studied the anxious, lost look on his young brother's face soberly. "Alex, two weeks ago you had no interest in settling down at all. Tell me what it is about her that's changed that."

"She's amazing and infuriating and completely wonderful. I feel like I'm on fire and drowning when I'm near her. I think about her all the time. She does and says things that drive me insane but I don't want to change anything about her." He flung himself back onto

James' bed and spoke to the ceiling. "She's beautiful, but it's the person inside that's burning me alive."

He sat back up and spoke hoarsely, "And I'm hurting her, James! Everything I say comes out wrong and I can't treat her like a brother would. I just can't! If I can't have her, I need to go away and never see her again."

James leaned back and hid an uncontrollable smile behind his hand. It was incredible to see this godling of sex and lust laid low by love and passion. Then the urge to smile disappeared as he wondered what advice to give. "I've never felt like that."

"What does it feel like? The way you love Lindy?"

"It fills me up. Every beat of my heart is for her. I wish I could take every pain and injury onto myself and spare her. I want to fill her life with beauty and love and happiness. And I want to destroy anyone that would ever hurt her."

Alex stared at him. "It's not how I feel but I understand now."

"Alex, what would happen if the power came back on now? Michael and Addie go back to work at the restaurant. What do you do?"

"I...I go back to school and get my degree. I could drive to the city every weekend to see her. And I'd be working for her." A look of determination took over his face.

"What about other women?" James asked quietly.

Alex laughed bleakly, "Don't you understand? There are no other women. Every other person I see has a label that says 'Not Addie'."

James suddenly had a glimpse of the man his brother could become if this went wrong; a harsh, bitter man who spread hurt all around him. Inspiration struck. "Here. Sit at the desk. Here's a stack of paper. Write to her. Tell her how you feel. Write poetry or songs, whatever. You can't say the wrong thing if it's on paper. Take as long as you need."

By the time James reached the door, Alex was already at the desk; his pencil dashing madly across the page. Downstairs again, James ate a lukewarm breakfast before going to the kitchen and asking, "Where's Addie?"

Pat looked up from the canning book she was reading, "Good morning. She's working on her inventory of the attic I think."

The blood drained from James' face as he thought of the old vents that filtered sounds from all the upstairs rooms straight into the attic. "Oh, hell!"

He ran up the two flights of stairs and looked wildly around the attic before spotting the small shape curled up on the floor over his bedroom. Addie lifted her tear-stained face from her knees and just looked at him. He stepped forward and held his hand out; she took it and let him lead her down to his bedroom door.

After closing the door behind her, James sank down onto the top step and thumped his head against the wall. Flinging himself into Lindy's arms and whimpering wasn't an option but was all he really felt like doing. No matter what happened, it was out of his hands now.

When the door opened, Alex looked up from the pages scattered across the desk and there was Addie. As he turned towards her, the question in his eyes, she flew across the room and into his arms. The following dialogue was mostly incoherent and only meaningful to the participants.

After they had calmed down, Alex looked at the mess on the desk. "I'll need to burn this."

"No, you don't!" Addie cried and gathered up each sheet, carefully smoothing out the crumpled rejects as she went. She chortled greedily as her eyes scanned different offerings. "I'm keeping it all. Are you going to finish this poem?"

"I think I wrote myself into a corner with that one."

"I especially like the limerick," Addie wrapped her arms around his neck and glanced at the bed. "Do you think James would mind?"

"Yes, he would definitely mind and before you ask, Adam is sleeping in my room. Anyway, we're going to do this properly and get married first."

"What! Why? You never waited before."

"This is different. This is *real*. I'm going to be your husband!"

"We're still going to fight. And I'll be a terrible farmer's wife."

"I know. And I can hire someone to slop the pigs and clean chickens. I want you just as you are."

Addie hopped off his lap with a determined expression. "Well! I have a wedding to plan then. Why aren't you sleeping? You still have to get up at 4:30."

With a laugh he pulled her back for another kiss. "Yes, dear."

"And we can tell everyone tonight?"

"We can."

After their day of sleep, when Alex stepped out of the barn into the hot afternoon sun, he found Adam fighting off an invisible attacker. "Should I even ask?"

"I'm practicing."

"Okay, why?"

Adam paused and wiped the sweat from his face. "Did you notice how Steve and Kat looked at us yesterday? Why am I even asking you? You probably only had eyes for your 'love'."

"Adam," Alex said in a warning tone. He had broken the news to his twin when they got up and Adam wasn't taking it well.

"Whatever. They looked at us like we were pitiful. Useless. Well, I don't plan on being useless any longer than I can help."

Alex's brow furrowed as he thought about the impatience in Steve's voice when instructing them. While it hadn't seemed important before, now it was embarrassing to recall. Also, he had someone to protect now. "Let me put the milk inside and I'll come practice too."

They had moved under the cottonwood by the house to get out of the sun and didn't realize they had an audience until a voice called out, "He's throwing you so easy because your center of gravity is too far forward. Shift back onto your heels."

Alex shifted position and called back, "It doesn't feel right."

"Just try it!"

This time Adam struggled to complete the move and after giving Alex a hand up, they both went to lean on the porch railing and talk to Frank. "How did you know that would help?"

"Oh, I picked up odds and ends of information all over the place. You boys are coming along well for beginners. Keep up the practice." Seeing their dejected expressions, he added, "You're already further ahead than the man who quit on day one. Just knowing that bit more could be the deciding factor."

The twins looked at each other and nodded. "Back to work for us then."

After the family had finished the daily defense lesson there was excitement of a different sort. Pat sank back down onto the lawn chair. Her mind was still whirling with the announcement that Alex and Addie has just made. While she watched the others talk excitedly, Jeffrey squatted next to her. "How are you doing, Mom?"

"Oh, you know me; I'm already worrying about their future. They seem so young. Isn't that strange? I married straight away after high school so why do I think they're too young?" She sighed. "It's funny how your perspective shifts when you get old."

"Did you think I was too young?"

Pat looked affectionately at her intellectual son. "I worried about you for completely different reasons. Everything you did was so logical and correct. You waited until you finished college. You chose someone very appropriate, but I worried about what would happen if you met someone passionate and inappropriate. It shows how silly it is to worry because it's never what you expect that happens."

"Hmm. Well, these two have all the passion I didn't and more. What I find strange is that none of us had a marriage like you and Dad. You two had so much love for each other but there was always more to share. Michael's marriage was so all-encompassing that there was no room for anyone else, mine was practically a business arrangement, I don't know how to describe Steve's romance and then there's these two."

Pat watched James talking to Lindy and Frank. "I don't know. James may be heading there. Thank goodness he has the patience to wait for her to heal; I'm afraid the emotional wounds will take longer than the physical ones."

Addie had stepped closer and overheard Pat's last words. "Lindy has nightmares every night. She's still terrified that John will come back and hurt us."

"Oh, dear. If only we could get some good news from the sheriff." Addie nodded agreement and went to accept Lindy's congratulations.

As Pat continued to look around the celebration, her gaze fell on Adam, standing alone with a frown on his face. "Poor Adam. They've always done everything together and now Alex is setting off on a new adventure without him. I hope he doesn't do anything rash."

"Like what?"

"Dashing off and marrying someone he doesn't love. It will be worse if Alex becomes a father right away." She turned to Jeffrey in shock, "Is that why you've been buying baby supplies? Did you know this was coming?"

He laughed, "No, I'm not a psychic. Actually, it was an experiment in statistics. With six young men and a limited supply of condoms, I believe it's inevitable that there would be babies. And since I was the only one thinking about it, I decided to get some supplies."

"Well! I do have some lovely, soft yarn. If only I didn't have this cast in the way."

"I think you have time. I overheard Addie telling Lindy when she arrived that she had recently got her shot. That's supposed to last three months."

"Oh. Well, that's good I suppose. I think it's best not to rush into parenthood when a marriage is still raw and untested. Babies!" She sat lost in her thoughts until Alex joined them.

28 SUNDAY

Addie burst into the room and announced, "The sheriff just pulled in!"

"Oh! Help me up! I want to hear what he says." Lindy cried as she swung her legs off the bed.

The sheriff had no trouble picking the victim out of the group that emerged onto the porch. Dressed in a tank top and shorts, her left shoulder was heavily bandaged and the arm strapped immobile to her side. She held her other hand up to shield her eyes from the sun but didn't try to conceal the ugly purple and blue bruising that swelled the side of her face around her temple. When she turned to say something to the girl standing close beside her, he saw the line of stitches crossing the back of her head. The muscles in his jaw spasmed as he clenched his teeth. Some things he would never get used to.

"Mrs. Stevenson," he nodded to Pat before turning to Lindy, "Miss. May I come inside?"

He followed them into the dining room and accepted a glass of water before addressing the reason for his visit. "I regret to say that we have not yet apprehended your assailant. He wasn't present when we raided the Grease Pit and nobody has admitted to knowing how to find him even in pursuit of a plea deal. We did, however, locate the informant, a Howard Biggedsly."

"Who?" asked Lindy in confusion.

"He's the owner of a business that sells and installs wood burning stoves and fireplaces. He's not an innocent who talked too much either. He went straight to the Pit and bragged about knowing where to find you before selling that information to your stalker for $500.

"Now don't any of you young men think you need to pay him a visit. I've charged him with accessory to kidnapping and tagged it for the FBI. He's currently a guest at the State Pen on a million dollar bond and because he has to wait for the FBI to confirm, he won't be going anywhere for a very long time."

He paused to sip his water. "This next part is off the record but I need to warn you to stay as far away from John's family as possible. In my opinion they're all bat-shit crazy. When I went up to pay them a visit, they shot at me and threw an explosive device at my car. Technically, they aren't in my county so I'm negotiating with the neighboring sheriff on how to deal with them. Anyway, they aren't your problem, but John still is and I urge you not to let your guard down at all. I wish I had more good news for you."

He stood to leave, but paused in the doorway and turned back. "By the way, I heard you all had a hand in fixing the mess at the nursing home. Thank you. My aunt is there."

Nobody moved after he had gone. Finally Pat said, "Well. I guess there's no easy resolution this time. Do you want to go back to bed, Lindy?"

"Not really. Is there a pair of sunglasses I could borrow? I'd like to go outside."

Kat trailed along beside her as Lindy strolled around the farm. She couldn't shake the feeling that this must be what it was like to have a professional bodyguard. Leaning against the pigpen, Lindy looked up at Kat's alert face; her eyes never stopped moving. "Did your father mind you moving out again so soon after you came home?"

Kat blinked at the sudden question, but continued to scan the tree line. "No. In fact..." she paused awkwardly. "He's not alone anymore. Emma Bucket moved in with him."

"Oh! Um, is that a good thing?"

Kat shrugged but didn't reply.

Lindy sighed. This conversation was an uphill battle. She had to stifle the sudden urge to shock a reaction by asking about Kat's love life. Instead, she forced herself to stick to a safe topic. "Is there anything I can do to defend myself now?"

A frown pulled Kat's eyebrows down. "Your current physical limitations are temporary. In fact, you're healing nicely. Another week and we can start on rehab for your shoulder. The light sensitivity and headaches may linger, there's no way to predict that, but eventually you will be back to full health and taking on an active role in protecting the farm."

"Do you think John will wait that long to strike again?"

"No, but he certainly isn't the only danger out there. Even after he is dealt with we will continue to train and guard."

"What other dangers? Nobody's mentioned anything else happening."

"Steve and I haven't broached the subject with the others yet. We felt the current threat was enough to get them into the habits they need to develop." When Lindy opened her mouth to keep asking, Kat held her hand up. "When the town runs out of food, they are going to start looking to the farms. Things could easily get out of control. Steve expected things to be held together well around here, but the nursing home fiasco proved that there could be serious problems."

Lindy thought about the situation and it seemed impossible. "How could it be handled? I mean if they put someone who knew what to do in charge."

"It would have to be someone innovative and authoritative."

"Well, that rules out the politicians."

Kat actually snorted in response. "That grocery store manager Juan mentioned might have been a possibility. He acted decisively and gave the store and his customers more time and resources. A team of people like that would be best; one for food, another for water and sewer, another for defense."

"Good luck getting the town council to step aside and let someone competent take over."

"Now multiply that problem all across the country. At least here food of some sort is plentiful."

"You'd need someone like a Minister of Food to set up rationing and education on how to make the most of what food is available and how to prepare it," Lindy said thoughtfully. "Making certain nothing is wasted and maybe allocating vitamins for the children if possible. Setting it up so farmers like Mr. Hansen never feel like their only option is to dump what they produce because there is no way to get it to market."

Kat looked down at Lindy in surprise. Although very likeable, she had never got the impression that the young woman was also capable and intelligent. "Would you be willing to work with Addie on brainstorming ideas to deal with this? I don't know if anyone would listen, but it would be good to have something prepared if the opportunity arose."

"Oh, I couldn't. It's not something I would be any good at." She faltered under Kat's skeptical look. "Well, maybe we could try."

At noon, Lindy quizzed Juan about any other stories he might have heard about people taking charge effectively and asked him to find out the name of the grocery store manager. That afternoon, Addie set aside her inventories and wedding plans so they could work on the Big Idea, as they called it. Recognizing that defense was beyond their scope, they dumped that section onto Kat and dug deeper into the food problem.

By the end of the day, they had broken the issue down into sections. Under the Minister of Food would be Deputy Ministers: one for rationing, one for education, one for preserving, one for growing and possibly one for enforcement. Occasionally, they dragged Michael or Pat in to answer questions and bounce ideas off, but mostly it was the two young women working towards solutions. Addie was in her element and Lindy was so caught up in it that she was able to ignore the headache that never went away.

That evening, Addie volunteered to stay up part of the night and learn what was involved in guarding the house. If she had planned to be awake all night, she would have spent the afternoon resting like Jeffrey had. He showed her how he patrolled the ground floor in the dark, not only listening and watching for trouble but also being alert to any unexpected odors. He verified that she knew where each of the fire extinguishers was as well as the buckets of water and damp sand near the doors. When the grandfather clock tolled one a.m. Addie gratefully climbed into her bed.

29 MONDAY

As the time slowly passed, Jeffrey wondered if they would be better off splitting the night shift in half. There was something about the hours between one and three that threatened to drag his mind into a stupor.

Biff was the first to notice the change in the night air and he alerted Jeffrey by whining at the front door. A sullen red glow grew as flames licked up the side of the porch.

"Fire! Fire at the house!" Jeffrey shouted into his radio.

Instead of the acknowledgement he expected, what he heard was one of the twins saying "Fire at the farrowing shed!"

Jeffrey grabbed the fire extinguisher and waited those agonizing seconds for someone to join him. He could barely hear the pounding footsteps upstairs over the pounding of his heart. Suddenly a hand slapped his shoulder and he pushed through the door to tackle the blaze.

James tore down the stairs on Steve's heels and had taken two steps towards the front of the house when he heard Mellow's sharp barks in Lindy's room. Spinning around, he charged in and saw a shadow hurl Addie away and turn towards Lindy's bed. "No!"

Leaping forward he tackled the shadow and, catching it in mid-turn, caused them both to fall back through the open window. Time seemed to stutter to a halt as a series of images flashed into James' vision. The angry red backdrop of the fires made the silver moonlight even more poignant as it reflected off the knife arcing towards his face. It felt like a cold fire sliding from the corner of his eye down his cheek. All his focus was on keeping his thumbs pressed into the throat beneath him. James gasped as the knife stabbed into his arm and side and felt himself slipping off. A boom sounded beside his ear and part of him wanted to laugh when the hot brass hit his face. As he fell onto his side, all he could see was Lindy standing over him like a vengeful goddess, pulling the trigger again and again, even after the slide locked back. Then everything spun sideways and faded away.

Pat reacted slowly when Frank pressed a cup of tea into her hand. Finding her voice, she said hoarsely, "Oh, thank you."

He patted her shoulder and looked down at James' still form on the couch. The bandages wrapped around his face were barely whiter than his skin and his arm and torso mimicked a mummy. His breathing was so shallow that Pat kept leaning forward to see if his chest had stopped moving.

"He's not going to die."

Pat jerked her head up, suddenly angry at the elderly man who was here when her life was shattered.

Frank met her glare with a look of compassion and understanding. "When they took my leg off, I saw so many wounded men brought in. Horrible burns, bodies mangled. After a while you learn to tell who will live and who won't. It's something you never forget. James will live."

Hot tears streamed down her face as Pat crumpled; finally giving in to the sobs she had held off all night. Pete walked in the front door and took in her distress with a glance. Hurrying to her side he knelt and held her as she wept out her fears and despair.

It had been a night of hell for the entire family. The farrowing house had burnt to the ground. The twins, barely able to keep it from spreading to the chicken coop, had to listen to the frantic squeals of the doomed pigs. At the house it had taken everybody's concerted efforts to keep the flames from engulfing the entire structure. As it was, it looked like a disaster movie with the ruined porch and blackened siding. The men were forced to keep close watch that a smoldering ember didn't reignite the blaze.

Addie had missed most of the excitement after throwing herself on the intruder and being knocked unconscious. Lindy didn't have any memory of the night, but Kat had found her frantically trying to staunch the blood flow from James' stab wounds. While Kat had worked with diligent efficiency to save his life, there was a haunted look in her eyes.

Jeffrey staggered away from the remains of the porch and fell into a lawn chair. His body ached with exhaustion; his lungs burned but he couldn't seem to stop coughing. When Michael sank to the ground nearby, he said, "One man. Just one man did all this to us."

They both turned their heads to look numbly when a voice called from the driveway. Neither moved when Juan jogged over. "Dios! Are you hurt? What can I do?"

What he did after talking to Pete was take a shovel and dig a grave next to the compost heap. Filled with a quiet fury, he kicked the body into the hole and spat on it before shoveling the dirt back in. He never would reveal where it was; only saying that the devil had come back for his own.

Afterwards, he took over watching the remains of the fire while everyone else collapsed into desperately needed sleep.

At 4:30, Addie turned away from the twins' room and determinedly went down to the barn. Her head still ached around the knot she had acquired when bounced off the wall, but she refused to wake Alex. She knew he had forced himself to milk the cows that morning, although later than usual, but it had to be done again. Having watched him milk, she vaguely knew what to do, but had never even touched one of the cows before. Forgetting to wash the udders quickly became irrelevant as the first one kicked over the pail and the second placed her hoof directly into it. She was in tears by the time she opened the door to let them back outside; her hands ached and shook from the unaccustomed labor as she struggled to latch the door again. Turning, her heart leapt when she saw Alex staring at her.

His mouth twitched into a smile before he rasped, "You really are the most extraordinary woman."

"You look absurd without eyebrows," she replied although her heart hurt to see the bandages on his arms and hands. Adam had been forced to pull him away when Alex had tried to reach the pigs.

"I love you too." He pulled her into a hug. "Why aren't you taller so I can bury my face in your bosom?"

Her responding laughter had a catch to it. So much had been lost, but so much more could have been.

30 TUESDAY

Lindy hesitated. Without the porch shading the windows, the moonlight danced across the living room, highlighting Pat's silent vigil at James' side. While it was the nightmares that drove Lindy from her bed, it was guilt and apprehension that froze her in place now.

A fresh breeze swept through the house, carrying the stench of wet, burnt wood and Lindy's stomach churned. Would she ever be able to move past the events of the night before? She couldn't remember what she had done, but her subconscious knew and in her dreams she was the killer.

A sense of movement behind her was a reminder that Michael was watching over the house. Instead of walking past, he paused and placed his hand on her back. That simple gesture of comfort undid Lindy's fragile control and she turned and burrowed into his shoulder. As her hot tears soaked into his shirt, he wrapped his arms around her shuddering body and murmured soothing words. Over her head, his eyes locked with Pat's.

When Lindy had run down to hiccoughs, Michael steered her back to her room and tucked her into bed. Joining Pat in the living room, he looked down at his brother. "A fine time for our only therapist to take a holiday."

"Oh, Michael," said Pat in a shaky voice. "Don't joke about it. I don't know how much more I can take."

Crouching down to bring himself to eye level, Michael said, "I don't have James' gift, but even I can see that girl is tearing herself up with guilt. Do you blame her on any level for his injuries?"

Pat replied instantly and vehemently, "No! Blame her? If she hadn't acted James would have died. She's taken on such a burden; she killed a man in our defense."

"She needs to hear it from you, Mom."

When Lindy woke again, the morning light was streaming through the window and a hand was holding hers. Looking up, she saw Pat smiling at her. Weariness weighed heavily on the face, but the eyes were gazing at her with the same affection as before.

"I need to thank you, dear, for saving my son's life."

"But it was because of me," Lindy cried. "If I hadn't..."

Pat interrupted, "No, Lindy. No regrets. Nobody else is going to mention this, but it's James' fault too. With all his good qualities, he's not a fighter. He didn't even draw his gun. He might have avoided any injury at all by shooting that bastard. Instead, he acted on instinct by putting himself between you and danger.

"I don't know how the rest of us would have reacted in the same situation, but I suspect most of us would have hesitated. Then you would have been hurt or a hostage." Pat chuckled ruefully, "The only one I'm certain would have shot first would be Steve. And that's just not how it turned out."

Pat's eyes unfocused as she considered something troubling. "When James recovers, don't let him blame himself for how it happened, will you? It would crush him to think he failed you. That you had to save him. He won't mind that you did, but the idea that he forced you into that position would eat away at him."

Lindy smiled tremulously, "I would never let him think that."

With a sigh, Pat heaved herself to her feet. "Well, I'm desperate for sleep. We should keep the chickens penned up today, but can you check on them this morning? By the way, has anyone mentioned how much your hair cut suits you?"

Lindy chortled, "Yes, a few have. Thank you."

The breakfast table seemed very empty with the twins, Michael and Pat having already gone to bed, but it was James' absence that was felt the most. Pete and Jeffrey discussed how many trips it would take them to retrieve all of Pete's supplies from town. They were going to meet Juan there. A lot of materials would be needed to replace the porch, but Pete refused to even consider not rebuilding.

Addie and Lindy were cajoling Frank into helping them flesh out their Big Idea while Steve watched Kat worriedly. She was pale and, although she shifted the eggs around her plate, she didn't seem to be eating much.

After breakfast, Addie quickly cleared the table while Lindy fetched their notes. Frank easily held his own in the discussion, shooting down some suggestions and offering alternatives.

Steve followed Kat outside where she avoided meeting his eye and turned away. He stood staring at her back, thinking about how she had avoided his touch last night and felt the rejection like a punch to the chest. For a moment he couldn't breathe, then he steeled his voice, "You're leaving, I suppose. The immediate danger is past, so why stay?"

Her shoulders stiffened, but when she spoke it was almost a whisper, "I let the family down. I was in the bathroom without my radio or gun when the call came. It was my duty to protect her and because of my weakness James almost died."

Steve moved a step closer. "I've never seen you move more than two steps from the bed without your gun. Why then?"

Kat gave a mirthless 'Ha!' before continuing, "I was throwing up. All I thought of was making it to the toilet. Weak! Stupid! Damn it."

"If you were ill…"

"No, I felt fine. I still feel fine, except…" Stumbling away a few steps, Kat heaved up the meagre contents of her stomach. Spitting to clear her mouth, she turned slowly around, her eyes wide. "Oh no."

Sudden comprehension hit Steve also. "Oh."

Pete cursed in a low, angry voice when he saw that the gate to his work site was busted down. Judging from the tangled metal and drag marks, someone had driven straight through it. Juan was waiting for them inside and shrugged at his boss's anger. "I don't know what they were looking for, but I don't think they found it. The office is trashed and some of the equipment got thrown around, but nothing seems to be missing."

The grunt he got in reply was eloquent enough and he and Jeffrey stayed out of the way while Pete stomped around. When he returned, he had calmed down. "Okay, it could have been worse but I want to take everything useful today. Juan, back the trailer in and let's start loading."

They had been working steadily for an hour when a police car drove in. The officer demanded that they prove their identities; tapping on his holster while he glared at Juan.

"Really?" asked Pete incredulously. "Where were you when my business was broken into and vandalized?"

This received some grumbles about increased crime and understaffing. Pete was unmoved and flipped his license out of his wallet while explaining that he had owned and worked off this property for thirty years and wondered where the police report was on the break in.

After the officer had left, Pete frowned at Juan. "Are you having any trouble here in town?"

Juan grinned back, "Not really. There's always a few bigots but most are decent enough if you don't stir up trouble."

"Hmm, well, don't keep your mouth shut if there are problems. I want to know." He slapped the side of the trailer. "Full load. Let's get this home and unloaded. Two more trips should empty the place."

Jeffrey stared out the window as they left town, tuning out the easy chatter between the two construction men. When there was a break in the conversation, he asked the question that had been nagging at him. "Will there be a way to get more lumber after this is used?"

"Possibly, but I wouldn't count on it. There might be a few indie loggers around who have their own portable milling equipment. You're thinking of rebuilding the pig shed?"

"Yes, we've always had hogs. And it was a horrible way to lose them."

Juan broke in, "It might be easier to put pens into the barn at New Farm instead of putting up a complete new building."

Jeffrey looked at him with surprise and Pete glanced over with approval. "Good thinking. We could probably manage enough lumber for pens from what we have now. Keep it up and I'm going to owe you a raise."

"I wouldn't say no to some bacon and chops when the time comes," Juan answered with a chuckle.

When Pete had said he wanted to empty the place, he wasn't joking. On the final load they filled boxes with all the scraps of previous projects: partial containers of screws and nails, special order windows and rafters that had been refused and everything else that had accumulated. There wasn't as much as might be expected from thirty years but Pete was an organized man who didn't care for clutter and cleared things out every few years.

"We're going to swing by and drop you at home," Pete told Juan when they finished. "I don't want you riding through this neighborhood with your groceries."

"Thanks, I don't mind getting home early either. We're putting in a community garden. Steve gave me some advice on what to plant this time of year and some extra seeds."

"Who watches your kids when you're both working?" Jeffrey asked with interest.

"My mother-in-law lives next door. She and Susan argue a lot but we don't have to pay for daycare."

"Do you need any help with the garden?"

"No. It's good for the neighbors to all work together on it. Everyone will enjoy the results more this way. If someone else did the work there would be many more complaints."

"Interesting philosophy," mused Jeffrey after they had dropped Juan off. "I wonder if it's true."

"Probably depends on the people. There always seems to be an exception to every rule, son." Pete looked chagrined. "Sorry, that just slipped out."

Jeffrey smiled easily, "Don't worry. As long as Mom is happy you can call me anything. I don't know how Michael or Steve would react, though."

"I'd rather not find out. I'll be more careful."

Steve had been watching all day for when his mom got up and, after she had a chance to check on James, he steered her towards the study at the back of the house. Once she was settled into a chair, Kat joined them and stood beside Steve.

"Mom, we have some news. Um." He glanced at Kat who raised an eyebrow at his hesitation. "We think we might be expecting."

"Expecting what?" Pat looked back and forth between them before catching on. Somehow the possibility that these two would produce her first grandchild had never crossed her mind. "Oh! But this is wonderful! Are you happy? Please be happy."

Kat flushed before admitting, "I think we're still in shock at the possibility, but I'm edging towards 'happy'."

Pat fussed, "I don't suppose anyone thought to pick up some pregnancy test kits."

"If anyone did, it would have been Jeffrey," Steve replied drily.

"We can bring the crib down from the attic, but how will you fit it into your room? Of course, I don't need such a large room anymore, maybe we could..."

Both Kat and Steve interrupted at the same time. "Absolutely not!" "We are not kicking you out of your room."

They exchanged looks and nodded agreement. Kat continued, "Maybe Adam would be willing to trade rooms after Alex and Addie move out. Or Lindy. We'll work something out. There's plenty of time yet."

The news spread quickly through the family. When Steve was helping unload the last haul from town and find room for it in the increasingly cramped pole barn, he caught Jeffrey eyeing him speculatively. "What?"

"I just never figured you for taking chances like that. Haven't you always been a strict condom user?"

"Not that it's any of your business," Steve growled. "But it was a heat of the moment situation the first time and Kat was on the pill. Weren't the odds against pregnancy?"

"Statistically speaking, yes. Obviously, you got lucky." Jeffrey had to duck the following punch but already knew his brother was really pleased.

31 WEDNESDAY

Kat frowned at the uncooperative yarn and the crochet hook that threatened to become the bane of her day. She transferred her glare to James when he commented from the couch, "The stitches are still too tight. You need to relax so you have space to work with on the next row. Why are you even bothering if you hate it so much?"

Dropping the needlework in defeat, Kat stared unseeing out the window. "Because it's something moms do and I can't do *anything* moms are supposed to do naturally."

"Mom?" mouthed James silently in wonder. He asked gently, "So, how old were you when you lost your mother?"

Crossing her arms and leaning back in the chair, Kat said defiantly, "I didn't *lose* her. She left. Walked out when I was three and never came back. She sent a letter when I was in high school; not even an apology, just gushing about her wonderful new family and how amazing those kids were. I tore it into little pieces and flushed it."

"Well, I can't imagine anyone less like you than that. You would never abandon someone."

With a little gasp, she locked eyes with him, then the shutters closed as she regained control. "I wish I knew for certain if I am pregnant."

"Are the bags from the shopping trip still under the table in the laundry room? There should be some pregnancy kits in one of them.

I remember grabbing a few boxes after Addie got all those condoms." James' eyes danced dangerously, but he carefully kept the smile off his face.

Kat stood abruptly, not noticing the ball of yarn rolling away.

"Go ahead. I'll be fine until you get back," James said.

A few minutes later, Lindy walked in and looked around the living room with a frown. "Why are you alone? What if you needed something?"

"Shh!" James waved her to silence. "Come pet me. History is in the making."

Scooting the chair closer, she felt his forehead. "Do you have a fever? You're not making any sense."

"No, no," he said, waving away her hand. Then he grabbed it and put it back on his brow. "On second thought, keep doing that. It feels good."

Lindy chuckled and finger-combed his too long hair back. He was practically purring with complacency when she murmured, "You know…"

"Hmm?"

"If you can stand the growing-out phase, you'd look good in a ponytail."

"I'll grow it out if you keep that sexy buzz cut." He grinned unrepentantly as her mouth dropped open and a flush spread across her cheeks.

Lindy pulled her hand back. "I don't know what's got into you today!"

The manic glint faded from his eye and he answered truthfully, "I'm so thankful to be here and I've never felt so alive."

She reached forward instinctively to stroke his unwounded cheek. "Doesn't it hurt to smile?"

"It hurts like hell." He captured her hand and turned to plant a kiss on her palm. When she jerked away, he released her.

Heart suddenly pounding, Lindy stood and backed away. She didn't even know why she was so frightened but desperately needed to escape. When the door opened and Steve and Kat entered, she slipped away and out the back; not seeing James' outstretched hand or hearing his 'Lindy?'.

Seething at his inability to follow her, James glowered at the oblivious couple.

Kat spoke first, "We wanted you to be the first to get the official notice that you are going to be an uncle."

"And we want you to be guardian if anything happens to us," Steve finished.

"Wha'?" James' mind raced to process the idea that they were already making plans for the orphaning of their unborn child; then, the enormous honor and responsibility they were bestowing on him. "I...yes, I will. Proudly."

But when Steve stepped forward to shake his hand, James pulled him down and whispered that he had damn well better be careful with himself.

Steve glanced at his brother's bandages and muttered, "You're a fine one to talk."

"Lindy, are you alone?" Adam's voice crackled out of her radio.

Stopping her breathless climb of the hill behind the house, she unclipped it and replied, "I need some time."

The raw emotion in her voice made him pause before saying, "Please stay in sight."

She sank to the ground there and buried her face in her knees. She didn't know how to handle the wave of emotion and desire she had felt. It was one thing to love someone quietly in a secret place, but when he looked at her like that...and how could she trust herself after believing she was in love with John? A quiet voice in the back of her mind whispered that she could trust James if not herself.

Adam looked at Addie questioningly. She shook her head and looked back up the hill. "I think we should try to give her what she needs. We can keep an eye on her from here, right?"

He nodded, although he suspected Steve would not agree. "Can you keep watch while I work?"

"Yes." Addie knew he was making an effort to be civil to her and she was glad, even if he was doing it for Alex. She was also grateful for a break from the filthy job of tearing off the remains of the porch. The twins had just gotten up and pitched in to help.

It was only half an hour before Lindy stood and slowly made her way back down the hill. Instead of returning to the house, she joined Addie and asked if they could work on the plans for the town. Addie slapped the soot off her jeans and happily agreed. She didn't notice the pause in the living room when Lindy and James stared at each other before they both looked away. Stepping into the dining room, they found Frank already had their notes spread out and was writing something down in his shaky, yet beautiful, penmanship.

"I think we need to make some changes to the plan," he began. "We started on the assumption that we could model after the system used during the war in Britain. It was a very good system for that time and place, but these people don't have Hitler breathing down their necks and aren't British. They won't put up with the same rules so we need to build in flexibility for independence."

Addie immediately argued the issue until Frank pointed out that it didn't matter how it 'should' be done if the people wouldn't do it.

Conceding the fight, Addie glumly turned to a fresh page of her notebook. "Okay, what have you got so far?"

They only stopped working long enough for a quick meal, then took over the table again. By the time the daylight was fading, they each sat back and looked at the others.

"This could work," said Lindy in wonder.

"It wouldn't be easy, but it could hold a community together," agreed Frank. "Well, a smallish community. Not a city."

"Who do we give it to?"

"Tomorrow," said Pat from the doorway to the kitchen. "You make some copies and a letter explaining the purpose. Then Juan can give it to his wife and she can pass it on to Doreen Sampson. We can hold onto a couple copies in case we hear of anyone traveling to other towns. Did you put in anything about defense?"

"No, and I don't think Kat has done anything with that yet."

"Probably just as well. Better that each town doesn't know how the next is planning to defend itself."

Lindy blinked to hear such cynicism coming from Pat, but Frank was nodding in agreement.

Pat walked around the table, pausing by each one to plant a kiss on the top of their head, not missing a grinning Frank. "I'm proud of all of you putting such an effort into something to help others like this."

32 THURSDAY

Addie rocked up onto the balls of her feet, studying the New Farm house with fresh eyes now that she and Alex were going to live there. With its new windows and bright white siding, the outside looked great; other than the sagging porch which would have to wait until the priority list thinned out. The inside, she knew, still needed a lot of work before it was ready for them.

"What can I do?" she asked Pete.

He smiled at her eagerness. "How about stripping off the old wallpaper in the living room? You'll need to wear a dust mask."

He paused as the distinct 'putt, putt' noise of Juan's moped could be heard approaching. "Juan and I will be working on the flooring in the addition. Once we finish that, we can get the kitchen stove in."

Juan joined them, "You're sure you don't want to keep working on the porch, Mr. Wilson?"

"Not today. I think it will rain. The boys can keep cleaning up that area this morning and we'll put in a full day of inside work here."

"If we had the generator for the saw, we could do the whole floor today. But cutting it by hand will take longer."

"I know, but they need it more. We'll get it done soon enough."

Juan shrugged and followed them into the house.

After a couple hours of peeling and scraping, Addie swung her arms around to ease the aching muscles. Deciding it was time for a break, she wandered back to the addition where the beautiful, golden bamboo flooring was being placed piece by piece. "Ooh! Nice."

Pete shifted back onto his heels. "Yes, Jeffrey has good taste. He knew we could never match the original hardwood floor in the old kitchen, so he went for a complete contrast. I thought he was making a mistake and tried to talk him into replacing it all, but he was right. It works."

Addie looked up at the faded orange roosters and green teapots on the old kitchen wallpaper and shuddered.

Pete and Juan both laughed at her expression. "No shortage of work for you."

"I'd better keep on then."

At noon, they headed down the drive to walk home. As they reached the road, Addie thought she heard a tinkling noise. Gazing around, she spotted a familiar looking horse and wagon coming towards them. Waving, she jogged forward. "Krista! Mr. Hansen! What a nice surprise. And your horse is wearing bells."

An unpleasant squeal sounded from the back of the wagon and Addie backed away in a hurry. Krista turned around, "Hush! You're supposed to be a surprise. Oh well. Surprise!"

Grinning at Addie, she continued chattering, "We heard about your fire. We hear lots of stuff on the milk run. My dad is donating a weaner to replace your hogs and when Mr. Schmidt heard that, he donated two! To be honest, his aren't great stock and I wouldn't keep them for breeding, but that little gilt my dad gave is a beauty. Definitely a keeper."

When Krista paused to draw breath, Mr. Hansen suggested they keep moving before the sun went down. Looking affronted, she sat back squarely and shook the reins. The mare wasn't in a hurry, so the others had no trouble keeping up.

Viewing the gifts at home, Steve said wryly, "I suppose we'll be building pig pens this afternoon."

"Yes," agreed Krista. "You'll want a separate pen for Xena, but the boys should be close enough that they can socialize."

"Xena?"

Krista blushed, "Well, she's awfully pretty."

"You didn't happen to name the other two, did you?"

She scoffed at the idea. "Bacon and Ham is good enough for them. You won't want to keep them around."

Pat broke up the discussion by thanking them profusely not just for the generosity, but that they took the time to deliver the gifts.

Hansen replied, "It was no trouble. I was sorry to hear about the fire."

"Oh! I almost forgot! My mom wondered if you were getting any extra zucchini. Ours got some kind of fungus and all died already."

"Just a moment," said Steve and gestured Jeffrey to come along. When they returned both had their arms full of a variety of sizes of zucchinis. Steve also handed over an envelope of seeds. "For next year. I jotted some notes down too on how to avoid that happening again. And, Krista, do you know if your mom saves seeds from her garden usually?"

"No, she doesn't. I heard her talking about saving from the tomatoes because they were heirloom plants, but nothing else was." Worry lines pinched her young forehead.

"You tell her that I'll save extra for her, okay?"

She looked from Steve to the zucchinis in the wagon and back to him before launching herself onto him for a hug. Then, completely business-like, she climbed back onto the wagon seat and announced that they needed to be heading back.

After waving goodbye to their visitors, Pat grew thoughtful. "I think we should plan on saving an overabundance of seeds this year."

Steve nodded, "I've already begun showing Lindy what to do and which we're keeping back."

Seeing her worried expression he added, "Kat hasn't seen any signs of infection in James' wounds, you know. She's been watching closely."

"I know, dear. It's all just been a bit much lately. I'm feeling tired again."

"Why don't you take a book and relax this afternoon?"

Pat sighed, "I know it sounds fussy, but I've read all my books. I wish I had something different."

Steve paused to hug Kat on his way through the living room and asked her if she had brought any books when she moved over. Eyebrows arching in surprise at the unexpected question, she answered, "Only a couple on field trauma. Why?"

Promising to explain later, he moved on. Addie only had a few magazines on winter sports, but Lindy offered up the two Amelia Peabody books she had brought on her original visit. "I'm sure she's already read them though. They're exactly the sort she would enjoy."

Soon Pat was turning over the worn paperbacks in her hands. "No, I'm not familiar with this author. But if Lindy wouldn't mind lending them…"

When Steve passed on his thanks, Lindy groaned. "This is so frustrating! I had the complete set in my apartment and I can guarantee that she's going to want to read them all once she gets a taste. There isn't even a bookstore in town anymore, is there?"

"No, they closed years ago. There's a hole in the wall shop that had used books, but they never seemed to be open normal hours even before the power outage."

Kat and James were listening in from the other side of the room. "I wonder if it would be worth a drive by next time someone is in town? I wouldn't mind a decent book while I'm stuck here," James mused.

Kat stood and stretched. "Well I need to get out and move around. Lindy, why don't you take over and tell the invalid a story for a couple hours."

An awkward silence fell as she and Steve left. Lindy edged over and gingerly sat in the chair. James said gruffly, "I'm sure you have more important things to do than babysit me."

"No, Kat insisted that you be watched over. A fast moving infection could be deadly unless it's caught early."

"Why didn't she worry so much about your shoulder then?"

"Because that was a slice more than a stab. Your wounds are deeper."

"Yeah, because I was too stupid to shoot first." James' voice betrayed how dark his thoughts had become and Lindy regretted avoiding him while she wrestled with her own demons.

Without conscious thought, she began smoothing the wrinkles out of the sheet draped over his legs. He watched her with a bemused expression until the light touch of her fingers got to be too much and, in a strangled voice, he said, "Lindy, *please!*" and reached out to grab her hand.

She looked up, startled. Her thoughts had been running in circles, but seeing his red face and embarrassed eyes, her mind caught up quickly and she flushed also. Then her sense of humor kicked into overdrive and she began to giggle. As suddenly as she had begun, she stopped laughing and studied his face. The sensible voice in the back of her head pointed out that there was nothing to fear here. Her eyes dropped to their clasped hands and, drawing his towards her, she placed a kiss in his palm.

When the rain drove Steve and Kat back inside, she frowned at the empty couch. "Where's my patient?"

Systematically checking each room, she looked inside Lindy's room and quickly shut the door again. "Never mind."

Drawing Steve to the vacant couch, Kat said, "We haven't discussed baby names yet."

"I had a friend...he was called Jemmie."

"He didn't make it back, did he?"

"No."

She snuggled against his side and placed his hand on her still-flat stomach, "Jemmie is a good name."

33 FRIDAY

Jeffrey leaned on the new pig pen and admired the weaners. They had lined the floor with freshly scythed grass, but needed to locate more straw soon.

Alex joined him and grunted playfully at Xena. "Krista knows pigs. That's as fine a red Duroc that I've ever seen."

Jeffrey laughed, "But she named her after a warrior princess!"

"True. I probably would have gone with Mabel or Betty, but Xena she is."

"I appreciate the gesture, but they're going to make a lot more work for us."

"We need to get some outside pens set up soonest." Alex kicked at a post absently. "I'd like to have a discussion about cutting back on the night patrols; I'm starting to feel like a vampire and there's so much to do."

"Hmm. It may not make the most sense to have our farmers sleeping all day. I'm afraid we're going to have to find a way to include New Farm in our patrols instead of cutting back though."

"I wish we had more dogs."

"How do you feel about geese?"

"Who has geese?" Alex perked up.

"Krista mentioned some. Maybe she could broker a deal."

"That girl is a force." Alex chuckled evilly. "If she were ten years older, she'd be perfect for Adam."

"No comment."

Alex was rendered speechless by an enormous yawn. "Ah, that's my cue. Can you arrange a family meeting for tonight?"

"Of course. Sleep well." Jeffrey watched his brother saunter out with a frown. Somehow they had to find a compromise between security and getting the work done. His mouth quirked into a smile as he looked back down at the pigs. Maybe he would take the time to ride over to Hansen's and have a chat with Krista later; for now, there was work to be done.

Pete and Juan soon finished the floor installation and shifted their attention back to the porch rebuild. Jeffrey was standing in the middle of the space, admiring the new, larger kitchen when he suddenly burst out laughing.

Addie popped her head in, pulling down her dust mask, "What? What's so funny?"

Jeffrey was leaning against the counter, gasping for breath. "I just realized. All this space. For a refrigerator. That we don't have and couldn't run if we did. And the laundry area, but nothing to wash with."

"That reminds me! I meant to ask if you could adapt an older washing machine to be run powered by someone pedaling. There's an old washer at the farm, not really old because it was still electric, but the motor was mounted on the back so I wondered if you could run a belt to it or something."

"Huh. Possibly. It might be worth looking into at least."

"And I wish you'd put up a guard rail around the basement steps. It makes me nervous to have an open hole like that."

"Yes, I was planning on putting up something basic today. I'll build a permanent one later when I have time to do it right."

Addie looked around approvingly. The hall opened directly into the expanded kitchen area and a door led to the enclosed laundry and basement stairs. The back wall was a row of windows bracketing the new back door that actually opened. "It did turn out nice though."

At lunch they gathered to eat at the picnic tables now under the cottonwood tree. Michael asked Juan if there was anything new happening in town.

"Trouble is starting." He shook his head. "People are getting upset. Smokers run out of cigarettes. Families are using the foods in the back of their cupboards and know there isn't more coming in. Water pressure is dropping. Bad times.

"You asked for more stories though. I heard one for you. The shop teacher at the high school is also in charge of the FFA group. When the power stayed off, he got all the FFA kids and took them out to the dairy farm south of town. They've all got tents and have camped out there ever since; doing chores but getting fed."

"What's FFA?" asked Addie.

"Future Farmers of America," chorused back to her and she chuckled.

"Did you hear how many cows there are?" asked Steve.

"Sixty! The farmer could never have done it without help."

Jeffrey approached Addie after the meal and asked if she'd like to ride along on a quick visit to Hansen's. "If you can handle riding a real bike, that is."

"Careful. Those sound like fighting words if the twins were up."

The Harley made short work of the three miles and they were soon riding past the meadow of complacent-looking cows. Krista stepped out of a barn door wearing a stiff white apron with her hair pinned up.

"Hi! You caught me churning butter but I don't mind taking a break. What brings you over? Are the pigs okay?"

Addie smiled. "They're fine. Jeffrey wanted to talk to you and I just came along to visit."

"You mentioned geese yesterday. Was it a large enough flock that they might want to sell some?"

"I bet they would! There must have been..." Krista closed her eyes and mumbled through a mental tally. "Twelve adults and at least twenty half-grown. What are you offering in trade?"

"Garden produce," Jeffrey responded promptly.

"Or fresh bread," added Addie.

"I'll talk to them tomorrow."

"Can you also keep your eye open for a farm or guard dog?"

"Sure. I could get my hands on a puppy easy enough, but if you want an adult... Well, nobody wants to part with a good one and you don't want a bad."

"Is everything else okay here and at home?" Addie asked.

"Yes, but," Krista lowered her voice. "When I told Mom about the seeds she started crying and I think Dad wanted to, but he thinks men shouldn't." She rolled her eyes at the general foolishness of men.

Jeffrey was chuckling when they were putting their helmets back on.

"What?" Addie poked him.

"I think Alex was right about that girl being a match for Adam if she wasn't so young."

"Huh. She'll make her own mind up when it's time."

They returned to New Farm to continue working and the afternoon proceeded in what was becoming routine. Pat retreated to her room to rest and read. Michael worked on perfecting his baking under Biff's watchful eye. Frank sat in the shade and supervised the reconstruction work. Kat asked Lindy to watch James again so she could go with Steve and try to buy more straw.

Kat paused long enough to murmur in Lindy's ear, "Don't let him overdo. Be gentle until he heals."

Taking in Lindy's pink cheeks and quivering smile, James demanded to know what Kat said.

"I'm supposed to go gentle on you."

"How did she know?"

"Um," Lindy thought back to a vague impression of the door shutting the day before. "I think she may have seen us."

"Blast!" Blushing fiercely himself, James met her amused eye. "It's not a spectator sport."

Lindy tugged on his hand. "Should we drape a sock over the doorknob? Or prop a chair under it?"

His expression brightened. "Really? You want to…"

"Come *on*, James!" He followed with a foolish grin.

This time, when Steve and Kat returned, it seemed to register with Steve that someone was missing. "Where's James?"

"Therapy."

"Oh. What do you want to work on now?"

"I think we better figure out how to restructure our security before tonight's meeting."

The family meeting took place after supper; it began a bit chaotic and tempers were rising before Pat firmly quelled them. "Let's hear what Steve has to say before jumping to conclusions on what is needed."

"This is a volatile time so what we decide today will probably have to be adapted as things change. But, for now, our greatest danger is over. I'm lifting the restrictions on having to move around in pairs. As long as you keep your radio on and let someone know where you've gone, spending time alone is fine.

"We're also stopping the patrols. There still needs to be someone on watch at night, but they can sit if they don't fall asleep. And splitting the night up into separate shifts is an option. Now, the tricky part; someone needs to be at New Farm at night. Not necessarily on guard, but at least on site."

"I wouldn't mind. I always enjoyed camping, but someone else would have to take over the morning milking." Alex looked around for volunteers; there were none.

Then Lindy raised her hand. "I'd like to help with the milking once I can use both arms again."

"Okay," Steve interrupted. "Setting some ground rules: nobody on the injured list gets to volunteer. Come see me when you're whole again."

"Then I'll camp at New Farm until Alex gets help," Adam offered.

"Thanks, Adam. Now who is willing to take a night?"

Frank surprised everyone by speaking up, "I'd like to. As long as the battery in my hearing aid holds out, I can probably hear better than anyone. I don't need much sleep at my age; I'm usually awake by 2:00 and the nights get pretty long waiting for the rest of you to get up."

"Well, with Frank's generous offer, that makes this much easier. Alex, I'm pulling you off night duties for now since you have to get up so early. That leaves Jeffrey, Michael, myself, Kat, Addie and Pete to take one shift every six nights. Any concerns?"

After the gathering had scattered, Lindy approached Steve with James' guitar. He raised his eyebrows in an unspoken question. "James asked if you would consider playing a little. He's missing music and since he can't play himself…"

"I haven't touched a guitar in years; not since I was stationed…" This time it was his voice that trailed off. The muscles along his jaw clenched and sweat dotted his brow. Recognizing the warning signs, Kat waved Lindy away, but Steve reached over and took the guitar. Turning his back to them, he sat down on the dining chair. At first, his hands shook too hard to use, but Kat placed her hand on the back of his neck and he breathed out some of the anxiety. The notes came hesitantly, then with more confidence. After about ten minutes, he stopped abruptly and said, "That's all."

Lindy noticed that he placed the guitar down on the table gently before walking away.

34 SATURDAY

James woke to fingertips trailing down his left arm. "Lord, woman! You're going to wear me out." He reached up and pulled Lindy down on top of him.

With a muffled laugh, Lindy tried to land so she wasn't near any of his wounds. "I'm not! I wasn't..." The rest of the words were lost in his kiss. Pulling back enough to speak, she said, "I had a nightmare and I had to see if you were okay."

"I'm okay, love."

"All right then." She began levering herself carefully up.

"Wait! Stay."

"Someone will see us."

"So?"

"What would Pat think of me seducing her favorite son after she took me in?"

"Is that what you did? You wicked, wanton creature. I'm helpless against your wiles."

"Stop laughing! I'm serious. What if she thinks I've betrayed her trust?"

"Oh, Lindy. She's been offering us up to you from day one. You could have had any or all of us as far as she's concerned. And you chose ME." The unabashed satisfaction in his voice made her shiver. "Are you cold? Come under the sheet."

She chuckled, then ducked her head shyly. "I only wanted you. I knew the night you were playing on the steps."

"I *knew* it! I should have serenaded you when I had the chance."

"Shh! Someone's coming." They froze as Steve walked in, stopped and swiveled around to stare at the couch. He shook his head and headed upstairs without saying a word.

"Did he see you?" whispered James.

"Of course he saw me!" she hissed back indignantly.

"No reason not to stay then," he said smugly.

The first thing Pat saw when she descended the stairs in the morning was Lindy curled up against James' side with one leg draped possessively over his. He watched from the corner of his eye as she clapped her hand over her mouth and slowly made her way into the kitchen.

Everyone else was gathered around with coffee cups, obviously waiting for her reaction. "Lindy and James," Pat said slowly. Then, looking up at her family with tears in her eyes, "I'm so happy."

"Lindy."

"Mmm?"

"You can wake up now. Everyone has seen us."

"What! What do you mean? I'm in my nightie!"

"Then you'd better get dressed before they all come trooping back through to congratulate us."

"Ack!" She practically levitated off the couch and sprinted into her room.

Lindy was still dithering around, avoiding going back out and facing the family when Addie bounced in. "Tell me everything."

"How did they react? God! What an embarrassing way to tell everyone."

"I could say they were horrified, but you know I'd be lying. Seriously, everyone here loves you. Falling in love with one of them isn't exactly an insult to the family honor. I don't even have to ask if you really love him; you've been dreamy-eyed for weeks. Although, if I didn't have such a thick skin I'd be upset. Pat wasn't exactly crying with joy when Alex announced our engagement. But you get caught in a compromising position with James and she's the happiest woman on earth. Humph!"

"Oh, Addie!"

"It's okay. Really. Once she gets used to the idea that Alex is truly settling down, she'll come around. I think she's gotten her hopes up before.

"Now then; why on earth were you keeping this a secret? I mean, we all knew James was madly in love with you, but not a hint from you. I figured it must have been Jeffrey or Michael you fell for because neither of them would have been right and that would have been painful. But James! When did you know he was the one?"

"How could it have been anyone else?" Lindy spoke with simple sincerity.

"Well, you had better get out there and rescue him then. He's facing them all alone."

"Oh!" Springing up, Lindy didn't hesitate this time and marched straight out.

After the fuss and the teasing had finally eased up, Lindy and James were alone again. He was stretched out on the couch with his head in her lap and she was twining his hair around her fingers.

"Your messing with my hair was how we got into this situation."

"Regrets?"

"Never." He smiled up at her happily. "Did you notice all the assumptions flying around this morning?"

"I noticed you didn't correct them."

"No, but I have to do this right. Give me a push, I want to get up."

Once upright, James promptly turned around and sank to his knees. "Lindy Aster DeVaney, I love you more than life itself. Will you marry me?"

The quiet little voice in the back of Lindy's head was shouting and doing cartwheels, but she still managed to say 'yes'.

Once James was settled back onto the couch, Lindy asked, "Just how did you know my full name?"

"I peeked at your driver's license. I was happy to learn that marrying me will improve your initials."

"LAD to LAS, sort of an improvement, I guess. What's your middle name?"

"Stuart. Named after Dad's best friend from high school."

"I didn't know adoptive parents got to pick names."

"It was either that or go through life as Baby Boy. They got me on day one."

"So somewhere in this house are pictures of your entire life…"

"You've already seen all of me, how much humiliation can one man take?"

"James," Lindy began with a dangerous glint in her eye.

"What?" he asked cautiously.

"I just accepted a marriage proposal from a man wearing only boxer shorts. I think I've earned a look at your mother's photo albums."

"Ah, yes dear."

The twins were loading fence panels, posts and wire into the pickup. "Steve didn't find any straw yesterday."

"Rats. Do we hope we get enough hay from the second cutting to use instead?"

"If we have to." Alex paused, then started laughing. "I wonder if he asked Krista."

"Why is that funny?"

"Because she looks like such an innocent child, but underneath is a cutthroat businesswoman."

"Oh, okay. You know, I'm really glad to be off the night shift. I feel like I've been cut off from so many of the important things happening."

"I forgot you haven't even met Krista yet. So, what's next on your to-do list after we get the pig fences set up?"

"I'd like to work with the vet some more. Going back to school seems unlikely and the experience is valuable."

"Back to an apprentice system already? See if you can arrange something where he covers your gas use."

"You aren't bothered about not finishing your degree?" Adam asked curiously.

"Not really. The newest farming practices I was going to learn are all heavily dependent on modern technology. Dad taught me the older methods he used. And Addie already has a business degree, so…"

They climbed into the truck cab and headed for New Farm. Adam stared unseeing out the window. "So much has changed."

"Yes and no."

"What do you mean?"

"You're talking about how much has changed because the power went out, right? Well, I've been thinking about that and a lot of the stuff that happened would have anyway. Maybe not so fast, but still. I think Steve and Kat would still have hooked up, Pete was going to court Mom no matter what, and we knew James had fallen off the deep end. Remember how prickly he was until he figured out we weren't going to steal Lindy away from him?" They both chuckled, then Alex continued speaking, "John would still have attacked. So the only real changes are Frank moving in, Michael coming home and…"

"Addie."

"Adam, it's not really different than Kat and Lindy joining the family, is it? I mean, I'm still just as much your brother as before." He looked anxiously at his twin. Neither made any move to get out of the cab.

"You're changing. And I don't want you to. It makes me think there must be something wrong with me if you have to change because we were the same."

Alex reached over and squeezed his shoulder. "It's not that. I'm changing because I'm taking another person in; I have to make more room in myself."

Adam looked at his brother in amazement, "Do you have any idea how completely bonkers that sounded?"

"Ha! I'm deep. You just wish you could make deep, philosophical comments like me."

"Idiot."

By early afternoon they had set up a pig run behind the barn and two separate pens opening up off it. They even threw together makeshift shelters so the pigs would be protected from the worst of the weather.

Now home again, Alex had gone off looking for Addie. Adam plunged his head into the cattle's water tank for some relief from the intense afternoon sun. Shaking the water off, he heard someone shout 'Alex!'. Turning, he saw a young girl running toward him. She stopped and said, with a suspicious glare, "You're not Alex."

"No, I'm his twin brother, Adam. But I'm just as nice."

She crossed her arms and gave a skeptical sniff.

"You must be Krista. I've heard a lot about you." Adam was beginning to wonder why the rest of his family seemed so fond of her. "Were you looking for Alex? He's probably in the house with Addie."

"No, I need to talk to Jeffrey."

"I'm sorry. He and Steve went to town. I don't know when they'll be home."

Krista's face fell. "Oh, I have to be back by 4:30 for the milking."

"There's still time for a visit then. Why don't you go up to the house and I'll move your horse into the shade and give her some water."

"Okay." She started away, then spun around to announce, "Addie is going to marry Alex. Isn't that wonderful? He likes cows, too." Turning, she ran the rest of the way to the house.

Adam leaned against the water tank, laughing helplessly. He decided Krista had redeemed herself by lumping Addie in with cows, even unintentionally.

Krista sat on the arm of the chair and leaned comfortably against Pat. "I wish my grandma didn't live so far away."

Pat smiled at her, "I'll be your spare grandma anytime you want."

"It's weird to be around so many grown-ups," Krista said wonderingly. "Mr. Hansen mostly leaves me alone to work now and there are too many kids at home."

Her eyes lingered on the couch where the two engaged couples were happily chatting. "I wish I was pretty."

"I think you're very pretty," Pat declared firmly.

"That's because you like me. Lindy must really like James." This was said in a slightly puzzled tone.

Pat struggled to contain her laughter. "Yes, Lindy loves him very much."

"My mom is going to have another baby," Krista confided.

"Oh!" Pat was dismayed at the thought of yet another child taking more attention away from Krista. Couldn't her parents see that she was reaching the age where she needed more time with them, not less?

"I'm never having babies." Krista's gaze soaked up the scene in front of her. "I might get married, but no babies."

"They're not all bad," Pat said fondly. "James was such a happy baby. Alex and Adam were a lot of work, but that's because there was two of them."

"Huh." Krista looked back and forth between the boys and Pat, clearly struggling to imagine them as infants.

The sound of a car pulling in distracted them and Krista hopped up to look out the window. "Jeffrey is back! I need to talk to him about the geese."

Three men climbed out of the car. Jeffrey stopped to talk to Krista, Juan headed straight over to where Pete was sawing lumber and Steve took some bags out of the trunk and headed inside.

Steve set the bags down near Pat and sank into another chair. "I had a good meeting with Juan's neighborhood gardeners. We talked about what they could reasonably expect to achieve in what's left of the growing season. I explained composting and the importance of fertilizing. I think they're going to try to work with that FFA guy and arrange something with the local farmers. There were even representatives from other neighborhoods there."

Pat was looking in the bags. "Are these...where did you get all these books?"

"You remember that funny used bookstore? I traded vegetables for these and there's a couple more bags in the trunk. I went a bit mad because I've been imagining winter without access to the library." Steve leaned forward with a laugh, "And our anonymous donation raid went without a hitch. We drove up the alley behind the nursing home, dropped off the box of food, I knocked and high-tailed it back to the car. Nobody saw us."

Addie leaned over to Lindy, "Would you like to walk over to New Farm and make plans? Or is it too hot?"

"Let's go. I haven't even seen the new kitchen."

They both put on floppy straw hats and sunglasses and headed outside. Krista waved to them from her wagon seat. "Do you want a lift? We can probably all fit if we squidge up a bit."

They climbed up beside her and Addie asked, "You aren't worried about driving around alone?"

"No. Mr. Hansen taught me how to shoot and gave me a shotgun to use. He said only pervs would bother someone like me and I should shoot those...um, 'bad guys' right down."

Lindy and Addie exchanged amused glances at Krista censoring her language for them. "It's too bad you don't have someone to keep you company though."

Krista sighed, "I wish I had a dog, but Mom won't let me. I've been reading a story about a girl and she has a dog. They go everywhere together.

"Well, here you are! I have to head straight back or I'll be late for the milking. Bye!"

"Poor girl. I can see why Pat got in the habit of taking in strays."

"I don't think her mother means to be unkind. She's just overwhelmed and has it in her mind that Krista can take care of herself. Come on. See what I've been working on."

They stood in the living room while Lindy admired the progress. With all the layers of wallpaper stripped away and the musty carpeting gone, it was transformed. "I'm glad we got all the paint ahead of time. This is going to be beautiful."

"I finished patching the plaster this morning. Then I started stripping the kitchen walls while it dries. I can paint in here tomorrow. You were thinking of the teal for this and the yellow for the kitchen, right?"

"Yes, exactly right. We got cream for all the other rooms because I couldn't imagine them fixed up."

"Come upstairs and we can decide which rooms we want. You know Steve wants our room for when the baby comes?"

Lindy chuckled, "I did get that impression. Does Alex get a say in which room you pick?"

"I already asked him and he couldn't care less. 'Is there room for the bed? What else matters?'" she quoted.

"Nice thick walls."

"Yes! I don't miss living in an apartment."

"You really don't mind a double wedding? I feel like we're imposing on your day."

"I might feel differently if I had spent a year planning it out with all the frills, but this makes it more special. Because we can't go abroad for a honeymoon or even have photographs taken, I was worried it would be just another day. You know; get up, do chores, take a shower, get married, do chores again. With both of us doing it together, it makes it The Wedding Day."

"Steve and Kat really don't want to get married?"

Addie laughed, "I overheard Adam asking her about that and she nearly took his head off. Don't go there."

While the girls were gone, Alex and James sat Pat down between them. "You know we want to get married as soon as New Farm is livable," Alex began.

"And we want it to be as much like a proper wedding as we can," continued James. "That's why Michael is going to walk Addie down the aisle and Lindy hopes you will do the same for her."

"Oh!" Tears filled Pat's eyes.

Alex leaned around her to glare at his brother. "I told you that would set her off. You should have waited 'til the end to ask."

Pat slapped Alex's arm indignantly. "I'm fine. Go on."

"They're going to wear dresses out of the stuff you got down from the attic."

"Oh, I wish I still had my wedding dress. I let a friend borrow it and it was ruined."

"Well, it might have been difficult with two brides and only one dress anyway."

"That's true. What else?"

"Hansen has offered to loan us his piano; it was actually his late wife's, but it's still a generous gesture. Jeffrey will play for the ceremony."

Pat nodded. Jeffrey was the only one who had stuck with piano lessons even though they didn't have one for him to practice on. "Who will you get to officiate?"

"We're still working on that, but it isn't what has us stumped. Neither of us has a ring to give."

Alex broke in to add, "And even if we could get the jewelry store to open for us we don't have enough cash left to buy any."

"This is a problem that I might have a solution for." Pat perked up. "People around here don't tend to be the types to bury jewelry with the dead. We're a little too practical for that. I have at least four wedding bands upstairs; only women's though. Your father was the first in his family to wear one and I, well, I'm not ready to part with that."

She got hugged from both sides; everyone getting a little choked up.

35 SUNDAY

Kat examined the wound on James' face closely. "This is healing nicely. I think it's time to take the stitches out."

"Hold still," she said when James started to speak. Using a tiny pair of scissors, each stitch was carefully snipped and slid out. "You will always have the scar, I'm afraid."

"There goes my modeling career," he quipped.

Kat moved on to checking his other wounds. Deftly prodding around the injuries, she watched him for any response. When he winced as she massaged his arm, she nodded.

"Kat, why does my arm hurt so much more than my side? He only hit it once, but it hurts constantly. The others don't bother me nearly as much."

"I expect it's because it went all the way through and caused massive muscle trauma. You really were incredibly fortunate; three stab wounds to your torso and he still managed to miss all your organs.

"Now then, since you're obviously steadier on your feet, I've got an assignment for you. I want you to start to practice drawing, aiming and dry-firing with your left hand. I know it will feel awkward, but you're going to be a leftie for weeks and you need to be able to defend yourself."

James' face shut down in an uncharacteristically grim look. "How can I learn to shoot first when I'm acting on instinct?"

"All I can suggest is practice until it becomes an extension of your arm. Learn to trust yourself with the gun."

He sighed. Then, gingerly touching his face, he stood, "I need a mirror."

"James." Kat paused until he met her eye. "Lindy will only see it as a reminder that you were defending her."

His eyebrows rose. "That bad, huh?"

She snorted. "If I wanted a pretty boy, would I be with Steve? You almost lost an eye. Keep it in perspective."

"Oh, hell." James stood in the bathroom and stared at his reflection. Involuntary tears blurred his vision. "What? I wasn't ugly enough before?"

Lindy stood on the front lawn watching Juan and Pete nail shingles onto the new porch roof. She felt a bit silly as she swung her arm around, but dutifully did the exercises that Kat had assigned her.

"Good morning, Lindy." Frank shuffled over to stand beside her.

She smiled cheerfully back, then cocked her head to the side as she looked at him. "Is it my imagination or are you getting around more easily these days?"

"It's true. I've got more reason to move about. I haven't felt this spry since I was eighty." His expression became wistful. "I'd like to see your new house one of these days."

"Of course, you will. It's not fancy, but it will be a good home."

"And how are the wedding plans going? You know, I've performed many a marriage in my day; none of them legal, of course, but no less real for the lack of that."

"But you never married yourself?"

"No, no. I was tempted a few times, but I knew my feet would start itching again. It was better not to make promises I couldn't keep."

"James!" Lindy called out as she entered the house. "Where are you?"

When he emerged from the bathroom, she ran to him. "Oh! Your stitches are out. Good."

He roughly pulled her hand away from his face. "How can you stand to look at me? Let alone touch me?"

Her smile faltered. "But James, I've been watching Kat change your bandages every day. Did you think it would matter to me?"

Her hand drifted to the ridged scar bisecting the back of her head. "Does this matter to you?"

"No! God, no! You could never be anything but beautiful to me." He pulled her close in a one-armed embrace. "I'm sorry. I'm being a bear and wallowing in self-pity. Please forgive me."

She relaxed against him, "Well, you could make it up to me."

He studied her face anxiously, then chuckled. "That is definitely your lusty look. I can't doubt you now, can I?"

Lindy purred and nibbled his ear teasingly before drawing back. "You know, I was looking for you for a reason."

"Not just to take advantage of me? Do tell."

"How important is it whether or not our marriage is strictly legal?"

James stiffened; his instinctive reaction was that it was very important, but then he wondered why. If Lindy had been as anti-marriage as Kat was, he would have accepted that without argument. He said slowly, "Maybe it doesn't really matter."

"I hoped you'd say that." Then she proceeded to tell him about Frank's history of officiating in an unofficial capacity.

"I like the idea of not bringing a stranger in; this keeps it personal. I don't know how Addie and Alex will feel about it."

"If they want someone else they can arrange that. I want Frank."

"Come sit with me, Lindy. We need to talk about Steve and Kat's baby."

"What about it?" she asked after they were snuggled together on the couch.

"They asked me to be its guardian in case they die and I said yes. I know you're okay with adopting, but needed to tell you this one could be ours someday."

"I hope it never happens, but any of your nieces and nephews will be welcome in our home. I want to adopt *lots*." She gave a happy sigh. "But not right away. I want to enjoy being your wife first."

Over at New Farm, Addie chuckled as she listened to the men grunting in the kitchen. They were installing the stove and she didn't envy them the job. She hummed to herself as the paint rolled onto the wall smoothly. The teal color was vibrant and rich. It even picked up and enhanced some of the colors from the stained glass. Privately, she was glad they hadn't replaced the old window, although she suspected she might change her mind in the winter.

Strong arms grabbed her from behind. "Hello, gorgeous. Is our room ready yet?"

"No, silly. I had to patch the plaster. I can't paint until it dries." She wriggled around to face Alex, carefully holding the paint roller aside. "You need to pull the carpet out, too. What are we going to do for a closet?"

"Oh, please say you're not going to make me wait until you have a closet!"

"You don't have to wait until I have a closet," she said through a series of kisses.

"Mmmmm. Do you want the carpet out before you paint?"

"Yes, please."

"Okay, I'll get Adam and Jeffrey to help and we can pull it out of all the upstairs rooms today."

"Is Jeffrey going to move in too?"

"Not right away. He said something about too many honeymooners for his sanity."

"Hmm, I wonder…"

"No matchmaking! I forbid it."

"You forbid it? Seriously? You just said that?"

"Well, not really." Alex looked sheepish. "But I'm asking you not to. How would you have felt if people had pushed you to be with me?"

"I would have run the other way. I nearly did anyway. Okay, I get your point; I won't meddle."

They were interrupted by Kat's sudden appearance at the door. She said, "I want to warn everyone that I took the bandage off James' face today and he's going to have a hard time adjusting to it. Please don't overreact when you see him."

Addie flushed when she realized that Kat was looking specifically at her. "I'm not that shallow!"

Kat's expression was sardonic as she looked from Addie to Alex before leaving the room with a parting shot, "You did pick a pretty boy."

Lindy noticed some tension when she and James accosted Addie and Alex on their return for lunch. Focused on asking them about Frank, she ignored it.

Addie brightened visibly at her suggestion, "That's a marvelous idea! Can we ask him together?"

Alex looked worried, "Wait. Addie, will you marry me legally when we can? Even if it's just a ceremony at the courthouse."

"Of course I will. This will be our real marriage and we can appease the government later for their paperwork." She smiled as he relaxed.

"Let's go ask him now."

Frank was delighted to agree. There was a touch of the showman in him and a wedding was always a performance.

Lunch was served under the cottonwood again. Addie made sure she and Alex weren't seated at the same table as Kat, although secretly she was glad for the warning. Even now it was difficult not to stare at James' injury; red and swollen and still pecked with holes where the stitches had been. She looked at Alex and tried to imagine him with that scar; she blinked in surprise as she realized just how ragged he looked with his hair scorched and his skin still peeling as if from a bad sunburn.

He met her gaze, "Is something wrong?"

Shaking her head, Addie leaned against him as she replied, "No, I was just thinking how much I love you."

The afternoon sun was beating down again, but the porch felt nice and shaded now that the roof was up. Pat stepped outside, absently scratching at her cast in a subconscious effort to reach the itch beneath it. Pete paused in measuring for the new railing and joined her. "How does it look?"

"It's perfect. Even better than before. I wish you weren't working so hard, though."

"I enjoy doing it for you. I'm only sorry I can't replace your flowers."

She squeezed his hand. "We will find new ones eventually. You're almost finished; will you take a break after this?"

"I'm not very good at taking it easy," he admitted. "I thought we'd do some patching up at the old chicken coop on New Farm. Maybe they'll keep Jeffrey's geese there."

"They'll have to be penned. Do we have enough wire?"

"I've been thinking about that," Jeffrey said as he climbed the new porch steps and set a wooden bench down. "There was an art professor at school, a true earth mother type with macramé plant holders in her office. Well, she ran a workshop on basket weaving that Melissa wanted to attend. She wasn't so happy when we had to go harvest our own materials from the river. Anyway, I rather enjoyed it so I made a point to watch for the other workshops and there was one on hedge building using willows and other pliable saplings. I think I could adapt the principles to apply to fencing."

Pete was looking over the new bench, but Pat was interested in Jeffrey's account. "Was she an artist? The professor, I mean."

"She sculpted."

Pat thought about the curiously powerful tree sculpture on Jeffrey's dresser. "Oh?"

He shook his head in amusement at her transparent thoughts and turned to answer Pete's questions about the bench. "It's only temporary until I can make some replacement chairs. I've got another one to bring up."

Pete nodded his approval. "It's solid. You'll want to take them over to New Farm eventually."

"I thought so, yes. A good place to sit and take your boots off."

Adam coughed through his dust mask as he yanked up on the musty shag carpet. "I don't blame Jeffrey for skipping out on this job. Yuck."

"Well, I appreciate you sticking around."

"You owe me a beer."

"I'll buy you a barrel."

Adam snorted in reply. Curiously though, neither of the twins cared for the taste of beer so it was just one of their private jokes.

"Have you and Steve figured out how you're going to rearrange the living quarters at home?" Alex asked curiously.

"I think so. I'm going to move into James' room and Steve and Kat will take ours. They'll have plenty of room for the crib."

"So the girls' room will be empty again?"

"Actually, I think Frank and Pete are going to take it. They'd have to move before winter anyway and the camper can get really hot during the day."

"That worked out well then. Are you still planning on checking in with the vet tomorrow?"

"Yes, any chance you guys can pick a date in case we set up a schedule?"

"I think we have. August 1st."

"Friday? You weren't expecting a bachelor party, were you?"

Alex laughed, "What would we do? Sit around and tell dirty jokes? No, when I think about it, I've been living a bach party for years. I don't need any more."

"Well, come on then, let's get this hauled out. It might take all week for it to air out in here."

Krista drove into the yard and spotted Jeffrey working on something at the picnic table. Hopping off the wagon, she ran over and leaned against him, breathing heavily in his ear as she looked at his papers. "What are you doing?"

With a chuckle he patted the bench beside him, "Sit and I'll show you."

He explained his process for designing a chair before he began cutting any of the wood. His patience and clarity were what made him an excellent teacher. Looking to see if she was understanding, he said in surprise, "Are you sticky?"

"Oh, sorry." Krista unabashedly licked her fingers. "We got paid with honey this morning. It tastes so good!"

Jeffrey laughed, "Well, you should wash up before going inside."

"Oh, I can't stay! I just came to tell you the goose deal is on. We can make the exchange in a couple weeks like you asked."

"That's too bad. I know Addie and Lindy wanted to invite you to their wedding this Friday."

"Friday...this Friday? Cool. That's my birthday too. I'm going to be thirteen; do I look almost thirteen?"

"You look timeless," Jeffrey responded solemnly.

"Huh. I suppose that's a riddle. Well, I'll probably see you when you come get the piano." She dashed back to her wagon and jumped aboard.

Jeffrey was still gazing after her wistfully when Steve straddled the bench across from him. "What are you thinking about?"

"Huh? Oh, just wishing." He met Steve's startled look with a shrug. "I really want to teach that girl. She's got enormous potential. Imagine what I could achieve if I got my hands on her now instead of waiting until she had her mind shoved into the narrow boxes today's schools use. What's so funny?"

"Nothing, nothing. Just laughing at my sun-addled mind. I forget sometimes how much you gave up when you moved back."

"Teaching is still my passion; I just have to work harder to find pupils."

That evening, Addie and Michael put their heads together to plan the wedding meal. They bemoaned the lack of exotic ingredients, but were confident in the menu they concocted.

Michael concealed his concerns about baking the wedding cake in the outdoor oven, but was determined to make it happen.

36 MONDAY

When Juan arrived in the morning, he brought the exciting news that the town was going to vote on whether or not to use their plan. They had been holding meetings the day before to explain the system and answer any questions. He was confident that it would pass. "Most people are happy to have someone stepping up and doing something. Especially now that the water has stopped running."

"Are you and your family okay?" Pat asked with concern.

"Oh, yes. Susan is mostly worried about her residents. I warned her that other arrangements will need to be made before winter. The nursing home used electric heat. If the vote passes, she will ask Mrs. Sampson what they should do. They will probably have to do something much sooner now without water."

Pat looked at Pete worriedly, "Rural water can't last much longer."

"There should be lines that ran into the basement from the pump at one time. They wouldn't be sound, but with a lot of digging and Lindy's help, we could replace them. In the meantime, we'll set up an outdoor shower; it's not like we're not all used to cold showers already. I'm afraid New Farm will be stuck with using the hand pump."

"And the toilet?"

"Oh. Right. Back to the outhouse. The twins are good diggers. That should probably move to the top of our list. We don't want to have to haul water in to flush for long."

Addie and Alex had already left to continue the work at New Farm, but Pete gathered the rest of his able-bodied workers and explained the situation. When he asked for suggestions, the discussion on where to place the outhouse began. It was finally decided to locate it in the backyard but on the opposite side from the clothesline.

Steve had an idea, "I know we don't have the time now, but eventually I'd like to build a composting outhouse. We could use the results on the fruit trees."

Michael laughed, "Well, it's not like everything going in won't be organic. Why not?"

Adam and Jeffrey began digging while Juan and Pete sorted through the supplies remaining. Pete asked hopefully, "Any chance of getting more in town?"

Juan shook his head. "The lumberyard and DIY store have both sold out of stock and shut down."

"Damn. I don't want to waste the quality lumber on outdoor jobs. Jeffrey can use it on furniture. I guess there's only one option, we're going dumpster diving."

"What?" Juan sounded dumbfounded.

"Hook up the trailer. We're going to repurpose all the siding we took off the New Farm house. In fact, I'm going to pull out anything I can possibly use before the weather ruins it."

Thus began a long, hard day. They were methodical; evaluating every scrap for potential, retrieving every bent nail. When they reached the bottom of the first dumpster, Pete looked in and swore long and fluently. Juan looked down and winced; it was a mess of shattered windows and jagged glass.

"Give me the heaviest gloves, Juan. I'm going in."

"I'm younger and lighter. Let me do it."

"Don't argue with me. I'm not letting you risk yourself in that when you have three kids dependent on you."

"Maybe it's not worth bothering with, Mr. Wilson."

"No, I can see intact panes in there. We'll need them." With that he heaved himself over the edge, cursing again at the cracking of more broken glass under his boots. By the time he finished his extremely cautious search he had found two entire windows miraculously whole and twelve individual panes. "Hindsight can be a real pain. If only I had put these aside to begin with."

Back at the house, Lindy slipped into the bathroom and looked over James' shoulder at their reflections. As she gently wrapped her arms around him, she murmured, "Brooding, pet?"

His eyes were bleak as he couldn't take his eyes off his cheek. "I'm hideous."

"James," she began thoughtfully. "Do you think I could have had Adam if I wanted?"

Now he looked wounded, but answered honestly, "I don't know about marriage, but he would have bedded you."

"What about Jeffrey?"

His voice roughened, "Yes."

"And yet, I chose you. I fell in love with you. Nobody else ever had a chance. What does that tell you?"

"That my face doesn't matter," he spoke in a whisper.

"Actually," she trailed her fingers around his head. "Your face matters a great deal. I find it incredibly attractive and sexy because it's full of life and your personality. This will add character, not detract from what you are. I'm the one who will be looking at you across the breakfast table for the next fifty plus years; will you please *hear* my opinion?"

His eyes darted from the raw scar to meet her eyes with a naked hunger that caused her to catch her breath. She held steady and refused to look away, sensing that this was a pivotal moment. Finally, he blinked and let his head drop; she felt the tension drain out of his shoulders. His voice held a hint of humor as he said, "Sexy, huh?"

Chuckling a little shakily, she quipped back, "Did I say that?"

Then she let her hands answer that question.

Addie moved the drop-sheets and paint into the next room, then shouted down the stairs, "Alex! Come look."

He bounded up the steps two at a time. "What?"

"It's our room. What do you think?"

"Mmm. I think we'll be very happy here."

"Yes, we will. I'll paint Lindy and James' room in the morning. Right now I'm going to come patch the holes you've been finding in the kitchen walls."

It was a weary bunch who met up for supper that evening. Even Adam looked worn out.

Pete apologized, "I'm sorry you didn't make it to see the vet today. I won't hold you back tomorrow."

Adam waved away his concern, "It's alright. I didn't have an appointment or anything. There's something really primitive about an outhouse that doesn't even have a proper toilet seat though."

James offered, "There are two brand new toilets at New Farm that aren't likely to be used. I can't see any reason not to take the seat off one of them."

This idea satisfied some need for a victory among the family; a victory, no matter how small.

37 TUESDAY

Lindy was busy making her bed while she and Addie chatted about their plans for the day. "I can come help you paint."

"Nah. We're good. You stay here and play footsie with Scarface." Addie's eyes widened, she slapped her hand over her mouth and stared at her friend's unmoving back. "Oh, Lindy! I'm sorry! I didn't mean that. It just slipped out. Please ignore me!"

Lindy discovered the meaning to the term 'a blind rage' as everything went red and all she could hear was the pounding of her heart. Stalking out and into the kitchen, she pierced Kat with her eyes. "I need an outlet. Now."

Kat gazed at her steadily before nodding and setting down her coffee cup. Snagging the Harley keys off the key rack, Kat led the way outside and in seconds they had roared out of the yard. Jeffrey still had his hand half-raised and his mouth open to protest when the sound faded in the distance.

James chose that moment to walk in cheerfully. Everyone stared at him until Pat demanded, "What did you do?!"

Kat pulled into her dad's farmyard and led Lindy into the barn. Swinging the doors wide splashed bright sunlight through the dancing dust in the air. Hanging to one side of the open space was a battered looking punching bag. After wrapping Lindy's hands with tape, Kat proceeded to talk her through the fundamentals. At first Lindy wanted to scream at her that this wouldn't help, but Kat paid no attention to the fury she was radiating. Finally, Lindy punched out in rage. The first flurry of strikes were mindless, but gradually Kat's voice began to penetrate and Lindy shifted with the instructions.

When Kat called an end, Lindy was drenched in sweat and her arms were shaking. Kat threw her a towel and waited while she caught her breath. "Well?"

"Well, what?" Lindy looked at her resentfully.

"Can you let it go or do I need to ask for your gun?"

Shock spun Lindy around, "You can't have my gun!"

A satisfied glint sparked in Kat's eye. "Good girl. Never give up your gun. I don't care what happened, but I need to know if you can move past it."

"But…"

Kat shook her head, "It doesn't matter. I won't stand by and watch my family get torn apart in a civil war. You have a responsibility to the family too. Can you let it go?"

Lindy straightened as the weight of responsibility turned out not to be a burden, but a support. "It was just words. I can let it go."

Looking back as the doors swung shut, she asked, "Can we do this again?"

"I'll come get it with the truck one of these days."

When they got home, James was waiting on the steps. Lindy sat next to him. "I'd hug you, but I stink."

He hugged her anyway. "Are you okay? Do you want to talk about it?"

She nodded then shook her head.

"Okay. I was worried."

"I know. I love you."

They were caught up in a kiss when Kat hopped over them. Her voice drifted back, "Don't injure my patient."

Lindy started giggling feebly, "She really grows on you."

Alex bounded up the stairs in the New Farm house to check on Addie's progress and found her sobbing in a corner. "Addie! Are you hurt?"

She told him the whole story.

"Oh, Addie!" He was horrified, but picked her up and cradled her in his lap. "Shh. She'll forgive you. It was a mistake. You forgave me for all the awful things I've said."

"What if she doesn't? Everyone will hate me for hurting her."

"Turn it around, hon. Would you forgive her a thoughtless comment about me?"

"Like what?"

"What if she called me a brainless gigolo?"

Addie gasped.

"Well? Could you forgive that?"

"Yes. I'd be really angry though."

"How could she make it up to you?"

"By sincerely apologizing and not mentioning it again." She sighed. "And there's my answer. Why do you pretend to be brainless?"

Alex rubbed his chin on the top of her head. "It shields me from people's high expectations."

"Too late."

"Oh, I plan on living up to your expectations. Shall we go home and face the music?"

"I don't want to. Yes."

Although it was a difficult conversation for both sides, they made a tentative peace and Addie received a timely reminder to guard her hasty tongue. The rest of the family speculated fiercely in their own minds, but Kat made it clear that the topic was closed. It had proven a disruptive event, leaving everyone feeling unsettled and none of the projects made much progress that day.

The only one who escaped the fallout was Adam who had left early to visit the vet. He returned with a backpack of anatomy books and an exciting account of assisting on an operation. The vet was equally pleased with the arrangement; he would teach and feed Adam as well as top off his gas tank on a flexible schedule of three days a week. In return, Adam would act as his assistant.

38 WEDNESDAY

"It's funny, isn't it?" Lindy murmured.

"What's that?" James asked. He wasn't in any hurry to get up this morning. Lindy had shifted the basics of her belongings up to his room the day before and spent the night with him.

"A wedding used to seem like a big deal. I would imagine the dress and flowers and everything that went with it. Now, though, it's turned out to just be a formality. I'm already your wife deep inside."

"Mrs. Stevenson."

"Mrs. James Stevenson."

"Do you not want to do the wedding?"

"I don't mind; it just feels like we're doing it for your mom mostly."

"And for me, too. I love that you already consider me your husband; I just have this need to declare us formally."

James studied her face for any lingering traces of the previous day's events. He didn't know the details, just that the young women's friendship had taken a beating. "Do you still want to move to New Farm?"

"Yes," she answered firmly. "I want to be somewhere less crowded and that house is your dream. I won't ruin your dream by holding onto a grudge."

"The house is A dream; you're THE dream," he corrected.

"Sing for me, please."

James softly sang a few lines, but broke off as she thumped him with a pillow. "That's not a real song!" she said indignantly.

"Honest truth! It's Hail Mary." Then he continued singing.

"Is it supposed to be reverent or naughty? I can't tell."

"No idea. It always felt a bit like both at the same time to me."

"Sing it again. I like it."

Steve and Kat were just passing in the hall when the sound of laughter drifted through the door. They smiled at each other and paused to share a kiss before descending the stairs.

Jeffrey, not a morning person, edged past, muttering, "Ugh, you can't move in this house without stepping in romance."

The morning light spread gently across the lawn, highlighting where Michael was patiently building up the fire in his oven. It also revealed that he was looking a bit rough around the edges. Running his hand over the stubble on his normally smooth pate, he reminded himself yet again to find time to shave before the wedding.

"Good morning, Michael!" Frank shuffled closer, looking cheerful. "It's going to be another scorcher today."

"Yes, it is. But somehow," he looked up into the clear sky. "It feels a bit thundery, too.

"Tell me, Frank, did you ever do any cooking in all your travelling years?"

"Oh, yes. Not well, mind you, but nobody died from it so that was good enough. There aren't many lines of work that I didn't try my hand at."

Michael looked interested and that was all the encouragement Frank needed to continue. "Have you ever cooked on a ship? No? That was an interesting time. I was working on a small freighter making its way down the coasts of Europe. It would have been easier if I didn't have a tendency to sea sickness myself. A squall blew up off the coast of Spain. The crew was wet and hungry, but just as I was about to serve, a wave tilted the boat back and forth and I lost it; threw up directly into the pot."

Michael laughed in sympathy. "Did you lose your job?"

"Yep. I was lucky the captain waited until we reached port to kick me off." He peered closer at Michael's face. "Something's bothering you, son."

Michael gazed up at the hill. "I have too much time to think. And everything seems to remind me of Amelia. I see my brothers moving forward with their lives, but it feels like mine is already over."

"Well," said Frank slowly. "I don't pretend to have the answers, but it sounds like this is the first time you've slowed down enough to grieve for your wife. That need doesn't go away just because you won't let it in. It waits and comes back for you."

Michael looked at him while his mind worked over what he had just heard. "Maybe you have more of the answers than you think."

"Tell me about her."

Michael did.

Everyone worked to make up for lost time. Adam only stopped in long enough to eat breakfast before heading to the vet's. Alex and Addie went back to New Farm while Pete was determined to get the outdoor shower up and working.

James stirred a pan of cream celery and sniffed appreciatively. Who knew something so basic could smell this amazing when homemade. "What are you going to use this in?"

Michael leaned over to check the consistency. "You'll just have to wait and see."

"Tease."

"Do you want some help getting spruced up for the big day?" He eyed his brother's scruffy whiskers critically.

"Would you?" James' face lit up. "It's crazy how hard it is to do the simplest things with my left hand."

"We'll have a men's spa that morning. We've all let ourselves get a bit seedy. I'll play barber, although it might be better if Steve lets us charge up the trimmer on his solar panel. What are you going to wear?"

James grimaced, "All I've got is my funeral suit."

"Me too. I just never thought to keep anything fancy here. You know the twins will be dressed to the nines."

"Of course. At least it will just be family; Lindy won't have to deal with the pity comments." Seeing Michael's expression, he said, "You know what people would say."

"People are idiots." He turned to the sink to fill a pot but nothing came out of the faucet. "Well, that's it. The water is off."

Their faces turned grim, not for themselves, but for everyone out there whose lives just got harder.

Lindy came inside early for lunch. She looked wearily satisfied. "We got the shower working. I didn't think it would be that difficult. Pete is putting up some sort of enclosure so nobody gets arrested for public indecency."

"Thank you, dear. Your hard work is very much appreciated." Pat bustled over and hugged her.

"Just say I can still come over and use it, please!"

"As if I'd ever say no to you." Pat smiled complacently.

At lunch, when everyone had grown tired of hashing over the water problems, talk turned again to wedding clothes. Pat offered to try to find something Kat could wear but was politely refused. "I've got some clothes in storage at Dad's. I'll find something there."

Alex was hauling the first of many buckets of water from the pump to the house when the low, throaty growl of thunder rumbled over him. Looking around in surprise, he stared at the mass of clouds that seemed to be whipping up out of nothing. Addie appeared on the porch and looked up.

"Oh, no!" she wailed. "I left all the windows open."

He handed her the buckets. "I'll run for it."

Lindy joined her on the porch in time to see Alex racing around the curve. "Wow! He's fast."

"I was airing out the house. The paint smell is so strong." Addie explained. They both watched the first, fat raindrops plop into the dust.

"Well, the garden needs rain, I just hope it doesn't..." Plinking noises began to mix in with the rain. "Hail."

They sat on the porch steps and watched the lawn turn white. The hail stayed the size of bb pellets, there was just so much of it.

"What are you thinking about?" asked Addie.

"I hope we don't lose too many apples." Lindy looked at Addie's tightly clasped hands and put her arm around her for a quick squeeze. "He made it fine. And he's sensible enough to wait out the storm. What a pair of legs!"

Addie chuckled weakly and squeezed her back. "Would you like to pick out our wedding dresses now?"

"Absolutely."

When the worst of the storm had passed, but the rain showed no sign of slowing, Kat took the truck over to her dad's farm. First she loaded the punching bag into the back, then went inside the house. Stopping to give a polite greeting to her dad and Emma Bucket, she made her way to her old room and dug around the back of the closet. Returning to the farm she now considered home, she took the items she had chosen up to Steve's room.

A few minutes later, Steve looked in, saying, "I thought I heard the truck pull in and...wow!"

He closed the door behind him and watched as she swiveled in front of his mirror. "Does it look okay? I can't see enough in this tiny mirror."

"You look stunning. I've never seen you in anything so impractical before." She wore a bronze-colored dress that hugged her lean outline. An intricate pattern of beading traced the hemline.

"I know, right?" She grinned back. "It's almost impossible to conceal a gun in this. Heels or flats?"

The four-inch spike heels raised her well above his height. "A bit tricky on grass? Of course if you want to wear them tonight for me..."

She slipped the shoes off and inspected the heels. "Hmm, I seem to have missed some of the blood."

"That would be completely unnecessary," he finished quickly.

39 THURSDAY

Michael, Steve and the twins took the pickup to Hansen's to collect the piano. The storm had blown through and the weather promised to be gorgeous which nicely reflected the men's moods. Michael was relieved that the cakes had baked evenly, Steve had found minimal damage from the hail and Alex was in a pre-wedding high. Adam was the only one not feeling particularly happy, but even he had accepted the changes and wasn't the type to brood.

Alex waved cheerfully when he saw Krista appear in the barn doorway. "Hey, Krista! Are you still coming to my wedding tomorrow?"

"Yes! I'm coming right after I finish the deliveries. And Mr. Hansen is giving me the whole afternoon off for my birthday."

"That's great. Addie was hoping you'd be there early enough to help her dress."

"Will she mind that I can't dress up? I outgrew my last dress and we haven't bought anything new for school yet. I promise to be very clean."

"She won't mind at all. Addie wants *you* there, not some clotheshorse."

He watched her think this through. "What's a clotheshorse?"

"Someone who only cares about having new clothes to wear all the time."

"It's sort of a strange expression. Horses don't even wear clothes. I wonder where it came from."

Alex laughed, "I don't know and I need to go help them load the piano now or they'll get mad at me. See you tomorrow!"

While they were busy with the piano, back at the farm Jeffrey and Pat were scouring the attic for useful items.

"It seems madness to try to furnish an entire house from the scraps up here," Pat fussed. "Here's a table for the living room, but it has a broken leg."

"I can fix that. What about this loveseat?"

"There's nothing wrong with it other than being horribly uncomfortable."

He tried sitting on it and immediately began sliding off the front. "I see what you mean; maybe I can replace some of whatever it's stuffed with."

"Here are the armchairs I mentioned. Oh dear, they look even rattier than I remembered."

"Beggars can't be choosers and it's better than sitting on the floor. Can I take this card table and the folding chairs for the kitchen?"

When there was no reply, he looked over to see his mother struggling with tears. She pressed her hand against her mouth and shook her head. Enveloping her in a hug, he said, "It's not that bad, Mom. Lots of newlyweds start off with hand-me-downs. This is better than what many college kids have. Anyway, they're taking their bedroom furniture and you know that's where they'll spend most of their time at first. I can guarantee that they'll be eating every meal here. Nobody is going to fire up that wood stove in August to cook breakfast and they don't have an alternative.

"Why don't you arrange to do a proper scavenger hunt up here with the brides in the next week or so? You can look for some pictures, spare dishes and other useful bits and pieces. Like that little bookcase over there. I'm sure they'd like that."

"You're right. I should think of ways to make this better instead of getting upset about what I can't change." Pat headed straight for a large trunk in the corner. When she raised the lid, the scent of cedar wafted out. Gently, she lifted out two beautiful quilts, one was cream and blues and the other white and yellows.

"These were made by your grandmothers. They used their wedding gowns in them."

"They're beautiful. It's the perfect gesture."

Frank eased himself down into the chair across from Addie. "You look a million miles away."

"Hmm? Oh, just thinking."

"Cold feet?"

"No, not at all," she chuckled. "But I can't get used to the idea that I'm getting married tomorrow and none of my family even know about it."

"Parents?"

"And aunts and uncles, oodles of cousins; they're scattered all over the country but we kept in touch. Weddings, babies and graduations were a big deal. My parents are in Corpus Christi; it seems so far away now."

"What would they think of Alex?"

"Mom would love him. She adores tall men and she's shorter than me. Dad, well, he never thought anyone was good enough for me and he would have gone through the roof when he heard about Alex's reputation."

"But you're not worried about that anymore?"

"No, we've talked it out. You see, with his past, if he strayed once I'd never be able to trust him again. He knows that boundary is there right from the beginning. We're either monogamous or we're not together."

Frank reached across the table and patted her hand. "I think you'll do well."

40 FRIDAY

Lindy woke with a gasp, heart pounding.

"Shh. Just a nightmare. We're safe." James voice soothed her.

She sighed into his chest; knowing from experience that sleep could elude her for hours.

"Do you want to talk about it?"

"No!" She shuddered with remembered horror. "Keep talking please."

"Would you like to know about when I fell in love with you?"

"Yes." Her curiosity was aroused.

"It took quite a while. We were washing dishes and you told me about your family moving all the time."

Lindy lifted her head in indignation. "That was my first day here! I thought you were seriously going to tell me."

"I am serious. Everything I did after that moment was designed to keep you here until you realized how irresistible I am."

"That's absurd."

"It worked, didn't it? I do believe you are marrying me today."

"I can't decide if it's incredibly annoying or adorable when you sound so smug."

"Adorable. Definitely adorable." She snorted as she laid her head back down on his chest.

"Mmm?" The sun was streaming in the window when Lindy blearily opened her eyes.

"Mornin', doll. The movers are here." James chuckled, "Apparently they're waiting for us to get up so they can take our furniture over to our new home."

"What? Already?"

"Well, we may have slept in a little. Adam said they've moved Alex's over; he sounded a tiny bit impatient."

Lindy yawned and stretched causing James' eyes to sparkle. "Of course, it would build his character if we made him wait longer."

"I heard that!" Adam growled through the door. "Get a move on, you lazy git!"

Laughing, they tumbled out of bed and got dressed.

"Good morning, sleepyheads." Pat pulled them both in for a hug.

"Sorry we're so late; I had a nightmare and had trouble getting back to sleep."

"That's okay, dear, we wouldn't start without you. You'll probably want to take your shower right after breakfast. When the boys finish moving furniture, there's going to be a line. And James, Michael is waiting for you."

After a quick breakfast, Lindy paused to kiss Pat's cheek. "Thank you for James. I'm the luckiest woman in the world."

Michael was surprised when James refused a haircut. He explained, "There's not much I can offer Lindy, so if she wants me to let my hair grow then that's what I'm going to do."

"Huh, you won't object to having it washed at least?" Michael had an array of buckets of water ready; one containing towels was steaming in the morning air. A small table held razors, scissors and the battery powered trimmer. One by one the other brothers joined them and soon the porch felt crowded as they jostled each other good-naturedly to reach the mirror.

Jeffrey sat next to James on a bench. "You know, you cheated."

"How do you figure that?"

"The rest of us were all following the rules and you swanned in and walked off with Lindy's heart."

"All's fair..."

"Seriously, I'm happy for you. Both you and Alex chose well."

"Do you think you might take the plunge again someday?"

Jeffrey shook his head. "Technically, I'm still married."

James looked dismayed, "But that's not real. You wouldn't let that stop you."

"No," Jeffrey took a deep breath and lowered his voice. "There is someone, but she already has a husband and I couldn't do that. *She* wouldn't do that."

"I'm sorry."

"It's an old story. Nothing that will take away from everything good happening today."

Pete and Frank joined the younger men and soon the group was roaring with laughter. Jeffrey sat at the piano and snatches of songs added to the merriment.

Adam stood next to Alex as they watched the others singing and said, "You know, we've been to a lot of bachelor parties, some of them really expensive and elaborate, but not a single one was as much fun as this."

"Those all sort of blur together in my memory, but I'll never forget this moment." Alex slung an arm around his twin's shoulders and squeezed. When Adam reciprocated, the last corner of worry dissolved from Alex's mind and he relaxed.

A familiar wagon pulled into the yard and Jeffrey switched to the Happy Birthday tune. Everyone belted it out as Krista stood listening with a broad grin. The she flung her arms out and spun around in a circle while declaring it 'the most perfectly gorgeous day'. Skipping into the house, she homed in on the chatter coming from Addie and Lindy's room. The women welcomed her into their party and soon she was sitting cross-legged on a bed while Pat painted her fingernails a delicate pale pink. She watched with fascination as the brides put on their vintage dresses.

Suddenly, Krista jumped up and dashed out with a shout, "I almost forgot!"

When she reappeared, she was hugging a bucket full of garden flowers. "My mom sent these. We all picked the prettiest ones."

"These are beautiful, Krista!" exclaimed Addie. "Gladiolas are my favorite flower."

Lindy caught Pat's eye and nodded. Pat said, "We've got something for you too, Krista. Happy birthday, dear."

Soon Krista was happily turning her arm to admire the pretty, little bead bracelet and patting her new hair clip. The bottle of nail polish was safely tucked into her pocket. The other women looked startled when Kat handed her a small knife in a leather belt sheath, but Krista was delighted. "Best day ever."

The wedding was the most simple imaginable, yet the emotions expressed were utterly sincere. While the small gathering sat on the dining chairs arranged on the lawn, Jeffrey played the wedding march. Michael was very serious as he led Addie down the aisle and placed her hand in Alex's. In contrast, Pat was smiling proudly through her tears when she walked Lindy forward. She and Michael sat and the couples stood hand in hand before Frank who played up the moment beautifully; telling jokes, then becoming serious and heartfelt.

After the ceremony was complete, rings were placed on fingers and the first married kisses exchanged. Kat leaned back in her chair and murmured to Steve, "Did you notice how well Frank projected? I wonder if he was ever on the stage."

"Maybe he's secretly Ian McKellen's real father."

"I think not. What's with the twins owning tuxedos?"

"Almost as glamorous as you." Steve had one arm across the back of her chair and the other rubbed her stomach. They shared a chaste kiss before he rose to help Michael carry out the wedding feast.

When everyone was sated and both emotional and humorous speeches made, Michael produced the wedding cake. There were cheers as both couples sliced at the same time. This was followed by laughter as the guineas protested the sudden increase in volume.

Jeffrey squatted next to Krista and slid a paper wrapped package next to her plate. "Happy birthday."

She tore the paper off gleefully. "A book? 'A Midsummer Night's Dream'. What's it about?"

"It's a comedy that was written hundreds of years ago and people still read and perform it today. I think you can figure it out, but if you get stuck, you can ask me." He added in a whisper, "You might read some of it to Frank, I think he'd enjoy that."

Kat gave in to her curiosity and asked Pat why the twins had tuxedos instead of renting like most men. Pat rolled her eyes derisively, "You know those charity events where people pay to attend? The organizers discovered that if they mentioned the twins would be there, ticket sales jumped."

"Oh, that seems a little sleazy."

"I just kept telling myself it was for charity in the end."

"They remind me of peacocks. Exotic and beautiful."

Pat smiled, but secretly thought the same could be said of Kat in her finery.

Later in the afternoon, Adam punched Alex's shoulder, "I'm giving you three days without milking chores, then you're back on the clock. So make the most of them."

"My honeymoon is three days of sleeping in; not exactly what I would have chosen in better times."

"In those so-called better times, you wouldn't be married at all."

"That's a terrifying thought." Alex nodded towards the other newlyweds, "James looks like he's about to burst with happiness."

"I hope they can hold on to that."

Alex turned to him in surprise, "Why wouldn't they?"

"Don't you think it will be hard on her when Kat has her baby? A daily reminder that she can't have any."

"Oh, and someday ours in the same house."

Adam paused, "When the time comes, be a better parent than ours were, okay?"

"I will," Alex promised gruffly.

The sunset was shading the evening sky purple when the newlyweds disappeared around the curve of the driveway. Pat stood on the porch watching long after they were gone. Pete had his arm around her waist and waited for her next move. Her voice was quiet when she spoke, "Have you ever noticed how the happiest times of your life can also be sad? I have no idea what's going to happen next. I just hope they can be strong and face it together."

He made no reply, merely held her closer.

EPILOGUE

Stacey sank wearily into a chair. She was the only nurse working in the Long Term Intensive Care Unit. Everyone else had moved to positions where they felt they could still make a difference. Only she couldn't leave these patients.

An alarm beeping jerked her awake. She looked around the dark room in confusion as more machines powered down and joined the first in sounding alarm. "Oh," she breathed out, realizing that the generator had finally shut down. Maintenance had kept it running an amazing five weeks.

Pushing to her feet, she cautiously made her way to the window and raised the blinds. The wan moonlight gave just enough light to find the power buttons and silence each machine. There was no reason to hurry; all her patients had been on full life support and no longer required her services. Sadly, she made her way around the room and draped the sheets over the still faces. Pausing at the last bed, she gazed at the young man lying there. He had always looked angry, even while unconscious, but now his face seemed to have softened. Gently drawing the sheet up, she walked away, shutting the door behind her.

Made in the USA
San Bernardino, CA
29 August 2016